"You don't like me."

Lorna continued w
Mr. Kittredge. Your
since Sonoma."

True. Yet Jesse hadn't ~~~~~~~~~ ~~~~~~ ~~~~ed out
for it. Miss Alderly ha~ ~ boldness all her own that
would be refreshing if it wasn't aimed at him. This
was not the boldness of the girls who worked the
dance halls. This was a boldness born of an innate
self-confidence.

"It's not that I don't like you, Miss Alderly." Far from
it. There was much to like about her—in a different
place and if he were a different man. "It's that you
don't belong here. Why would you leave all that for
this?" They'd reached the gate of her cottage and
he gestured to the weathered exterior of her home.
"You had everything back East."

"I didn't have one thing," she argued. Now who
was being the contradictory one, Jesse thought
but wisely held his peace. "I didn't have a purpose.
There's purpose here. There's work to do and I
intend to do it."

Elizabeth Rowan lives in the Pacific Northwest, where she works as a professor. She enjoys taking long morning rambles with her dog, Bennie, and talking through her next writing project with her husband. Elizabeth plays the piano, loves to watch her three kids pursue their passions and enjoys being part of her local church.

Books by Elizabeth Rowan

Love Inspired Historical

The Major's Family Mission
Their Inconvenient Marriage

Visit the Author Profile page at LoveInspired.com.

Their
Inconvenient
Marriage

ELIZABETH ROWAN

LOVE INSPIRED
INSPIRATIONAL ROMANCE

LOVE INSPIRED®
INSPIRATIONAL ROMANCE

Recycling programs for this product may not exist in your area.

ISBN-13: 978-1-335-49851-9

Their Inconvenient Marriage

Love Inspired
22 Adelaide St. West, 41st Floor
Toronto, Ontario M5H 4E3, Canada
www.LoveInspired.com

Printed in U.S.A.

For I know the thoughts that I think toward you, saith the Lord, thoughts of peace, and not of evil, to give you an expected end.
—*Jeremiah* 29:11

For Ellen H.,
who always helps me find the most interesting things.

Chapter One

Concord, Massachusetts, March 1851

The First Parish Church of Concord was filled to over-flowing; eight people to a pew and every square inch of standing room claimed by persons, progress and positivity. Lorna Alderly could fairly feel the energy of such a combination thrumming through her as she sat on the edge of her seat, heart, mind and body craning toward the words of the speaker, Mrs. Grace Elliott of the Society for Women's Westward Migration. The message of domestic feminism, of women reforming society from inside the family and working outward into the currently untamed communities of the west, was just the sort of message the good people of Concord warmed to—and Mrs. Elliott did not disappoint. Tall and angular, simply attired with dark hair lightly striped with gray pulled back in a severe bun, the woman was saved from plainness by the twin qualities of a piercing brown gaze and a voice that commanded and carried as she spent the better part of an hour elucidating the charms of California.

In California, as Mrs. Elliott put it, a man might find gold, but a woman could aspire to something more valuable: freedom. In California, a woman might run her own business, might participate in the community, might make her own money and her own way. In short, a woman could be her own person with her own legal rights without relying on a husband. For Lorna, after a year of attempting to gain employment as a teacher with her newly-minted teaching certificate—a year in which, other than a few short-term positions at her father's school, she had utterly failed to achieve a post on her own—California sounded like the Promised Land.

Be patient, her mother had counseled when each rejection letter had arrived. *The Lord has a plan for you.* In theory, Lorna believed that was true, but in practice her patience was waning. It made little sense to her that the Lord would leave willing hands and hearts like hers idle for so long. There seemed little purpose in it. Each day the inertia of her life chafed a bit more. But tonight, listening to Mrs. Elliott, Lorna felt something awaken. Was *this* the plan? Was the Lord moving in her life, bringing her to this meeting so that she could be called to California where her teaching skills would be welcome? Where she might have the chance to live out the beliefs of equality she'd been raised on but so far had been unable to practice in her hometown?

"Mrs. Elliott's quite good," Theo whispered beside her, shifting his long legs for comfort in the crowded space the pew allotted. He ran a finger between his collar and his neck, sweat starting to stand out on his brow from the crush of people. Poor Theo. What a good friend he was. He'd come tonight because she'd asked and that was what friends did. They supported one another unhesitatingly, even if their interests might not quite align, even if it meant spending the evening crammed into a pew with an overwhelming desire to stretch one's legs.

She flashed him a smile of appreciation before returning her attention to Mrs. Elliott, not wanting to miss a word. "Educated. Virtuous. Competent." Mrs. Elliott enunciated each word in crisp authoritative tones. "These are the qualities the Society is looking for in women who are interested in going to California and bringing a civilizing influence."

The church might have been filled to capacity, but Lorna felt as if Mrs. Elliott's words spoke directly to her. *She* was educated, with the certificate to prove it. She was virtuous—though admittedly, it was hard not to be in Concord. People came here, lived here, so that they could write, think and dedicate their lives to reforming the world in ways that bettered the human condition.

The methods they took to achieve that goal might be sometimes controversial, but they were not unvirtuous—not in the way other vices were, like gambling and drinking. People searching for vice went into the world, they didn't come here. Or if they did, they rarely stayed long.

Other than a few visits to Boston, she'd never really left Concord. She loved her home at Garden House with its rambling acres, and she loved her family; her parents, her three younger brothers. But she was certain there was more to life than Concord and Garden House. To be twenty-one, to be educated to think for herself, taught to dedicate her life to making the world a fairer place for those without certain advantages of birth, and to be trapped here, unable to act on those teachings, seemed a bitter pill. She was meant for more than the quiet roads of Concord.

Hunger for the adventure promised by Mrs. Grace Elliott had swelled to overwhelming proportions within Lorna by the time Mrs. Elliott concluded. The crowd rose to its feet with applause as the tall woman made her way down the aisle to the back of the church, where she'd receive her guests as they filed out. Lorna tugged at Theo's hand. "Come on. I want to meet her." She pulled Theo through the throng to join the queue already forming.

"You enjoyed that, didn't you?" Theo laughed. "You're all lit inside, like a lamp." His velvety brown eyes gave her a soft look. "It's good to see you so happy." They both knew she hadn't been truly happy for a long time. She'd confided her disappointments over the teaching positions to him with growing frustration.

She hugged his arm as they waited their turn. "I *am* happy tonight." Happy was too tame a word. She was engaged, alive, awakened. She felt truly herself, her *best* self—not the weary, resigned creature that had taken hold after that long string of rejections. When they reached Mrs. Elliott, Lorna shook her hand. "Is it true that schoolteachers are in high demand? Even female teachers? I'm a schoolteacher myself." She worried that, in her excitement, she'd simply misheard. "It sounds too good to be true, Mrs. Elliott. Miners merely dipping their pans into the Sacramento River and coming up with a fortune in gold sounds far more plausible than a place where women might act on their own volition." Lorna gave a breathless laugh as Mrs. Elliott gave her hand a squeeze that said she understood precisely why Lorna was asking.

"It's absolutely just as I described." Mrs. Elliott's sharp eyes gave her a kind, considering look. "The Ellsbridges are hosting me while I'm in town. There's to be a tea tomorrow afternoon where those who are interested in learning more can talk informally about opportunities. Perhaps you might care to come? If so, you are welcome."

Lorna practically danced her way outside, the cool night air fanning her cheeks. She gave a little whirl once they were free of the crowd. "Did you hear that, Theo? She invited me to tea!"

Theo laughed and tucked her arm through his as they began the short walk to Garden House on the outskirts of town. "Are you really considering going?" It was said lightly, but Lorna detected a hidden tone of disbelief beneath it and her temper flared.

"Why, yes I am," Lorna replied staunchly, not liking the doubt in his tone, as if he found the idea of her traveling out West to be too fantastical to be believed. She felt stung by the implication that to be more than excited over the evening's material, to *act* on that excitement, would be somehow impractical. "It sounds like a place with more opportunity than what I have here."

For a moment confusion flickered across Theo's brow, replaced by incredulity, his words coming slowly as his thought caught up with him. "I meant the tea, not California," Theo clarified. "Are you're truly thinking about following in Mrs. Elliott's footsteps? You can't be serious, Lorna. California is half a world away."

She stopped walking and faced Theo. "Why should I not be serious?" Now that the idea had taken root, she would defend it, even against Theo. "Did you really think I'd stay here forever? That I wouldn't want something more from my life? You're barely home from four years of college, and you're leaving again for Boston to work with your uncle in his business. Your life is starting, but mine is not. Why shouldn't I go somewhere, too? Why shouldn't I take up the calling for which I was trained?" It was not like Theo to disagree with her. He'd always been so supportive of her dreams—why not this one?

He stepped toward her, reaching for her hands. "Because you don't have to." His eyes were alight with a new earnestness. "As you said, I am going to Boston to learn my uncle's business so that I can take it over when he retires in a few years. But it was never my intention to leave you behind. I am doing this for us, to make a life for us."

"Us?" It was her turn to be perplexed. This was Theo, her best friend since they were eight. But he wasn't talking like a best friend tonight. He was talking like a… suitor and it made her uneasy, unsure.

Theo gave one of his easy smiles, but it did not allay her growing concern. "I am botching this incredibly." He gave a laugh. "I did not expect to be having this conversation in the middle of the street, but now I think we must have this out without any further delay." He drew her to the side of the street, away from others walking home. "I was going to talk with your father when I returned from Boston in a few months."

"About what?" The Todds had made their fortune in dry goods and retail. Perhaps Theo was hoping her father might make an investment with him.

"Why, about us marrying, of course." He gave her a look that said surely she'd guessed such a thing was in the offing. She felt as if she had missed a step on the staircase in the dark. The world that was meant to be steady under her feet had somehow turned upside down.

"Marry? You and I?" she said, careful to leave out any incredulity that would sound like mockery. There was uncertainty in Theo's eyes now, and she hated to see it. He was suddenly unsure of himself and she was aware that he'd laid himself out for her, bared his soul, without any clear assurance of reciprocation. She needed to treat his disclosures with the gravity they deserved. She would not laugh at them. But neither could she agree to them. They were friends, not sweethearts, and they could certainly never be husband and wife. She simply could not picture it.

"Surely, you've thought of it?" Theo argued. "We've been friends for ages, we know each other's foibles, and I can think of nothing better than marrying my best friend, than sharing my life with her, than raising a family with her." He broke off with a sly laugh. "But I can't do any of that if she's thousands of miles away in California." He chuckled nervously. "Say something, Lorna. You've gone quiet. That's not like you." Nor was it like Theo to talk so much. Neither of them were behaving like themselves at the moment. Something was changing between them, and she was terribly afraid that they'd never be able to change it back.

She tried for a smile. "It's a lot to take in all at once, Theo, and you must admit it's been sprung on me rather suddenly." If Theo recognized that California had also been a rather sudden idea and *it* had not disconcerted her, he was too good of a friend to say anything. They did not speak much the rest of the walk to Garden House, where lamps shone in the front windows. Her father was still up, likely preparing lectures for classes tomorrow. Perhaps her mother was still up, as well, working on her latest poetry collection. How blessed they were, living the lives they wanted. Shouldn't she have the same chance?

"Did you want to come in? It seems my parents are still up," Lorna offered, although she hoped he would not accept. She wanted time to think—without him there to be hurt by the direction her thoughts took.

Theo shook his head. "No, not tonight, I think. Thank you for the offer, though. Give your parents my best." He offered a half smile. Perhaps it was meant to be reassurance that their friendship would survive these past few moments. "Tell me how the tea goes tomorrow. I shall be eager to hear." He made her a small bow and turned down the lane to make the short journey to the Todd residence.

Lorna stood on the front step for a while, watching Theo fade into the dark. After a year of stagnation, everything was starting to happen at once; California loomed large with opportunity, and yet there was Theo to consider in a new way. If she refused him, what would that mean for their friendship? It had been a mainstay of her life for so long, and she hated the thought of it being altered or diminished in any way. But it seemed clear now that something would have to change. If she went to California, would she have to give him up? It seemed unfair to have to choose between friendship and the future, and yet that seemed the very choice she was going to be required to make.

Chapter Two

The tea was a revelation. Lorna would not have thought she'd ever have an epiphany while sipping tea in Mrs. Ellsbridge's much vaunted gold parlor, let alone have two, but that was indeed what happened. The first was that she truly wanted to go to California. Even after twenty-four hours, the excitement of the prior evening still lingered within her. If anything, it had only grown stronger and more sure.

She'd lain awake last night, thinking and praying. Could she really do it? Theo was not wrong; it would take her far from everything and everyone she knew and put her into circumstances she'd never encountered before. She'd be alone, entirely dependent on her own abilities. There would, no doubt, be numerous obstacles to overcome that would test her strength of will and character. It would not be easy, no matter how lovely of a picture Mrs. Elliott painted. Even with all of that considered, though, she still wanted it—and that was because of epiphany number two.

If she did not go to California now, *this* would be her

life: attending evening lectures, sitting in Mrs. Ellsbridge's parlor sipping tea, listening to others talk about adventures and causes, offering money to those causes because she could offer nothing else. She would marry eventually, because it was expected and because there would be nothing else to fill her life. And once she had a husband and they started a family, there would be no more opportunities for anything else. A wife or a mother couldn't pack up and follow Mrs. Grace Elliott to California.

Another thought trailed in its wake: if she stayed, she would be a wife and a mother sooner rather than later. Theo was making plans for them, and she knew in her heart that if she stayed in Concord, she'd eventually convince herself marriage to Theo would be an acceptable choice. It would be unbearable to think of staying in Concord and *not* having the comfort and security of Theo's friendship. She would marry him, because the only other option would be to lose him entirely and be left with a life even narrower and quieter than the one she had now.

Marriage to Theo would not be such a hardship. She'd thought about that, too, in the long night spent staring at her ceiling and thinking. Theo was her best friend. They would have a good, enjoyable life together, one of ease and likely one free of any trial that could not be overcome with money and prayer. The Todds and Alderlys had plenty of money and faith between them. One of the families would gift them a house as a wedding present—probably her family. Theo's family would furnish the house, gifting them a shopping trip to his uncle's emporium so that she could select whatever she liked.

There'd be a lovely early autumn wedding at the First Parish Church. She'd wear her mother's old lace and carry her mother's white Bible. Theo would be handsome and calm, waiting at the altar, his dark hair brushed back, one lock already trying to escape his efforts to tame it into place. Their children would be baptized at that same altar, married at that same church, her grandchildren baptized there, too.

Lorna willed her thoughts to stop. She could see it too well: time marching on in a predictable pattern, life following a well-ordered sequence of events, until those events led straight to the church one last time and then to the cemetery just beyond. An entire existence in one confined sphere with everything so predictable and settled that she could visualize the next half a century with ease. Was that all the Lord had planned for her? To marry Theo. To raise a family. To never leave Concord except to perhaps live in nearby Boston? The world was bigger than that. To never put her skills to use? To hear about places like California but never see them? And then die without…without so much. That simply couldn't be all there was to life. To *her* life. Not when she had so much more that she wanted to do and be and give. Panic rose, making her pulse race and stomach churn.

"My dear, if you grip that teacup any tighter it will shatter." Mrs. Grace Elliott approached and took the vacant seat beside her. "Please tell me my stories have not been the cause for such anxiety." The woman did not disappoint up close. She was in fact even more impressive in a smaller group than she'd been last night speaking before the crowd. There was a sincerity to the woman as she covered Lorna's hand with hers. "Miss Alderly, the schoolteacher, correct?" She reached for the tea tray, helping herself to two slices of lemon cake. She offered one to Lorna. "Cake is a grand cure for almost anything." Her smile was warm and friendly. Lorna felt the knots within her ease. "I've been watching you today. You have much on your mind since we spoke last night, and your agitation today tells me you're wrestling with something momentous. Perhaps you'd care to share with me?"

She did want to share, Lorna realized, and the words tumbled out. "If I don't leave now, I'll be sitting at tea parties forever. My life will be over." She searched Mrs. Elliott's gaze, hoping she didn't sound like a desperate lunatic.

"Your young man doesn't like the idea of you going so far away?" Mrs. Elliott divined. "He has proposed, perhaps prompted by your strong response to last night's events? You do not return his sentiments?"

Lorna gaped. "How did you know? It's not that I don't return his feelings, it's that I hadn't even thought of feeling anything more than friendship for him, and now that he has declared his intentions, I don't know what to do."

"He looked sweet on you last night, that is all," Mrs. Elliott nodded patiently, her eyes holding Lorna's. "As for the rest—it's a more common story than you might realize. I've seen it often enough to recognize the signs. Believe me, you're not the first young woman to be in that situation. I can't make your mind up for you, however, I can tell you this. If you are running away from something, if you're looking to escape, California is not for you. Your troubles, your doubts, *will* follow you. Changing locations won't solve any problem that you're seeking to evade. But, if you're running *to* something— a hope, a dream, a purpose, a calling—well, then, California might be the answer."

Lorna felt a rush of relief. A hope, a dream, a purpose, a calling. *Yes.* That was exactly what she was looking for. Exactly what she knew she would never find if she stayed.

"There are opportunities to make a different life," Mrs. Elliott continued, "but it will be difficult." And expensive. California was an investment in herself. Mrs. Elliott had been quite clear that two hundred and fifty dollars per person would be required for travel to California. The philanthropic society might pool funds and sponsor an individual or two, but anyone else would need to pay their own way. What a tragedy it would be to spend the money and then fail at the endeavor.

"I have the funds," Lorna said quietly. "I have a trust from my great-aunt. She left it to me with the strict instructions that I use it to do something extraordinary." Lorna gave a small half smile. Would Auntie approve of California? Lorna rather thought that she would.

"It takes more than funds, although I think the Concord society here would offer partial support." Mrs. Elliott eyed her seriously. "Allow me to speak plainly, Miss Alderly. You live in comfort here." She gestured to Mrs. Ellsbridge's locally famed gold portieres imported from Paris, France. "San Francisco is a growing town that I believe will become a fine city one day, but it currently lacks the luxury and sophistication that you take for granted on the East Coast," Mrs. Elliott warned.

"It is true that I'm accustomed to a certain lifestyle, but that does not mean I require it. I can adapt. I am hardy enough. I am resourceful. I have three younger brothers—I have to be," Lorna assured her with a little laugh. Resourcefulness could be learned and expanded on. Whatever she might currently lack in skills for the West, she was certain she could pick up through observation and common sense.

"I know what you mean. I have brothers, too." Mrs. Elliott smiled kindly and reached into her pocket. "I brought this today, just in case you came. I was thinking about you last night after the talk." She handed Lorna a folded sheet of paper, a much-read letter. "The people of Woods River are in need of a schoolteacher. Woods River is a five-day journey by coach from San Francisco, but it's near a county seat, a town called Sonoma, so you would not be entirely isolated there," Mrs. Elliott offered that last bit in a tone of optimism.

"Is it a boomtown?" Lorna asked, thinking of the stories she had heard of towns springing up nearly overnight surrounding a place where gold or silver had been found.

"It started that way," Mrs. Elliott admitted, "but I think that even when the gold rush passes, places like Sonoma might last, might be more than a mining town. It could be exciting, Miss Alderly, to be part of that initial building process for the area. New towns lay out more than streets. They lay out laws and ways to live. You could make an impact there from the start." Lorna knew the impact Mrs. Elliott meant, since she had spoken of it so eloquently the night before: the impact of feminism, teaching women they had rights and teaching communities to acknowledge them.

Lorna stared at the paper, taking in the small details. There were up to twenty or twenty-five children in need of various levels of education. The school shared space with the church, the same building serving both functions depending on the day of the week. There'd be a small salary and a home of her own provided at no charge. A thrum of excitement hummed through her. Seeing the words made the possibility more tangible than ever.

Fifteen children were the most she had ever taught at one time, when she assisted at her father's school. The prospect of twenty or twenty-five was a trifle intimidating. But it was also intriguing—a challenge. An opportunity. She'd have her own classroom, design her own lessons. She was already imagining telling her pupils stories about the great explorers, artists, musicians and writers, how they might put on a play at the end of the year featuring those historic figures for their parents.

The prospect of her own house was a powerful enticement, too. She would do her own cooking and baking. She would bake on Saturdays, perhaps plant a vegetable garden or flowers… "It sounds like a perfect opportunity," she enthused to Mrs. Elliott.

"Keep the letter and think on it, Miss Alderly. You don't have to decide today. In fact, I prefer you didn't. Talk to your parents. Talk to your young man. Think of questions you might have. I will be in town until the day after tomorrow, then I leave for Boston to make the final preparations before we sail the first of May. I want to be in San Francisco the end of August, in time for any of the schoolteachers I might bring to get settled and start the term in the fall. I have engaged passage on a clipper ship. We'll make good speed, but the voyage is still anticipated to take one hundred and ten days." Mrs. Elliott laid out the timeline, careful to provide her as much subtle detail of the rigors of the position and the environment as possible. Those rigors would be immediate, beginning with a three-and-a-half-month journey at sea.

Not the rigors, Lorna amended. The *adventure*. There would be wondrous stops on the way when they'd put in to resupply. In just a quarter of a year, she would see more of the world than she had experienced in all her years that came before. Mrs. Elliott rose. "I would love to have you join our troop, but only if it's right for you."

It *was* right for her. Lorna knew it with a confidence that grew every step she took on the walk home. This was what she'd been waiting for. Her parents would understand. They were always telling her and her brothers to follow their hearts, to look about the world and see what needed to be done. Just think of all the good she could do in Woods River! Children to teach, and even women with whom she could share the message of equality. Surely, this was what God intended for her. She was already making packing lists and shopping lists by the time she reached Garden House.

"Lorna! There you are." Her mother met her in the foyer, beaming, her hands outstretched. "Oh, my dear, we are so happy for you." Lorna took her mother's hands, smiling to cover her surprise. Surely, word of the post in Woods River had not beaten her home? No, how could it have? It wasn't as if she or Mrs. Elliott had made any sort of announcement. The conversation had been just between the two of them. But then whatever could her mother mean?

"Theo's been here to talk with your father." Her mother squeezed her hands, eyes misty. "I'm so happy for you. Theo is a wonderful young man with a bright future."

Lorna's own happiness faded. She pulled her hands away, a sense of unease flooding her. How could Theo do this? He'd promised her time to think. He knew what going to this tea meant to her. He knew she was considering California. It felt like a betrayal that he had gone to her father without giving her a chance to decide what she wanted. "Mother," Lorna began solemnly, "I am not sure I want to marry Theo, at least not right now." Perhaps it would be best to get her announcement over with. She drew a breath and plunged in. "I went to Mrs. Ellsbridge's tea today with the intention of speaking to Mrs. Elliott about journeying West with her when she departs. I've decided I want to go to California and teach. There's a position for me and I want to take it."

Her mother sobered, her gray eyes resting solemnly on Lorna's face. "I see."

Lorna thought she *did* see; that Theo's proposal was rushed because he feared her leaving, that she was intrigued by California because the last year in Concord had been nothing but a string of disappointments for her, and that she needed to leave because if she stayed, nothing would change. Where some parents might have argued in disbelief over such a drastic course of action, her mother simply said, "I'll get your father and make some tea. It seems the three of us have a lot to talk through and a lot to pray about."

* * *

In the end, it was much more difficult to tell Theo about her decision than it had been to tell her parents. Her parents wanted only the best for her, and they saw God's hand in this opportunity in Woods River. But Theo wanted something also for himself. He wanted her love, her commitment—her future, pledged to him and the path he had chosen for his life. As much as she cared for him, she simply couldn't give all of that to him.

On the other hand, she wasn't eager to hurt him, and this *would* hurt him. The Lord was moving in his life, too, in wonderful ways through his opportunity in Boston, but the Lord was not moving their lives onto a path together. It would be hard for Theo to accept. It was hard for her, too. These new paths couldn't help but impact their friendship

She had to refuse Theo. That scared her as much as the thought of California excited her. And in truth, beneath the fear of losing Theo there was an unworthy anger, too. She was angry at him for putting her in this position, for making her decide what happened to them. She was angry at herself, too, for not seeing this coming. California or not, a change in their relationship had likely been inevitable. They were both adults now. They both had futures to look after. The opportunity of California was merely a catalyst, bringing the issue forward perhaps by a few a months. Still, it would be hard to tell Theo and she procrastinated, putting it off until the last moment as if she could hold onto childhood a bit longer.

She waited until after church on Sunday as everyone was filing out to their usual post-service gathering places in the churchyard, the Alderlys with the Todds, the Ellsbridges with the Emersons, although Mr. Emerson would inevitably make his way over to speak with her mother about poetry once everyone gathered outside. He always did. People had been sitting in the same pews and filing out of church to gather outside in the same clusters and have the same conversations in precisely the same way every Sunday she could remember for the last twenty-one years. Lorna wondered if she would miss that predictability when she was gone. Or did the people of Woods River sit in the same pews every Sunday, too?

She stepped into the aisle, falling in beside Theo. He was neatly turned out in a dark suit as always, but he looked…tired. Weary.

"Good morning. You look pretty today, Lorna." Theo met her gaze hesitantly. She had not spoken to him since she'd come home from the tea. That had been on Wednesday. She didn't recall the last time she'd gone five days without seeing him, without talking to him. Even when he had been away at college, she had been able to rely on his letters, as regular as clockwork. "You always look good in blue." He offered her a smile, but it was not one of his easy grins.

She touched a hand to his coat sleeve, keeping her voice quiet. She didn't want her brothers interrupting and pulling Theo away. "Can we talk for a moment under the elm?" It was where her parents and his always met after church to exchange news. Hopefully by the time they reached the tree, she'd have found the right words to share her news as gently as possible. *Please Lord, help me find words that won't hurt him.*

"Are you angry with me, Lorna?" Theo leaned against the tree trunk, arms crossed over his chest, worry in his gaze. "Is that why you've not spoken to me for five days?"

She shook her head. "I *was* mad, Theo. I felt betrayed. You went behind my back by speaking to my father without my permission and you *knew* better. But I understand why you did it, and I forgive you."

Theo nodded, resignation in his gaze and his tone. "I had hoped it would change your mind—that you would see how happy the prospect made our families and would decide that it was what you wanted, as well. But I fear this is the part where you tell me you're going."

"Yes." He was making this too easy for her. She hadn't had to find the words, after all. But from the look in his eyes, it was clear she had *not* succeeded in sparing him pain. "I leave tomorrow. I'll have two days in Boston for shopping and then we sail." Her trunks were packed and already awaiting departure in the foyer of Garden House.

"Be sure to shop at the emporium. My uncle will give you a discount." He tried for a grin and halfway succeeded. He shifted his feet and thrust his hands into his trouser pockets. "I am scheduled to go to Boston at the end of the week, but I could push it up and go with you tomorrow. We could travel together," he said hopefully, but Lorna knew she had to decline the offer.

"I think this is something I'd like to do alone, Theo. But thank you for the kind offer." It wouldn't help to let connections to home linger unnecessarily, and that's what would happen if Theo came to Boston with her. She also felt certain he would try once again to change her mind, which would result in a very uncomfortable journey after she told him no again. When she left Concord tomorrow, it would be best to leave it all at once. She needed to focus her attentions on the future, not the past.

"May I write to you?" Theo asked.

"Of course. Friends may write to one another, and I will always be glad to hear from you." This she could allow. A letter from home with news of friends and of his own progress in Boston would be most welcome. "You may write to me, Theo, and I will write to you, although the news will be months old by the time it reaches you. I want to hear all about Boston and how things are going with your uncle's store." Impetuously, she squeezed his hand and smiled. "You are going to be marvelous. Write to me, Theo. Tell me all about it, but don't wait for me. I don't want to hold you back in your new life." Their eyes held for a long moment, the silent meaning of her words passing between them.

Theo stepped back and straightened the lapels of his jacket, a shadow moving in his brown eyes before a curtain seemed to come down in his gaze. He was not shutting *her* out, but something else she couldn't quite grasp. The distance stung a little, but she understood and respected his need for it. They would never again be the children who had been so close…but it would be foolish to expect them to be. No one could stay a child forever.

"I will miss you, Lorna," he said, his tone as warm and gentle as ever. "I wish you all the best in California. I hope it is everything you believe it will be. You deserve it." He gave her a short nod, and she understood with heartbreaking suddenness that this was the goodbye she'd been dreading the most. She would not see Theo in the morning or even later this afternoon. Her throat tightened as he left her beneath the elm. He would never know the willpower it took not to call him back, not to change her mind, although she knew she'd regret such an impulsive reversal. Perhaps this was the first of many tests in the new life she'd chosen for herself. Perhaps this was the first temptation to resist—the urge to stay, to take the safe path offered in Concord. She'd not thought the temptation would be so great.

Theo did not look back and she did not call out. Now she understood the shadow in his gaze. He'd drawn the curtain on childhood and perhaps the dreams of childhood today. New life, adult life with new dreams, awaited them both. This was a moment she'd waited a long time for. She'd never imagined it would feel so bittersweet, but this was the price of adventure and she'd been warned.

Chapter Three

This was the price of doing his share: sitting on the hard seat of a buckboard, waiting for the San Francisco-Sonoma stagecoach to arrive, when he could be working. The monotony of waiting around like a lump on a log rankled, but it was necessary. He'd preferred to pay his portion of investing in the new schoolteacher by bartering his time and skills instead of relinquishing what little money he had. Still, that, too, came with a cost. This little jaunt into Sonoma had cost him a half day on his day off when he could have been working on his own place. He'd have to find a way to make up the time later—though how he'd manage that, he truly couldn't say.

Jesse Kittredge shaded his eyes with his hand and squinted into the distance, hoping to catch signs of the stage. If it was on schedule, he might make it back to Woods River in time to at least put in a few hours before supper. His one consolation was that he'd still have his cash when the new teacher quit and went home or took a better post in Sonoma with its comparatively more urban luxuries. This whole exercise was a waste of time, but at least it wasn't a waste of money. Or rather, not *his* money.

She *would* quit. That was a given as far as he was concerned. No prissy East Coast debutante had any business coming out here. The newly formed town council of Woods River should have known that. They should have insisted on a man with experience not only with rowdy young boys—of which Woods River had more than its fair share—but experience with the rigors of the West. But no, the council had gone and hired the exact opposite: a woman from the East Coast who had only taught a few sections of the "Classics"—whatever those were—at a private academy. *You could have sat on that council and offered an opinion. You were asked,* his conscience reminded him. And he'd declined. He had better things to do with his time than go to meetings. Now they had Miss Lorna Alderly coming to town, and she sounded like a prim schoolmarm, exactly what the children of Woods River didn't need.

Jesse lifted his hat and pushed a hand through his hair before replacing it. He hoped he didn't have to wait much longer. It was getting hot. He reached under the seat of the buckboard for a jug of water and took a swallow before returning to his musings.

The children of Woods River were miners' children. What would they do with a "classical education"? The boys would grow up to be miners like their fathers and the girls would marry them. Boys needed to know how to read a vein of gold, how to light a fuse, how to dig enough gold out of the rock to keep a mine open. If not, it would mean moving from strike to strike, from gold to silver, perhaps gems, hopefully not coal. Coal was nasty stuff to mine. The dust got into the lungs until a man couldn't breathe. It was why he'd headed West, away from the mines of his home that had laid so many men low. *And yet if you'd stayed in the Appalachians, Evie might still be alive. That* wasn't his conscience speaking—it was his guilt. It never seemed to shut up, either. Especially when he knew it was right. A little coal dust on the lungs seemed a fair trade when put that way.

Evie would have been excited about the new teacher. She would have been proud her children were going to have more learning than the two of them had had. It was because of Evie he was letting Lotte and Adam attend what was bound to be a short-lived school. He could feel the ghost of her beside him on the buckboard. He could hear her whisper at his ear, *Get those children to school, Jesse. The world's changing. They're going to need more than we had to get by. Don't you want more for them?* To what end, though? Where would book learning take them out here? Straight to disappointment, that's where. No sense in getting hopes up—it only made it that much farther to fall when reality set in.

There would be disappointment when Miss Alderly left, disappointment when Lotte and Adam realized they couldn't change their destinies, that it wasn't how much learning a person had but how much money and power a person had that mattered, and Jesse had very little of either to give them. Not enough to change his family's situation. A cloud of dust rose in the distance. The stage at last.

Jesse watched the disembarkation with a cynical eye. The usual allotment of hopeful miners come to try their chances at striking it rich climbed off the cheap seats atop the coach roof. Men began handing down trunks as the passengers inside stepped out. There were five of them in all, three women and two men, all of them dressed with an air of the city about them.

One couple was an immediate, obvious pair. The other man went inside the building that acted as the coaching station. That left the two women—one who was plump of figure, stern of face and in the middling years of life. The other was of medium height, dressed in a blue two-piece traveling outfit and not nearly old enough, Jesse thought, to be out West alone. Her family should be ashamed of themselves, letting her come out to a place like this on her own.

He ought to concentrate his attentions on the older woman, who seemed the most likely candidate to be Miss Alderly, exactly the type of woman the philanthropic groups were always sponsoring to come West. But his eye was repeatedly drawn to the woman in blue. She'd moved to the rear of the coach and was offering polite directions for retrieving her trunk. No, not just one trunk. Jesse watched in something akin to amazement as the men unloaded *three* trunks, all belonging to her. Who had that much? What could she possibly have to fill that much space? His whole household would barely fill one trunk.

The driver came to help with the last trunk, dusting off his hat along with his manners. It was clear to Jesse that the woman in blue had everyone charmed. The men were quick to do her bidding and seemed to be dazzled by her smile. The driver trotted beside her. "Miss Alderly, is anyone coming to meet you? I might suggest the hotel down the street if you need rooms for the night."

That was Miss Alderly? Oh, it was worse than he'd thought. A pretty, charming young woman would be eaten alive in Woods River. The town was rough, still haphazard in its formation, not fully transitioned yet from mining camp to mining town. This elegant, citified woman couldn't have stood out more if she'd painted herself green and stuck chicken feathers in her hair. There was not a single thing about her that looked like it belonged.

She would need a whole lot more than her smile to survive here. She'd need actual skills: cooking, cleaning, washing and providing for herself instead of flashing a smile at someone else to do it for her. If one could not do for oneself in the West, one either went home, found a way to do without, or died. *You could help her, Jesse.* That was Evie whispering again, Evie with the kind heart who helped everyone, even those who didn't deserve it. *Who are we to decide who deserves anything, Jesse? That's the Lord's work, not ours.* He hadn't much respect for the Lord's work these days, not when that work included taking Evie from him.

"Someone from Woods River is meeting me." The woman in blue shielded her eyes and looked about the street.

"If someone doesn't come, ma'am…" the driver said but Jesse was already reluctantly in motion. He could wait no longer. He'd given his word to bring the teacher back and he always kept his word. It was the one thing he had to give, the one thing he owned that had value anymore. He jumped down from the buckboard.

"Don't go fretting. I'm right here. I'm Jesse Kittredge from Woods River. I am to drive you up, Miss Alderly." He fished the folded letter out of the depths of his coat pocket as proof, for whatever that was worth. He could imagine what the letter said even if he didn't know exactly. Some people set a great store by written words. He wasn't one of them.

"Mr. Kittredge, I am so pleased to make your acquaintance." Miss Alderly turned her wide smile his direction, and his first thought was that her eyes were impossibly blue, the exact same shade as her jacket. The second was that there was no doubt Miss Alderly was what one might call a "cultivated woman." His third thought was that he had absolutely no doubt he'd be making the return trip to Sonoma—with this woman and her three trunks—in six weeks or less.

He nodded toward the stack of trunks. "Is this all you brought?"

If she'd heard his sarcasm, she gave no sign of it. Instead, she smiled even brighter. "It is, but there are a few things I want to pick up at astore . I thought I'd take care of those last bits while you loaded the trunks."

For a moment, Jesse was dumbfounded. "You're going shopping? Now?" He could see his afternoon slipping away before his eyes. So much for his hopes of being able to squeeze some work in after all.

She fixed him with a concerned stare. "Would it be better to come back later and make a second trip?"

"Let the lady shop, Kittredge," the driver put in, offering Miss Alderly his arm. "She's just spent five days traveling from San Francisco—and a long boat journey from back East before that. Come, Miss Alderly, let me show you the merchants." He gestured to two men idling by the coach. "Both of you help with the trunks."

Jesse gave a curt nod and asserted what authority

he had. "Quarter of an hour is all I can spare, though, and then we leave."

She was punctual, he'd give her that. Fifteen minutes later, Miss Alderly strolled out of the store carrying parcels while the driver hefted two large bags on his shoulder like a besotted lackey.

"Did the store have what you needed?" Jesse raised a brow. As if there could be anything left to purchase not already in one of those three heavy trunks. He was glad he'd hitched up both horses today. The weight of the trunks would have made the route home a challenge for one horse.

She settled her parcelsand , bade the driver farewell. She brushed her hands against her skirt. "I didn't want to take up space in the San Francisco coach with staples, and I wasn't sure what the situation might be in Woods River, so I thought it best to get flour and sugar here." She flashed him a smile that said she'd heard his sarcasm and she was delivering him a polite set down.

"Well, it's not a bad idea," Jesse admitted begrudgingly. "Prices are higher in Woods River on account of the extra distance."

"I'm glad you approve, Mr. Kittredge," she said drily, climbing up to the seat by herself in a show of independence. "Shall we be off?" Jesse stifled a growl and slapped the reins. This was going to be the longest six miles of his life.

Jesse Kittredge was the largest man she'd ever encountered. A fact evidenced by the amount of seat space he took up. He was also the hairiest. Long, sun-streaked hair trailed in thick waves from beneath his wide-brimmed hat, brushing down past the collar of his well-worn shirt. Stubble lined his jaw, and the sleeves of his worn cotton work shirt were rolled up to reveal a dense thicket of dark blond hairs on his muscled forearms.

This was a different type of masculinity than what she was used to, but she was not unprepared for it. Mrs. Elliott had spent the one-hundred-and-eleven-day journey (they'd not quite made it in one-hundred-and-ten) educating the ten women under her care about the nature of the California miner they were soon to encounter: surly, coarse, given to few words and likely fewer manners, all consequences of having lived alone outside of civilized community for so long.

If this man was any indication of what the population of Woods River would be like, then Mrs. Elliott had not been wrong. Lorna had a thousand questions she'd liked to have asked about the town that would be her new home to fill the time as they traveled, but she recognized the stubborn set of his jaw and decided it would be wiser to let him have his silence. She had tried his patience enough already, although that had not been her intention.

Everything she did seemed to irritate him, from simply having three trunks, to wanting to purchase staples, to thanking the stagecoach driver. Even her attempts to be polite to him had been met with resentment. And some of her not so polite attempts, too. He had gotten under her skin with the barb about needing to shop. She'd liked, too much, giving him that little set down, and she sent up a little prayer of repentance for letting herself be driven by pride. She promised God that she would try to do better—but also reminded Him that she could make no guarantees. She would have to wait and see how severely she was provoked.

Meanwhile, if he wanted to journey in silence, she resolved that she would enjoy it, taking in the surroundings of her new home. The scenery *was* breathtaking. Mrs. Elliott had not exaggerated on that score. The wild beauty was entirely new to her—and all the more stunning for it.

Granite cliffs soared high into a bright blue sky. Tall pines grew in abundance along the roadside. "Road" was something of a generous term. It wasn't paved or even that well packed down. It was more of a path, wide enough only for one wagon at a time. It was rough country, but it was also beautiful country. One had the impression that few people passed this way, that this was pristine, untouched landscape rarely traveled.

And the air—oh, the air was a treat with its crispness now that they'd gained some altitude. *Be still and know that I am God.* The verse seemed apropos for the journey, and having no other choice, Lorna gave herself over to it.

The next time Mr. Kittredge spoke it was to tell her to climb down. Apparently, they'd have to walk until the wagon made it up the incline. Six miles had not seemed a great distance when they'd left Sonoma, but it was starting to seem as arduous as a transcontinental journey. The environs of Sonoma felt a world away. She was doubly glad now that she'd insisted on shopping when she had the chance. She did not know when she'd be able to make the trip to Sonoma again, and she certainly wouldn't be making it on her own. She had no horse, no wagon, and even if someone was willing to lend theirs to her, she'd surely get lost without any road signs.

She was panting a little when they reached the top of the incline, and the view that awaited her stole the rest of her breath. Before her in the distance rose three peaks like jagged teeth jutting toward the sky.

"That's Castle Domes," Mr. Kittredge offered, bending down to check the horses' hooves. "That creek down there is Woods River where it picks up with the south fork of King's River."

Lorna wiped a hand across her brow. "Does that mean we're nearly there?"

"Just another mile to go. You can ride again." Mr. Kittredge climbed back onto the buckboard seat, and she gladly did the same.

Mr. Kittredge seemed in a better mood, so she ventured a question. "What's Woods River like?" She found herself gripping the seat as they made a slow, careful descent.

Kittredge made a dismissive sound in the back of his throat. "It's just a place, Miss Alderly. It's nothing special. Just a mining town like a hundred others. Don't get your hopes up." It was hardly a rousing endorsement. But Lorna decided that she disagreed with his assessment. It *would* be special—even if only to her—because it was the place where she was going to start her life, the place where she was going to have her own home and her first classroom. How could such a place not be special?

The last part of the journey took them along the banks of the creek, and Lorna felt her excitement start to grow again. There were people in the water, wet to the knees, panning for gold—the first people they'd encountered since leaving Sonoma. They were nearly there! There were haphazard collections of tents gathered in clusters and canopies under which men sifted ore. Lorna spotted a cook fire here and there with a woman minding it. Among the stands of tall pines, children gathered wood. There were a few log cabins interspersed with the tents but most of the dwellings were of the canvas variety.

Gradually, the canvas town gave way to wooden storefronts done in new pine but hastily constructed, and the semblance of a street took shape. Lorna read the shingles and the makeshift signs advertising a clothier, a bakery, a saloon, another saloon, a dance hall from which the sounds of a tinny piano emanated out into the street, a dry goods store, another saloon. The street was dry and dusty today, but she could imagine it as a muddy morass after a good rainfall. At the end of the street rose an all-wood, whitewashed structure with a steeple on top, stretching to the sky. Her hopes rose with it. "That must be the church-cum-school." She couldn't help but smile. After months of travel, her journey was nearly over.

They drove past the wood building and turned left, heading out the other side of town. There were more tents, more cabins and a collection of small cottages along the roadside that shared the same hasty construction of the main street but not the main street's newness. These buildings had been here longer, perhaps the first ones built, she thought, when the mine had first opened. They showed their age, their timbers gray. Kittredge pulled the buckboard to the side of the street in front of a weathered, gray cottage whose front door didn't quite fit the frame. "This is your cottage, Miss Alderly."

Her cottage. This was what she'd traveled three thousand miles for. She fought back the wave of dismay that nearly swept away her excitement. Three of those cottages would fit inside Garden House. She'd been prepared for plain, for modest—but she had at least expected the building to be sturdy. Part of her wondered if the house would fall down at the first wind.

"Well, Miss Alderly? Are you getting down?" Kittredge had immediately started unloading her trunks. "Best get inside or be prepared to give the people of Woods River something to look at. News is, no doubt, already working its way through town, with tongues wagging from one end of Main Street to the other, now that people have caught a glimpse of you as we passed through."

He was watching her, judging her, just as he'd judged her at the stagecoach. He was expecting her to balk, to fall apart at the first obstacle. It gave her the spine she needed to climb down. She might be cringing inside at the condition of the cottage, but she would absolutely not let him see that disappointment.

"As I said, Miss Alderly," he added, sounding a bit smug, "this place is nothing special." He hefted a trunk and carried it down the short path to the cottage door, shoving the door open with his broad shoulder when it stuck in its awkward frame. She squared her shoulders and was about to follow him inside when two towheaded children pelted toward her—and then right past her.

"Pa! Pa! You're back and you've brought the school-teacher!" the youngest, a girl, yelled with excitement as Mr. Kittredge returned for the second trunk.

Lorna wasn't sure what surprised her the most: the knowledge that the taciturn Mr. Kittredge had children, or the sight of him embracing them while his stoic face broke into a smile. He looked up and she noted that his eyes were green and theycrinkled at the edges when he smiled.

"Miss Alderly, allow me to present two of your new pupils. This is my daughter, Charlotte, who is eight and my son, Adam, who is twelve."

Well, wonders never ceased. Mr. Kittredge was a family man. She would not have guessed it. Nor could she guess what sort of woman would put up with him. For the woman's sake, she hoped Mrs. Kittredge was a strong one.

"Isn't the cottage grand, miss?" The boy, Adam, spoke up, his eyes, green like his father's, were wide and round. He was all lanky arms and legs and tall for his age. Much taller than her own brother who was the same age. "Pa and I did all the repairs ourselves. We're in charge of the cottage. It's our part of helping the new teacher," Adam offered with visible pride.

Lorna held out her hand to Charlotte and found a smile. It would help buoy her own spirits to see the cottage from the children's excited perspective. "Why don't you take me inside and show me around? I'd love to see everything you've done."

She could only hope that the inside seemed more stable than the outside. If the house ended up need-ing regular repairs, the situation could quickly become uncomfortable. She couldn't imagine what it was like dealing with Mr. Kittredge on a regular basis, but apparently she was going to find out.

Chapter Four

The cottage was as gray inside as it was outside. There were two rooms: the main room, which served as parlor, dining room and kitchen all in one, and then a smaller room at the back set apart by a curtain, which was to act as her bedroom.

For a moment, Lorna's determination deserted her as an unbidden, angry thought arose in her mind: She'd traveled three thousand miles for this? To live in a weather beaten cottage with a door that didn't quite fit its frame? To associate with people like this taciturn bull of a man who did *not* like her? She was not used to anyone not liking her any more than she was used to the squalor of the cottage.

"You even have a cookstove!" Charlotte tugged at her hand, drawing her forward. Her exuberance was the reminder Lorna needed that beauty was in the eye of the beholder. Charlotte thought this place was wonderful. And Lorna should, too. The townspeople had done their best for her. *Their* best. She lived by their standards now. Mrs. Elliott had warned her there would be hardships and that the standard of living would be substantially different. She had assured the woman that she could handle it—and she did not intend to go back on her word.

"A cookstove, yes, how splendid." Lorna knelt beside the girl, letting Charlotte show her the door that opened to the oven.

"The former owners left most of their furniture," Mr. Kittredge said as she rose, his comment directing her eyes to sweep the room, taking inventory. There was a table, two benches and a chair. That table would do triple duty as a place to prepare food, serve food, and plan her lessons. There was a rough-hewn credenza for dishes and utensils. A settle resided beneath one of the cottage's two windows. But there was no rug on the plain plank floor and there was no bookcase.

"Is something wrong, Miss Alderly?" Mr. Kittredge's inquiry hid a note of challenge beneath the seemingly innocuous question. He was daring her to find something wrong with the cottage. In voicing that complaint she would prove to him that his assumption was correct: that she was too citified, too female, too delicate in her sensibilities to be effective in the West. She didn't know which bothered Mr. Kittredge more, that she was from back East or that she was a woman. But she *did* bother him. That had been obvious the moment she'd stepped off the coach.

She met his green gaze evenly and offered a polite smile. "Nothing is wrong. Everything is wonderful." She hoped the lie wouldn't be held against her at Judgment. She would simply have to strive to make it true—to come to see this cottage as everything it should be.

The cottage and its furnishings were, no doubt, the best the community could provide. People had put effort and time into providing a place for her and she would not belittle those offerings. "Once I settle in, I will see about getting a bookcase." Perhaps she might even contrive to build one on her own if she could find the nails and the wood. How hard could it be to build a square with shelves? This was, perhaps, in line with what Mrs. Elliott had meant by being resourceful.

Charlotte was tugging at her hand again. "You also have your own bedroom. Come and see."

The back room was small. The size made Lorna wonder what sort of living accommodations Charlotte had if she was so impressed by this. The room might have been a lean-to at one time before it was enclosed to earn the moniker of "room." It held an iron bedstead, bare except for the mattress, and a chest of drawers.

"You have four whole drawers all to yourself for clothes," Charlotte said in solemn awe. But there was no clothes press or wardrobe, only pegs on the wall. She had money. She could remedy any shortcomings in her furnishings by ordering what she needed from Sonoma or San Francisco *if* there was room for it. She doubted there'd be space.

Back in the main room, Adam and Mr. Kittredge had lined her trunks against a wall. Charlotte eyed them with undisguised interest and curiosity. "Shall we help you unpack?" the girl asked hopefully.

Lorna was torn by the offer. She could see from the child's expression that to help would be a treat, but she'd also seen the girl's reaction to the run-down cottage, as if it were a tiny paradise. Lorna thought about the contents in her trunks. They were nothing luxurious to Lorna's eyes, but to Charlotte, they would be treasures. And to Mr. Kittredge, they would be signs of Eastern softness. "I appreciate the offer, Charlotte, but I am sure your father needs you at home. I've taken enough of the Kittredge family's time already. I wouldn't want to impose any longer."

"But what will you eat?" Charlotte insisted, flashing her gaze in her father's direction. "Miss Alderly must come and eat with us tonight, right, Pa?"

Kittredge shifted uneasily on his feet rather than responding, the idea obviously discomfiting him. Lorna could guess the reasons, although Charlotte's hospitality spoke well of the girl. Whatever graces her father lacked, Charlotte possessed them in plenty. Likely due to her mother's influence. A mother who didn't deserve to have an unexpected dinner guest foisted on her when she'd already sacrificed so much of her husband's time by sending him to get her. No, she couldn't bring herself to impose. Especially if food was scarce for the family.

"Charlotte, I'll be fine," Lorna declined politely. "There will be plenty of other opportunities for us to dine together."

Charlotte brightened at the prospect. "Yes, especially since we are neighbors. Our cottage is just three down the row. We'll pass by your house on the way to school every day."

Lorna smiled. "I shall enjoy being your neighbor, Miss Charlotte, Mr. Adam." She lifted her gaze to Mr. Kittredge and sobered. "Thank you again for your time today." She hoped for a little acknowledgment from him in turn. After all, she was being gracious, and she'd done a lot of conversational work for him, saving face for him by declining Charlotte's offer to help and her offer for dinner.

All the big man could manage was a grunt and, "Come along children. We're burning daylight."

The little cottage seemed strangely empty after the children and Mr. Kittredge left. It was a silly feeling to have about such a small space. How could two rooms— *one and a half rooms*—feel empty?

But in truth, it wasn't the emptiness that hit her as she stood in the center of the cottage, it was the sheer aloneness of it all. She was three thousand miles away from home, from family and friends, from everything she'd known all her life. She'd sailed around Cape Horn, endured storms at sea and one hundred and eleven days aboard a ship, five days stuffed into a coach jolting over dusty roads, but the whole time she'd been surrounded by people. In Boston and on board ship, she had had company from Mrs. Grace Elliott and the other nine girls who had come with her. On the stagecoach, there had been the other travelers. Everyone had been kind, everyone had been encouraging. She'd been full of hope that all would go well, and that she'd feel at home at once.

But now, she was completely alone, completely unknown to anyone else, after three and a half months of being with others. The darker sides of this adventure had suddenly gotten very real.

There was no one she could turn to, unless one counted Mr. Kittredge, and she didn't think she should count him. He hadn't said it outright, but his conclusions about her were in his eyes every time he looked at her. He was certain she would fail. Maybe he was right. When she looked at this cottage, the prospect of building a home for herself here *was* daunting. This was like no place she'd ever lived and these were like no conditions she'd ever lived in. Maybe she couldn't do it. *You can do it, but you have to want to do it,* her conscience whispered.

She *did* want it, she reminded herself. She was giving up too easily. These were the moments Mrs. Elliott had spoken of. This was the first of many challenges. She would not give up at the first obstacle. She put her hands on her hips and surveyed the room. Of course this place was dismal. It had no life to it. Its former owners were gone, and she had yet to put her own stamp on it. She would unpack and that would keep her busy while also making the place feel more like it was truly hers. It would feel good to do something productive. Idle hands and idle thoughts created all sorts of mischief she could not afford.

Lorna went to the first trunk and unbuckled the sturdy leather straps. Lifting the lid was a little like Christmas. It had been over three months since she'd packed in Boston, every item carefully selected from Todd's Emporium and then gently wrapped and stowed. At the memory of her shopping trip at the Emporium she thought of Theo and hoped he was doing well. She could imagine him eating as an honored guest at Boston's finest homes, dressed in well-tailored clothes, dazzling hostesses with his company. Would he laugh if he could see her now? If he could see this cottage? Would he say "I told you so"? Of course not. Theo wasn't like that. But he had tried to warn her that California might be a bigger challenge that she expected—and that once she was there, she would be very far indeed from the help and comfort of those who loved her.

Well, here she was. There was no going back—quite literally. She couldn't find her way on her own to Sonoma, and even if she did somehow manage it, there would be the issue of catching the stage and finding a ship, followed by another three months at sea.

No, going back wasn't an option. There was only going forward, there was only making the best of things. "Lord, give me strength," she prayed as she tied on an apron. Strength for all of it: for setting up house, for finding her way in this new community, for teaching the children. There was so much she needed strength for.

The first trunk held household goods. Blue and white dishware she placed on the shelves of the credenza along with a pretty vase for flowers. She filled the white canisters she'd brought with her purchases of flour, sugar, tea and coffee from Sonoma. Already, her brief time in Sonoma seemed to have happened ages ago, much more than an afternoon away.

In the drawers of the credenza she arranged flatware and cooking utensils. In the cupboard beneath, she put her skillet and her pans and a bowl for mixing. There was a little space left on the right side and she had a moment's inspiration. Why not put the books there until she could get a proper bookcase? That made her smile. Her books were like her—they may not have quite the home they'd expected, but at least they had a safe place to rest.

She put her kettle on the cookstove, noting that the barrel beside the stove was filled with water. She had not noticed that earlier. She would have to thank Mr. Kittredge for that particular thoughtfulness. She'd have had no idea where to fetch water from at present. She made a mental list of things to find out tomorrow— that was at the top.

Lorna opened the next trunk, and the scent of her mother's lavender and vanilla sachets fill the room. That, too, made her smile. It felt good to have the scent of her mother nearby. This trunk contained her linens. On top were two tablecloths. A blue-and-white-checked cloth for every day and a white linen cloth for special occasions. She would keep that one wrapped and in the trunk. There were cloth napkins, too. The everyday ones could go in one of the credenza drawers. She unfolded the blue-and-white-checked cloth and gave it an unfurling snap, settling it on the table. She stepped back. Already, the room looked better, more homelike.

There was a blanket that would do well for the settle, so she draped it over its back. A lamp with a chimney was positioned at the center of the table. She could use one of the trunks for seating along with the settle and one of the others as a "coffee" table of sorts. She smiled at her improvising. She was getting the hang of this, of making do with what she had; seeing different ways to use items.

Back home, empty trunks would have been returned to the attic awaiting the next trip. But here, these trunks could be repurposed as furniture, and they could also be used to store extra items until they were needed.

She carried the remainder of the linen to the bedroom and set about making the bed, finishing it off with a bright multicolored quilt and pillows stuffed into pillowcases she'd embroidered herself. Even this small space was starting to look better. She dragged the last trunk into the bedroom and positioned it to the side of the bed where it could double as a bedside table. Then she began to unpack her clothing.

Not all of it, she reminded herself, eyeing the meager four drawers. Her winter clothes could stay in the trunk for now. She would swap out her clothes as the seasons changed. She placed her last lamp on top of the chest of drawers, although she suspected she'd move it to the top of the trunk, given that she liked reading bed.

Lorna surveyed the room, pleased with her efforts. Her summer dresses hung from the pegs, and her personal items were arranged across the top of the chest of drawers, along with a white ewer and basin for washing. Her smile diminished a little at the thought of washing. There was no tub. There was no space for a tub. How would she wash? She added that to her list of things to find out. Tomorrow she'd look around and see what others did for washing. She also added a tub to her list of things to order—or buy, if she could find it locally. Based on space, she'd have to choose between the wardrobe and the tub. She'd choose the tub. Perhaps she could store it in the front room next to the stove. She was already imagining how many kettles of hot water it would take to fill a tub. She might never have a hot bath again, or at least not until she made a trip to Sonoma.

Don't think on it now, her conscience warned and she pushed the thought away. She thought instead of the verse that had sustained her through the difficult year she had spent in Concord before deciding to leave. Matthew chapter six, beginning at verse twenty-six.

Consider the lilies of the field... Even Solomon in all his glory was not arrayed like one of these. Wherefore, if God so clothe the grass of the field, which today is, and tomorrow is cast into the oven, shall he not much more clothe you, O ye of little faith?

God provided. He'd provided her a way out of Concord, a way out of the routine that had stagnated her life. He'd brought her here. He would not let her fail after having brought her so far. There was extreme comfort in that thought as Lorna went into the front room and struck a match to light the lamp for the first time in her own home. Shadows were falling, the evening of late summer was gathering. It was time to make a meal, to say the blessing even though she'd eat alone, and to make a list for tomorrow. She had much to be grateful for. All year she'd been praying for her life to begin and now it had.

"What do you s'pose Miss Alderly is eating for supper?" Charlotte asked as Adam finished the blessing. The children took turns saying it, just as their mother had taught them. As for Jesse, he was done with blessings. He ladled leftover stew into their bowls. "Nuthin' hot, I reckon."

Charlotte frowned her displeasure his direction as she took the bowl from him with two hands, careful not to spill. He knew she was wishing the teacher had joined them, but he was relieved the woman had had the manners to turn the invitation down. It was the third night with the stew and there was just enough for them. How could he have invited someone to supper knowing there was so little to serve them? Especially *that* someone.

Miss Lorna Alderly, of the three trunks and blue traveling outfit that managed to still look fresh after five days in a stagecoach.

Jesse filled his bowl last and reached for the last loaf of bread until baking day on Monday. He sliced a piece for each of them. "She'll likely have bread and cheese and do just fine for herself," he assured Charlotte. *She* would no doubt have found their stew and bread supper meager. She would find his home meager, too.

Jesse glanced about the cottage. For the first time since Evie died, he felt the lack of his home—or perhaps it was the lack of domesticity that he felt. He took a big bite of the crusty bread and chewed.

"You're becoming a fine baker, Charlotte. This bread is even better than last week's," he complimented, partially because it was true but also to direct the conversation away from any more questions about Miss Alderly. "Your mama would be proud, Lotte." So proud, Jesse thought—and so sad about all the responsibility that had landed on their young daughter's shoulders. But there hadn't been any other option.

Out of necessity, Charlotte had become quite the housekeeper in the two years since Evie passed. Charlotte managed the cooking, the cleaning, the mending and even some light sewing like buttons on shirts and letting down hems. He sent the laundry out to Mrs. Andress and traded work for the other tasks Charlotte couldn't manage, like putting up preserves for winter. But Charlotte did well. She was the woman of the house at eight, far too young of an age for such a role. Jesse grimaced when he thought about it. He'd failed to give

Charlotte a childhood. Perhaps it was another of his failings to add to the list.

"Pa," Adam began solemnly, "I was thinking this fall, I could work on your crew in the mine instead of going to school. The extra money would come in handy, and I remember you said there's an opening on your team. Jasper Kinney is joining his pa's crew and he's twelve, same age as me. I figure I'm almost too old for school, anyway." He gave a casual shrug of a rangy shoulder he likely wouldn't grow into until he was twenty. But Jesse was not fooled by his son's attempt to act casual. He remembered being twelve. This was no idle conversation to a boy that age who hovered on the edge of adolescence and, in this world, manhood.

At twelve, Jesse had been providing for his family—his mother, his injured father, his two sisters. At thirteen, Jesse had seen Evie for the first time. At fifteen, he'd married her. *At twenty-eight, he'd lost her.*

Jesse nodded, treating the topic with the seriousness it deserved. He didn't want his son to feel belittled or dismissed. "Almost too old is right," he said carefully. "But not quite." It took all of his restraint to not shout the words, "No, not on your life!" But what would a show of temper solve? It would only make the boy want the mining job all the more.

Jesse did not want his son in the mines—not now, not ever if he could find any other path for him—but the fastest way to drive him there would be to shut him down, to not listen. Adam was tall and lean for his age, blond with green eyes. Looking at his son was like looking at his younger self and it scared him most days. "No need to rush it. You have plenty of time ahead of you to work and, as you say, little time left for learning. Best make the most of it while you can, while we *have* a schoolteacher. Don't know how long such a luxury will last." He didn't give Lorna Alderly six months. *She might be tougher than you think,* his conscience prodded him. *She wasn't afraid to stand up to you in Sonoma and she walked up that hill without a complaint.*

Adam wasn't ready to give up. "You started when you were twelve," he persisted. Our first adult conversation, Jesse thought. He couldn't get angry at the boy for pressing the point. He wasn't exactly arguing, just discussing, just standing his ground. Evie would have been proud if she could see him like this.

"It's not that I don't want you. You'd be a fine addition. It's that your Ma wanted school for you both," Jesse replied sternly. "I made her promises and I intend to keep them." He'd never broken a promise to Evie. He'd kept them all, except one. "Do you understand that, son? A man keeps his word." Particularly when it was all a man had to offer.

"Even to the dead?" There was a hint of cynicism beneath Adam's words that Jesse didn't like to hear. It was one thing for him to be disillusioned, but he didn't want that for his children. But he supposed it wasn't really something he got to choose. The last two years had been hard on all of them. Evie's death had scarred them in different ways.

"Especially to the dead," Jesse answered solemnly. "They're counting on the living to carry out their tasks for them."

Adam looked downcast, and Jesse reached out briefly to squeeze his shoulder—a small consolation, but it was all he had to offer. "Do school this year, son, and we'll revisit this conversation next summer, alright?" Jesse offered. Every year he could keep Adam out of the mines the better. From where he sat at the moment, a year was a long time from now. Who knew what might happen by then?

"Tomorrow is Sunday." Charlotte sopped up her stew with a chunk of bread. "We should stop at Miss Alderly's and offer to walk with her to church. She'll be all alone in a new place. It's the neighborly thing to do." It certainly was, and although Jesse would like to argue with the suggestion he couldn't.

Chapter Five

The knock came at half past nine in the morning, just as Lorna was tying the ribbon on her hat and gathering her resolve to make the walk to church alone. The church was only a few blocks down the street, and with the steeple pointing into the sky, she could hardly get lost. Still, she could feel butterflies fluttering in her stomach at the thought of facing the townspeople on her own. *Hello, I'm Lorna Alderly, the new schoolteacher.* She'd practiced the line over and over in her head as she'd dressed. The knock jolted her out of her internal reflections as she hurried to answer it.

"Miss Alderly, we've come to walk you to church." Charlotte Kittredge blurted out the words the moment Lorna had the door open. The sight of the girl standing there—her gaze direct, her words forthright—brought a smile to Lorna's face and quieted the butterflies.

"Miss Charlotte, I am so glad you've come. I was just thinking how much I'd like a friend to sit with for church and to show me how to go on here," Lorna said truthfully. She truly did feel a surprising amount of relief at the thought of facing her new church community with a friend, even if that friend was an eight-year-old girl. Charlotte tossed a smug look over her shoulder to where her family stood a few feet back from the door, as if to say "I told you so" to some private family debate that had taken place previously. It was crystal clear to Lorna whose idea it had been to call for her—and whose idea it wasn't. She noticed, too, that there was no Mrs. Kittredge among them today. For the first time, Lorna realized that there might not be a Mrs. Kittredge—not anymore. Surely, if there was, she'd be with them for church. Lorna's heart went out to the little girl. Eight was a young age to be without a mother.

Lorna grabbed her shawl and reticule from the peg beside the door and stepped out into the sunshine of a Sunday morning in Woods River. The sky was blue, the day still cool, the air holding on to some of its evening crispness from the night before. And, oh, what delicious air it was! Mountain air. They didn't have that in Concord.

"You look very nice this morning, Charlotte," she told the girl as they joined Adam and Mr. Kittredge. The family looked neat and clean even if their clothes were worn. The checked pattern of Charlotte's dress was faded except for where the hem had been let down, and the Kittredge men wore only shirts and work pants; no coats, no waistcoats or neck cloths. "Thank you for coming to collect me. It was truly kind of you. I was just preparing to set out on my own, but this is much nicer." Lorna fell into step beside Mr. Kittredge, Adam and Charlotte walking ahead of them.

Kittredge shot her a strong look that held a hint of

disapproval. "You should not be walking around town unescorted, Miss Alderly. I would not advise it. We might have a few wooden buildings and storefronts and cottages, but we are still a mining town. Mining towns are rough places for women. The men here are not like the men you're probably used to from back East."

"Your sense of honor is admirable, Mr. Kittredge, and I thank you for your concern, but I can hardly hide in my cottage waiting for someone to come escort me before I go anywhere. I am certain I can take care of myself walking the two blocks to church in broad daylight." She smiled to soften the scold even as she did take his words to heart. She'd need to think twice about roaming around after dark.

In all honesty, she'd never really thought about whether it was safe for a woman to wander on her own—in Concord or California or anywhere else. Back home, she'd always had Theo with her or been surrounded by friends as they went to and from evening entertainments. Going somewhere alone simply had never been an issue, and no one had ever mentioned any concerns for her safety.

The situation was quite different here, of course. She would have to be cautious and sensible. Nothing was to be gained by taking foolish risks. That said, she would not let a man or men dictate where she could go or when she could go. "I believe a woman should have as much freedom of movement as a man, Mr. Kittredge. We ought to live in a society where we are civil to one another, where we can control ourselves to the extent that no one is afraid to go out."

"Well, that's a nice dream, Miss Alderly." Mr. Kittredge's tone suggested it could be nothing more than that. The street grew busier near the church as the townspeople converged on their destination. Several glances were directed Lorna's way, and she was glad to be attached to the Kittredges, even if Jesse Kittredge thought she spouted nonsense. A few families approached and Mr. Kittredge made brief, taciturn introductions.

"This is Peter and Kate Kinney and their sons, Jasper and Malcolm." The boys appeared to be about Adam's age and they seemed to be good friends. Adam smiled when he saw them.

"I am pleased to meet you," Lorna enthused. "We'll have a good collection of older boys for the school with you three. I'm sure you'll be wonderful role models for the others."

Jasper shifted on his feet and his father put a hand on the boy's shoulder. "Thank you for the offer, Miss Alderly, but we've decided Jasper will start work on my crew at the mine this fall. You'll have Malcolm though for the year. He's ten."

Lorna acceded diplomatically, not wanting to start her relationship with this family with conflict, although everything in her wanted to argue that Jasper should come to school with his brother. She saw a stubborn look pass between Kittredge and Adam. Perhaps a similar discussion had taken place in that household, too. "You are welcome any time, Jasper, if you change your mind."

A man in a black robe came out of the church and rang the bell, signaling for everyone to come inside. Other introductions and conversations would have to wait until after the service. Kittredge ushered her and his children to a pew set in midway back, giving her a good view of the room. The pews were full if not tightly packed. She wondered how many of the townspeople chose not to attend church? She wondered, too, how many more discussions would she have like the one with the Kinneys?

There was a rustling at the back and heads began to turn as a party of three entered after everyone else was seated—two men, one older, perhaps in his fifties, and one younger, in his early thirties if Lorna had to guess. Both were dressed nattily in suits that had "back East" stamped all over them. The woman they were escorting was older, too, probably the wife of the older man, and she was also dressed fashionably in a black-and-white-plaid gown with a black silk bonnet. The younger man's gaze landed on Lorna, a smile curling on his lips as he gave a brief incline of his head. She felt her cheeks flush as she dropped her gaze. Beside her, Kittredge gave a grunt of disapproval. For her or for the late arrivals?

"Those are the Carringtons," Charlotte whispered from her other side. "They own the mine," she managed to say before her father shot her a silencing look.

Sermons were a good opportunity to survey a congregation and Lorna took full advantage. That was not to say the reverend was boring. He had a pleasant, deep voice and seemed warm and sincere in his message. But like most sermons, it went on too long after it had already made its point. Lorna let her gaze carefully count the children present and note their ages. They were all dressed similarly to the Kittredge children: faded calico dresses for the girls, plain shirts and work pants for the boys. Many were barefoot, most faces were clean but not all.

If all the children present here came, she'd have fifteen children, not to mention those whose families might not have come to church. But of course, it was likely that not all of them would come to school, as illustrated by the Kinneys. Still, fifteen students was quite a lot. She'd only ever had fifteen boys at a time once at her father's school and they'd all been at the same learning level. Her students here would be scattered among a range of different grades. Lorna began to imagine them sitting in these same pews, balancing slates on their knees. It wouldn't be ideal.

The reverend gave the benediction and Lorna bowed her head along with the children, although she noted Mr. Kittredge didn't bow his head. He just stared straight ahead until it was done. Had he bowed his head for the other prayers? She'd not thought to look—but she suspected the answer was no.

Afterward, the congregation filed out to gather in the churchyard. Just like home, Lorna thought. At least something was familiar. There were more introductions to make, this time to the families of the men who worked on Kittredge's crew. "Pa's a crew chief," Adam told her proudly between introductions. "He's the best one. If there's a vein, he can find it." Lorna tucked that piece of information away along with the other she'd learned today. Now she knew two more things about the man who'd picked her up in Sonoma yesterday: he was a widower, a crew chief and the best ore finder in Woods River. And he didn't like her. Her list of things she knew about Jesse Kittredge was growing rapidly.

By the time the sleek, dark-haired Carringtons approached, Lorna's head was swimming with names and ages of children from all the families she'd met. "We are delighted to have someone of your caliber teaching in our little burgh." Carrington the younger bent over her hand as if they were at a dance. "Charmed to make your acquaintance, Miss Alderly." When he looked over her hand, his blue eyes twinkled as if they were sharing a private joke. Lorna felt her cheeks heat again. "I'm Jack, and this is my father, Hamish Carrington, and my mother, Eleanor." His eyes flashed with a spark of sudden insight. "Has anyone taken you to see the schoolroom?"

"There's a separate schoolroom?" Lorna echoed in surprise. "I was told that the church building was used as the school, as well, and I thought the children would just use the sanctuary."

Jack Carrington slanted Kittredge a sly look and chuckled, only to be met with a narrow-eyed glare from Kittredge. "You haven't shown her. Shame on you, Kittredge. You'll have her thinking we're complete barbarians." He crooked his arm. "Come with me, Miss Alderly. Allow me to show you just how civilized we are."

He led her back through the empty sanctuary and to a side door on the right. "We have added a new annex, if you will, for the express purpose of schooling." His hand dropped to the small of her back as he ushered her through the door to a room that still held the faint scent of fresh pine.

After the disappointments of yesterday, the room was a delightful surprise. "It even has a window!" Lorna exclaimed, noting the light that flooded the room. Best of all, beneath that window was a small three-shelf book-case, one shelf already lined with primers. Her books would have a home after all. She could bring them here. For a moment, it was enough to simply stare at the book-case and its bounty. Jack Carrington wanted to show her more, though.

"There are desks and two long tables. The benches are moveable so you can configure the room as you'd like. There's a desk for you, too." Jack Carrington ges-tured to the desk set in the front right corner of the room near the window on one side and near the stove on the other. *My own desk*. Lorna couldn't help but smile as she ran her hand over its surface.

"I don't imagine your cottage has much space for doing schoolwork," Carrington said as if he'd read her mind. "Last but not least, look behind you."

Lorna turned to face the front of the room and gasped in delight. "A blackboard!" She'd given up on having such a thing and had already been planning ways to work around its absence. It felt almost like Christmas to have it here after all—it was a present she hadn't dared hope for.

"My family had everything brought in from San Francisco," Jack Carrington announced proudly. Per-haps too proudly, Lorna thought. One should not be boastful. "Though there's no one of school-age in our family, we still feel it's our duty to make a significant contribution to the education of the community. We un-derstand how important education is because, of course, we've had the benefit of being educated ourselves. We know the difference it makes." He wasn't wrong, but his words only heightened her impression that he was too prideful. Lorna sensed a streak of noblesse oblige beneath his words, and it made her a trifle uncomfortable. Still, she was grateful for all that his family's generosity had wrought.

"Thank you. This is much more than I'd hoped. It will make a great deal of difference for the children."

"And for you, I hope?" he favored her with a long look from those blue eyes. "We want you to be comfortable in Woods River, Miss Alderly." He paused and gave her a considering, conspiratorial look. "How is your cottage, by the way? Kittredge was supposed to make repairs."

"My cottage is fine. Mr. Kittredge has done nicely." Lorna replied, feeling both wary and defensive on Mr. Kittredge's behalf. Even though Mr. Kittredge didn't like her, he had still done well by her—bringing her safely to Woods River, preparing her home, escorting her to church. She was grateful—all the more so since he didn't seem to demand gratitude or praise in recompense.

"Kittredge is my lead crew chief. One of my best men. I'm glad to hear he's seen to it that you're comfortable—or as comfortable as you can be, anyway," Jack Carrington's smile was as sleek as the rest of him. "I hope cottage accommodations will be alright until something better can be arranged. The town council insisted on making all the arrangements, and since we'd already put money into the school, it seemed a bit too heavy-handed to insist on taking your housing over, as well. The townspeople did the best they could."

Again, she felt her defensiveness and protectiveness rise on behalf of people she barely knew. Beneath his words was an insult for the hardworking people of Woods River. "My cottage is more than adequate," she assured him. "I want to be part of the community, not above it." She smiled as she added that last bit. "I find it helps instill confidence and build trust."

He beamed at her. "You are exactly the right person for this position then, Miss Alderly." It was hard not to like Jack Carrington despite his pretentions and privilege. He was quick with a smile, unlike the taciturn Mr. Kittredge, and his genteel manners and fine fashions were potent reminders of home. Just looking at him made Concord feel less far away. After weeks of living among sailors in culottes and the dust of stagecoach travel, it was a type of pleasure to gaze upon someone well-dressed and well-groomed, like coming across an oasis in the desert. Jack Carrington was definitely that—an island of elegance in a sea of plain.

Carrington was taking his own sweet time showing off the schoolroom. It was a single room with not much in it. Here's the desks, here's the chalkboard. School starts September first. What else was there to say? How long could it take? Jesse shifted impatiently on his feet. Most of the other churchgoers had left by now. He was eager to leave, too, to get home and get up to his place in the hills. He'd finally started to make some progress on his little mine just when the bottom seemed to have fallen out of his world, his precious free time sucked up with driving into Sonoma, and now waiting around for Carrington to stop flirting with the new teacher.

He was just about ready to send Charlotte in with an excuse to flush them out, when they exited the church,

Carrington smiling and beaming down on her, her arm tucked through his as she laughed at something he'd said. They looked good together, he in a dark suit with a snow-white shirt and she in a delicate, flimsy white dress patterned with tiny blue flowers. In Woods River, where the streets were constantly full of either dust or mud, white was a color for rich people, the color of the frivolous who had more clothes than sense. Of course they looked good together. They were alike. They had a lot in common: both of them educated, both of them familiar with refinement and elegance. They could probably both sit around and make references to Greek gods and that dead Austrian fellow, Mozart, with their pinkies sticking out on their teacups.

But that was where the similarities ended. Did Miss Alderly see that? Although there were many things about her that irked him, he was not blind to her good qualities. Beneath her pretty dresses was an inherently good person, even if she was misguided and in over her head. Inherently good people often were prone to be led to those deep waters by their very nature. Evie had been like that. Too decent for her own good, always giving away whatever she had to help others: her time, her love, her kindness—even when people didn't deserve them, even when such giving left her weakened. But she hadn't known how to protect herself—hadn't been able to be anything other than open and generous.

He'd recognized that quality in Miss Alderly yesterday—the way she'd been with his children, the way she'd hid her disappointment over the cottage and how she'd saved face for him when Charlotte had asked her to dinner. She'd declined more for his sake than for her own. She'd not forced him to be the villain and refuse his daughter. Good people weren't always the ones who threw their money around furnishing schoolrooms and telling everyone what they'd done. The ones who felt the need to make a show of their goodness usually had very little of it in the first place. Good people spent time, spent kindness, put others first in small ways that no one ever knew about or bragged about. Lorna Alderly was that kind of person—and that made her dangerous to herself in this town that would eat such good intentions alive.

Jesse narrowed his gaze, squinting against the sun. Jack Carrington was nothing like Lorna Alderly, no matter how well matched to her he appeared on the surface, with his fine suit and pristine white shirt. He was vain and prideful, and those were just the man's personal faults. When it came to business matters, he was also greedy and headstrong, willing to gamble with others' lives for the sake of his bank balance. There were those that admired a man like Jack Carrington, a man whom some might feel was a self-made man of fortune. But Jesse thought the man Lucifer incarnate: glorious on the outside, corrupt on the inside.

"I've shown her the schoolroom and I venture to say she was impressed, to my humble relief," Carrington returned Miss Alderly to the Kittredges with a wide smile. He groped in his pocket and came up with two peppermints. "One for each of you." He handed them to Charlotte and Adam, whose eyes widened at the sight of the rare treat. Jesse would like to refuse the gift on their behalf but it would only make him look like an ogre. He could rarely afford to provide them with such luxuries, and he hated to deprive them—no matter how it rankled to take handouts from such a man.

"Yes, the schoolroom is splendid. I think we'll have a marvelous time learning there." Lorna's smile was wide and genuine, its very own sun, warming everything in its path.

"Marvelous? What does that mean?" Charlotte inquired.

Lorna took the girl's hand. "It means something is good, extraordinarily wonderful. Do you like words? I have a whole book, called a dictionary, full of them—with a definition for each one. You can learn a new word every day." Jesse's heart constricted as Charlotte's face glowed at the prospect.

Jack Carrington laughed appreciatively. The man had a laugh for everything. "Your girl's a bright one, Kittredge. Looks like we got a teacher here for her just in time." Carrington slanted a look Adam's direction, and Jesse went immediately on alert. "What of you, Adam? Are you going to go to the school like your sister? Or are you eyeing that spot on your Pa's crew?" He clapped a manly hand on Adam's shoulder. "I can tell that you're going to be tall and big like your Pa, too. I'd be proud to have such a strapping miner. You'll be drawing a man's wage sooner rather than later with that build. You're strong—that's good. A miner has to be."

The man was playing to Adam's pride in the most dangerous way possible. Jesse wanted to punch that silky smile right off Carrington's face. *Stay away from my son.* "We've decided Adam should attend school for another year," Jesse put in swiftly.

"Nothing wrong with that. Learning is good for a

man," Carrington said equably. He made a small bow in Miss Alderly's direction. "It was a pleasure to meet you. School starts in a few days. Please let me know if there's anything you need once you take stock of your pupils. Do you have plans for Sunday dinner? If not, might I offer an invitation to dine with us at the Hill? It's our home, just a little ways out of town. The reverend will be there and there's always room for one more at the table. I could drive you up and back."

"She has plans to dine with us," Jesse put insuddenly, his gaze holding Carrington's with a private challenge. If Miss Alderly wanted Carrington's attention, she at least deserved to be warned first. Then she could decide for herself. He turned to Miss Alderly. "Of course, you are welcome to postpone our supper if you'd prefer to dine at the Hill." Where there would be china and crystal and four courses.

Miss Alderly's gaze flashed between the two men before settling on his. "Of course not. We've already made plans and I am looking forward to them." She turned to Carrington with a soft smile. "Thank you, but I must decline for now. I do indeed have plans."

Jesse felt momentary relief pass through him before it was followed with another less favorable feeling: self-doubt. Why in the world had he done that? He was no more interested in having Miss Alderly to dinner tonight than he had been last night, and he even had less to serve: a half loaf of bread and whatever fish he could catch at the river. He grimaced. He knew what Evie would say to that: Jesus had fed far more than four with less. But Jesse just didn't have that kind of faith anymore.

Chapter Six

Lorna knew why he'd done it. Kittredge hadn't wanted her dining with Jack Carrington. What she didn't know was the reason for it. Perhaps it was nothing more than an attempt to win some kind of male posturing competition. She could tell that Kittredge had not liked the proprietary air with which Carrington had placed a hand on Adam's shoulder. Nor had Kittredge liked the way Carrington had attempted to claim ownership of Kittredge himself. *One of my best men.* As if Kittredge were something or someone to be owned.

Such a gesture might flatter a lesser man. But Lorna could have told Jack that it would only alienate Kittredge with his fierce independence. She already could tell that Jesse Kittredge was a proud man. One only had to be in his presence a short time to know that. His was a quiet pride, a pride that did not need to be advertised or proclaimed. *Unlike Jack Carrington's,* came the un-looked-for comparison.

It was Kittredge's quiet pride that propelled Lorna to fire up the cookstove and bake biscuits, despite how uncomfortably hot it made her tiny cottage on the warm afternoon. She could *not* show up empty-handed to the Sunday supper table even if the invitation was unplanned. On principle, it was bad manners. She'd been raised better than that. Concord hospitality demanded it. There was a practical reason, too. The offer to dine had been a spontaneous one. Both she and Kittredge knew the invitation had been invented on the spot. Which meant there would have been no time for Kittredge to plan what to serve.

She had gotten the sense from the previous evening's awkward dinner discussion that perhaps food was not a ready commodity at the Kittredge household, or at any household in the town, based on what she'd seen at church. Guests at the supper table were luxuries that only families like the Carringtons could afford. Charlotte's sweet invitation the night before had been a reflection of the girl's kind heart rather than an indication that the family had any surplus to spare. And she highly doubted the Kittredge pantry had suddenly restocked itself overnight. Biscuits were a must on all accounts.

At half past five, Adam knocked on the door, come to collect her for the short walk three cottages down. She'd have to disabuse Mr. Kittredge of the notion she couldn't take herself anywhere—but that could wait for now. She wouldn't vent any of her indignation on the boy, not when he was only obeying his pa.

"Something smells good." Adam sniffed appreciably as he stood politely on the threshold while she wrapped the biscuits in a white linen cloth and put them in her market basket.

She held out a spare biscuit to him and smiled. "Would

you like one before supper? I'd say you'd spoil your meal but I know better. I have three younger brothers, one of them your age, and nothing spoils their appetites."

"May I?" he took the biscuit gingerly as if it were a gold nugget. "Perhaps I shouldn't. It wouldn't be fair to Lotte. She wanted to come but she had to finish making dinner."

"There's plenty," she assured him. "I baked two dozen. Charlotte can have an extra one with her meal if she likes, and if it makes you feel less guilty." She reached for her hat and Adam insisted on taking the basket for her. The boy had good manners and a kind nature, just like his sister. From their father or their mother? She wondered. Jesse Kittredge struck her as a strict parent, and yet she did not forget how he'd smiled at them yesterday, his whole grim face lighting up as if they were the sum of his world.

The Kittredge cottage was much like her own, like *all* the houses in the row: built with the primary goal of speed instead of attention to detail. The only difference between hers and theirs was that theirs was home to three people instead of one, a fact instantly demonstrated by the bed that stood against one wall with a glimpse of the trundle underneath that Lorna imagined was pulled out every night. Clearly, this was where the children slept.

On the opposite wall was a cookstove, and a table with two benches took up the center of the room. Like her cottage, a pair of curtains closed off the small room beyond. With a family occupying the cottage, those curtains offered the merest slice of privacy.

"You're here!" Charlotte turned from the stove, wiping her hand on an apron like a little mother. In a way, that's what she was, Lorna realized. At Charlotte's age, Lorna had only been playing at keeping house, following her mother around and learning to bake alongside Cook because it was fun, *not* because the household depended on her to make anything edible.

Mrs. Elliott had warned her it would be like this in the mining towns. Children were little adults in this gold rush world as families struggled to make ends meet while they waited to strike it rich. However, seeing it firsthand was far more impactful than hearing about it.

It did make Lorna appreciate the cottage that much more. Yes, it was small and plain, but the floor was swept and the table was set. Guilt pricked at her. Had Lotte given up what would have been an afternoon of freedom to take on the extra chore of preparing the house for a guest? "I am happy to be here, Charlotte."

The girl smiled almost shyly. "We are happy to have you. We're neighbors. And because we're neighbors, you can call me Lotte. All my friends do, and that's what we are. We are friends."

The gestured touched Lorna unexpectedly. She swallowed once and then twice to gain her composure. "Thank you, *Lotte*. That is too kind. I hope it wasn't too much work to have me as a guest? I don't need anything fancy. I am just glad to be invited." Lorna held out the basket to the girl. "I've brought biscuits for dinner if they suit or if you'd rather, they'll keep for breakfast."

Jesse Kittredge chose that moment to enter the cottage from a back door. His hair was damp at its long blond ends and the shoulders of his shirt bore evidence that he'd been washing up. At a pump perhaps? "Biscuits were unnecessary, Miss Alderly. There's plenty of food." His eyes met hers, a silent duel ensuing. She answered that stubborn quiet pride of his with a raise of her brows and serene smile.

"I did not mean to imply any insult to your table, Mr. Kittredge. It's a hostess gift, nothing more."

"Hostess gift." Charlotte tested the words out with interest. "What is that?"

"It's a way for someone to express gratitude to one's hosts for having them over. Usually one brings a little something to add to the meal or something that the host could choose to keep until later, like bread or biscuits, pie or even a bouquet of flowers. Nothing fancy, just something simple and heartfelt to show appreciation. That's all." She said the last with a pointed glance at Kittredge.

"I think hostess gifts sound wonderful." Charlotte sighed and sniffed at the basket. "And I think we should eat these at once. I'll get a plate for them."

Minutes later, the biscuits sat in pride of place in the center of the table, stacked on a pewter plate next to a pitcher of milk and a platter of fried river trout. Lorna was informed that the trout had been caught courtesy of Adam and Mr. Kittredge and cooked by CharlotteLorna took a place on the bench beside Lotte. Adam and Mr. Kittredge sat across from them on the other. They bowed their heads and Charlotte offered a short blessing. Mr. Kittredge's gaze met hers as if daring her to comment on his table . "No sense letting the food get cold," he commented, passing her the platter of fish.

"Miss Alderly has three brothers," Adam said, clearly impressed with that fact, as everyone filled their plates.

"You have a large family, then?" Mr. Kittredge asked.

"I suppose so if a family of six is large." Lorna split her biscuit open. "My brother Andrew is sixteen, Gregory is twelve and Georgie is nine." She smiled. Just saying their names conjured a feeling of happiness, as if thinking of them brought them a little closer. She'd been surprised to find how much she missed them, nuisances that they were.

"You don't have any sisters?" Lotte asked.

"No, only brothers. But they're good brothers and I miss them more than I thought I would," Lorna confided. "Everywhere I look I see something that I want to tell them about. These mountains would astonish them. They'd want to hike and climb and fish in the rivers. This would be glorious country to them."

"Are there no mountains in Massachusetts?" Adam asked, interested.

"There are," she told him, "but if you were to see them, compared to what you're used to, you might think they're more like hills. Everything is bigger here." Everyone laughed—even Mr. Kittredge *almost* laughed. The meal evolved into a spirited conversation of questions about her family, about her home, about Massachusetts and how far away it was. The children were avid listeners and Lorna asked her questions, too, wanting to learn as much as she could about Woods River. They stayed at the table long after the last biscuit was gone, sharing tales and, best of all, laughter.

The room darkened until a lamp became necessary. Kittredge rose to fetch one, but Lorna worried that a lamp in the summer was a luxury most families probably didn't employ with the long daylight hours. "Don't bring out a lamp for my sake. I should be going, anyway." She rose, too, suddenly remembering it would be Monday tomorrow. A workday. No doubt, Kittredge would need to be up early. She'd likely overstayed her welcome. "Thank you for a lovely evening, everyone."

"I'll walk you back," Kittredge said with long-suffering gruffness.

"I can manage," Lorna protested.

"No, I won't hear of it. I will walk you back." Kittredge's tone brooked no debate as he handed her the empty market basket. She was learning quickly that no one argued with Jesse Kittredge—at least, not successfully. A more stubborn man she had yet to meet, even though she suspected he was trying to be on his best behavior. If this was his best, she could scarcely imagine him at his most, ah, entrenched. There would be no shaking him then. He was immoveable as the mountains of Woods River and as silent. It was almost astonishing that she could have shared such a pleasant evening with such an intractable man. She ascribed it to his lovely children. *They*, at least, were a delight.

"It's so quiet, and peaceful." Miss Alderly stopped in the middle of the street and lifted her face to the purple sky above the mountaintops, her eyes closed, a smile curving on her lips as she inhaled deeply, contentment etched in her expression. Naivete was etched there, too, Jesse thought. Her contentment was displaced. There was no peace here. He knew that better than most.

"*This* end of town is quiet at night. But the main street will be noisy until dawn," Jesse pointed out. "The dance halls, saloons and other entertainments will run all night with no regard for the Sabbath." Jesse didn't hold with such activity but that was how life was. In these new mining towns that were booming one day and bust the next, everything seemed to happen faster, harder, and with greater intensity. The miners indulged in extreme pleasure to offset extreme pain—the pain of loneliness, of loss and disappointment that came in so many different forms. That pleasure was a pathway to vice, but there were few men who would hesitate to indulge themselves, just for the sake of morality. Who wouldn't choose to feel good if only for a short time instead of bearing pain day in and day out with no relief in sight?

He'd nearly succumbed to such temptation when Evie had died. If it hadn't been for the children he likely would have. Most of these men didn't have the anchor of a family to pull them back from the brink.

She opened her eyes and favored him with a smile. "Well, it is beautiful here, all the same. God's country to be sure."

"Hmph," he grimaced at the comment. "We'll see what you think halfway through the winter. It doesn't seem very godly then." Or beautiful, either, when the snows were smudged with mud and the residue of mining. It was quite ugly, in fact, and it did ugly things to people who didn't have enough to eat.

She faced him then, hands on hips, impatience flaring in her eyes. "Are you always so glum, Mr. Kittredge? Do you take pleasure in looking at the worst, grimmest side of every situation? Or is it simply that you enjoy contradicting everything anyone says?" She speared him with that gaze, contemplation rolling through it as she reached a conclusion. "Is that why you invited me to dinner? You wanted the pleasure of contradicting Mr. Carrington?" Her gaze flickered with challenge and his hackles rose.

"I am not glum, I am realistic—and I do *not* do that." He took the bait, seeing the trap too late.

"Really? You just did. *Again.* I'm beginning to believe it's a compulsion for you. I think I could say the sky was blue and you'd disagree."

"I would if it wasn't true." Jesse stood his ground, arms crossing over his chest automatically. This woman got under his skin like a sliver beneath a thumbnail—an unlooked-for inconvenience that caused enormous aggravation despite its small size. "I am not going to agree with someone just for the sake of not disagreeing. Sometimes people are just flat-out wrong." Like Miss Alderly. She was in the wrong place at the wrong time. She had no business here. This kind of place would ruin a person like her and some part of him did not want to see that happen.

"I suspect people are wrong quite often around you," she retorted. Jesse gave a begrudging chuckle. No one would call Miss Alderly short on fire.

"If you must know, I invited you to dinner because Carrington is a man to be warned about. One does not turn him loose on unsuspecting strangers without giving them a choice first."

"I'll have to dine with him eventually since he's apparently part of the welcoming committee, as it were." She cocked her head. "What exactly is Mr. Carrington's great failing in your opinion?"

Jesse thought for a moment, choosing his words carefully. A woman this naive would look for the kindest explanation for everything. If he said Carrington was greedy, she'd likely just say that he was being a good businessman. If he said that Carrington was prideful and boasting, she'd point out that he had a right to be proud of what he'd done. What could he say that would get through to her?

"He's ambitious, Miss Alderly. He doesn't let anything stand in his way—including good judgment—when he wants something." She considered his response for a moment. She looked as if she was about to ask another question but he shook his head. He didn't want to talk about Jack Carrington. One did not bad-mouth one's boss and "live" to tell about it. Word always got back somehow. He didn't countenance gossip any more than he countenanced the Main Street entertainments operating on the Sabbath. He'd given her his warning, and that was the most he could do. He hoped that she would take heed—but he didn't have much faith that she would.

"That's all I'll say on the matter, Miss Alderly." Although there was plenty he *could* say. Carrington ran the mine and the town, he controlled everything from prices to wages, who worked and who didn't. That control was not always ethically exercised, in Jesse's opinion. Carrington risked men's lives as if they were chips at a card table. "It's better to let a man's own actions speak for him than another man's words."

"Is that so? Would you apply that to a woman, as well?" she asked as they began to walk again.

"What do you mean?" The question caught him off guard. He'd been expecting her to try and pry more information out of him about Carrington. Women liked hearing about Carrington.

She shot him a quick glance, a "beware" smile twitching briefly at her lips, and he braced himself for whatever he'd walked himself into. "I mean, I want a fair chance, too. You say that a man gets to prove himself with his actions instead of having people decide the limits of his capabilities. Shouldn't a woman have the same opportunity? I want that chance, Mr. Kittredge. From you."

The last startled him. "From me?"

"You don't like me and I think that's rather unfair. You don't know me well enough to dislike me." She silenced him with a smile. "Come now, Mr. Kittredge. Your disapproval has been evident since Sonoma."

True. Yet he hadn't expected to be called out for it. Miss Alderly had a boldness all her own that would be refreshing if it wasn't aimed at him. This was not the boldness of the girls who worked the dance halls and such. This was a boldness born of an innate self-confidence. "It's not that I don't like you, Miss Alderly." Far from it. There was much that he was sure he would like about her in a different place and if he were a different man. "It's that you don't belong here. That should be as plain to you as the moon in the sky. I can't help but wonder why you *are* here at all? Your father is a headmaster, your mother a poet. You have a family that cares and provides for you. Back in Massachusetts, you had every comfort. Why would you leave all that for this?" They'd reached the gate of her cottage and he gestured to the weathered exterior of the shabby building. "You had everything."

"I didn't have one thing," she argued. Now who was being the contradictory one, Jesse thought, but wisely held his peace about pointing it out. "I didn't have a purpose. There's purpose here. There's work to do and I intend to do it. Starting tomorrow." Her reply was resolute.

"What are you doing tomorrow?" Jesse asked, experiencing a fleeting sense of alarm. He had to work tomorrow. He couldn't play nursemaid and follow her around.

"I am going to visit families at the encampment we passed entering town and invite them to send their children to school. It will be a good chance to introduce myself to those who couldn't come to church." Couldn't come? More like *didn't* come, by choice. Not everyone in Woods River was God-fearing. He certainly wasn't, not anymore. He went for the children's sake, not for his own. Jesse didn't correct her assumption. There were other battles to fight and he suspected one had to pick them carefully with Miss Alderly.

"How do you plan on doing that?" He leaned on the gate.

"I'll walk. I have two perfectly good feet and it will be a chance to see the town."

"Hmph." He made a sound of disagreement for the sake of voicing his disapproval but said nothing. "I'll send Adam over at nine tomorrow morning. He can go with you. We can't have anyone mistaking your purpose in town." It was the nicest way he could put it. One look at her in her fancy dresses and some men would draw the wrong conclusions. Decent women in town didn't have fancy clothes except for Mrs. Carrington. "Fancy" generally indicated "loose."

For a moment he thought she'd protest. Then she nodded. "I appreciate all you've done with fixing the cottage and picking me up. You do not need to put yourself out for me. I do hope we can be friends, though. While I was able to meet many people at church, it still feels like you're the only person I know in town. I haven't spent more than a moment or two with anyone else."

"It's my job to do those things," he corrected gruffly. "Friendship is not required." The last thing he needed was to be friends. "The other women will come around soon, inviting you to their circles and such." Hopefully, she wouldn't need him so much in a week or so.

"And warning me about Mr. Carrington? Is that part of the job, too?" She fired a parting salvo with a smile. She did that a lot—smiling to soften the blow of her words. But then, she had a very pretty smile, so it was more effective than it had any right to be. "Tell Lotte again how much I enjoyed the dinner."

Jesse waited until she was safely inside before he shut the gate and walked himself home, her comment rattling about his mind. Women and men being friends was dangerous, ambiguous ground. Not just for them, but because of what those around them were likely to think. Such a friendship was never viewed as a neutral association, and he was not in the market for something more. He never would be again. Evie had been his one love. A man didn't get two.

Chapter Seven

The days before the school year began passed in a whirlwind of activity for Lorna. Some of that activity was self-appointed, like setting up her classroom and visiting with families at the encampment. Those visits had gone well and Lorna was anticipating a number of those children showing up. Some of that activity, though, was driven by external forces, such as meeting with the town council that also acted as the school board.

All the members were men, Lorna noted, a number that included Jack Carrington and his father, Hamish. The rest of the board consisted of the reverend, who attended all the meetings but did not vote out of respect for the separation of church and state, he said; the town mayor, Bill North; the town banker, Elmer Cleveland; and three businessmen who owned various establishments in town. John Putnam of Putnam's Dry Goods, Joseph Knight who ran the Red Slipper Saloon and Parker Hudson, proprietor of the Golden Nugget dance hall. All in all, it was a very distinguished group, but there were no miners among them.

The council had been impressed with her proposed curriculum and had encouragingly nodded their heads when she explained her plans to them. The women had come around, too, as Mr. Kittredge had predicted. The mayor's wife, the banker's wife, the reverend's wife and the wives of the shopkeepers extended an immediate invitation for her to join the Ladies Auxiliary, which met on Saturday mornings at the church.

It was on these high notes of approval and acceptance that Lorna approached the first day of school. She dressed circumspectly and modestly in a plain gown of dark blue with just a hint of white lace at the throat for trim, her blond hair pulled back into a snood at the nape of her neck, her only ornamentation a small watch pinned to her bodice. "Dear Lord, guide my instruction. Give me the wisdom to be what these children need," she prayed as she gave her appearance a final glance in the small mirror, a tremor of excitement rippling through her. Today, she'd finally realize her dream of being a fully independent teacher, presiding over her own school.

The Kittredge children collected her early so she'd have time for any last-minute preparations. She could hear them playing outside in the churchyard as she picked up a piece of chalk and wrote Wednesday, September Third, in precise letters on the board. At ten minutes until nine, she went outside to ring the bell for the first time, announcing that school was about to begin.

Though she'd heard the sounds of other children arriving as she'd gone through her preparations, the churchyard was far less populated than she'd anticipated. Well, there was still time, she encouraged herself. The bell was only the ten-minute warning. But when she rang the bell the final time, there were still only a handful of the expected students.

Aside from Malcolm Kinney and the Kittredges, all the others had parents on the school board: Tommy and Alfie North, the mayor's children; Eliza Cleveland, the banker's daughter; Katie Putnam, whose father ran the dry goods store; and Joshua McClain, the reverend's son. Everyone ranged in ages from seven to Adam's twelve. Just eight students when she'd counted on at least fifteen of the possible twenty-fiveShe'd been so sure they'd all come. Their mothers had sounded enthusiastic when she'd visited the encampment.

"Miss Alderly, is something wrong?" Adam inquired as they all took a seat on the benches surrounding one of the long tables.

"Not at all." Lorna found a smile. "I am so pleased to meet all of you. We will spend today getting to know each other. I am interested in figuring out where each of you are in your learning. There is no wrong place to be, but I want to be sure I create lessons that are useful to you. I thought we'd begin with the alphabet and move into reading." Lorna passed new primers to each of the students. Her first day of teaching was underway.

That day went well. They moved from the alphabet to reading before lunch, and then dealt with math and geography in the afternoon. At the end of the day, Lorna spread a map of the United States on the long table and anchored it with two big rocks. "One way we can get to know each other is to know where we all come from." California was full of first-generation settlers. Few people in the mining camps and towns had actually been born here. Everyone had come from somewhere else.

Lorna took a small pebble out of a jar and passed the jar around, encouraging the others to do the same. "I'll start," she offered as a way to model the activity. "I am from Massachusetts in the northeast. My family lives in a little town just here. That's where I was before I came to Woods River." She put her pebble down near Boston. "Who would like to be next?" Eliza Cleveland put her pebble down in St. Louis. The North boys put pebbles down in the newly organized Minnesota Territory. The Kittredges were the last to put down their pebbles, but they hesitated, looking down at the map in confusion.

"Where are the Appalachian Mountains?" Charlotte asked, her brow furrowed as she studied the map. "I don't see them, but we're from there."

Lorna nodded patiently. "It depends. The Appalachians cover quite a lot of ground, you see. They run from southern New York, here—" she gestured to the place on the map "—to northern Georgia, here. And in doing so, they run through parts of several states." She pointed them out. "Do you know which state you came from?"

"We're from western Virginia, right here on the Kentucky border," Adam said quietly, placing his pebble.

"And where are we now?" Lorna asked. "Can anyone find where California is on the map?"

Katie Putnam pointed to the state right away, picking out the letters. She'd proven herself to be a strong reader earlier and those skills served her well with the map. "Very good, Katie," Lorna praised. "Now, who can tell me where in California we are? This is a big state." She looked about the table.

"The north," Tommy North put in jokingly, and everyone laughed. His brother, Alfie, punched him in the arm. The day was getting late, and the students were getting fidgety. Lorna moved to wrap up the lesson.

"That's right. We're right here, east of San Francisco." She showed them.

"But our town's name isn't anywhere on the map," Eliza Cleveland commented with a pout.

"It can be. Would you like to put us on the map before we go?" Lorna handed her a pencil. Eliza had excellent penmanship, although her spelling needed a little work. "We can all help spell it. Alfie, you start. What's the first letter?"

With Woods River successfully added to the map, Lorna dismissed class. She saw her students out the door and turned back to discover Charlotte still at the table studying the map. "We came a long way, all of us," Charlotte said, looking up at her. "How far is Woods River from the Appalachian Mountains?"

"About twenty-five hundred miles." Lorna came to stand beside her and look at the map. "You're very brave to have come so far."

Charlotte considered Lorna's pebble in Massachusetts. "You're brave, too. We've both come a long way, but you came all alone." She paused before asking, "What gave you the courage to come so far?"

Lorna thought for a moment. "Prayer. When I told my parents I wanted to come here, my mother told me to pray about it, to ask God to help me find the right direction, to show me His plan for my life. They prayed, too, for wisdom to guide my decision and to abide by whatever decision I made."

Charlotte nodded. "My ma prayed a lot, too. So did Pa—back then, anyway. They prayed about coming here. But he doesn't pray anymore. I think it would make her sad to know that." Ah, so her mother had made the journey West. Had she died on the journey then or after they'd arrived? Lorna was curious but didn't want to pry.

"Did you come by wagon or by ship?" She gently shifted the conversation to something she hoped was more neutral.

"We came by wagon. I don't remember too much since I was so young," Charlotte said in a very adult, matter-of-fact tone. Lorna suppressed a smile, since Charlotte was in earnest about thinking she was now grown-up. "I do remember the stars, though. At night when the wagons were circled, I'd lay on my blanket and stare up into the sky. There were so many stars, fistfuls of them, and they were so close it was like I could pick them out of the sky. Ma would lay next to me and tell me stories until I fell asleep. It was the best part of the day." Charlotte gave a sad smile. "I miss her."

"I'm sorry, honey. She sounds like a wonderful mother." Lorna's heart twisted at the girl's simple words. Sorry that she'd lost her mother, sorry that in losing her, Charlotte had had to grow up much too soon. It no longer seemed a laughing matter that Charlotte thought she was "old" compared to the girl who'd crossed the plains. That six-year-old used to have a childhood of sorts, a mother who told her stories. By the time she turned eight years old, she had needed to step into that role, to cook and to clean for the family. How soon had that happened? At what point had she lost her mother and her childhood?

"Are you coming, Lotte?" Adam poked his head into the room.

"She was just helping me clean up," Lorna explained. "Do you have time to come to the store with me or do you need to get home?"

Adam shrugged, careful not to betray any excitement a visit to the dry goods store might evoke. "Sure, we can go."

And that was how Jack Carrington found her at the store, two children in tow, a short while later. "Well, if it isn't my scholars," Carrington boomed. "How was the first day of school?"

"Wonderful!" Lotte supplied. "We had a map of the country and we all put pebbles on it to show where we'd come from." The enthusiasm touched Lorna. The activity had clearly been a good one if that was the first thing Lotte wanted to talk about.

"And you, Adam? How was your day?" Carrington smiled in the boy's direction, but Lorna felt that the inquiry was not entirely sincere. She remembered the tension from that first Sunday in the churchyard when the mine owner had seemed to be goading the boy into taking a job rather than going to school. Was Carrington fishing for something or trying to egg the boy on? Or was she reading too much into it?

"School was fine, sir," Adam replied politely if succinctly.

Carrington chuckled. "You're as tight-lipped as your father, son. No unnecessary conversation from you Kittredge men. That's fine. No harm in it. I'm glad you enjoyed it." Was he, though? Lorna felt as if his words were meant to convey just the opposite. "Might I have a word with Miss Alderly, children?" He had a hand at her elbow, leading her away to a quiet corner of the store before she could say anything against the idea. Not wanting to cause a fuss, she complied.

"Is everything alright, Mr. Carrington?" She was instantly concerned.

His eyes twinkled mischievously. "No, it most certainly is not. You've been here almost two weeks and you haven't had supper with me yet."

"I've been busy getting things ready for school." Kittredge's warning buzzed through her head. "Besides, I am not sure it would be seemly for me to dine with you. Schoolteachers are often held to a high standard of conduct." Back East, female schoolteachers were not permitted to fraternize with men while they held a post. Here, the council had laid down no such strictures when they informed her of her duties, but perhaps they didn't know better. Still, Lorna would not abuse such freedoms.

He gave her a teasing look. "I understand that is indeed the case in many places. But this is a mining town in the middle of nowhere. Those old-fashioned rules of etiquette hardly apply here. If anyone made a fuss, I'd tell them we were meeting to discuss schoolboard business, and it wouldn't be a lie. I'm sure we could find something to discuss about the school. How about tomorrow night, early, at five, so I can have you home at a decent hour. I'll have a table reserved for us at the Golden Nugget. We'll have dinner and see the show."

"We'd eat out?" The idea was both tempting and terrifying. She'd thought it would be dinner at the Carrington house with his parents present. But he must be at least thirty, and likely used to moving about on his own as he pleased. No doubt he'd laugh at the idea that he required a chaperone. Besides, in a public setting, it wasn't as if they'd be truly alone.

"Of course." His eyes were twinkling again. "We might be a mining town, but we have a bit of dash. I'll show you. Until tomorrow, Miss Alderly."

He tipped his hat and moved off, leaving her misgivings fluttering aside the butterflies of excitement in her stomach. She was looking forward to going out, but was it the right thing to do?

Chapter Eight

Whatever misgivings Lorna had about dining with Jack Carrington quickly evaporated in the wake of his excessively good manners and her own enthusiasm about being out. This was an entirely new experience for her and in an entirely new place. Back home, she'd only eaten in a restaurant a few times and then only with a large group, usually in Boston when the Todds and Alderlys would go up together for some shopping. Never before had she been out for an evening with a man on her own. It felt extraordinarily sophisticated and grown-up.

Tonight, they'd both dressed the part. Jack was dressed to great effect in a dark suit with a gray silk waistcoat embroidered with maroon leaves and vines, and a neck cloth held in place by a ruby stickpin. She'd chosen one of the fancy dresses she'd brought with her: a cerulean-blue taffeta gown with an off-the-shoulder neckline that she'd worn once to the theater in Boston. She'd worn her grandmother's pearls, too—a gift from her parents on her eighteenth birthday.

"You look splendid." Carrington complimented her, his voice low and close at her ear in order to be heard above the noise as he escorted her upstairs to their box at the Golden Nugget, his hand a light, guiding pressure at her back. "Here it is, the best seat in the house, for the prettiest girl here tonight."

The "box" was more of a niche. It was draped with red velvet curtains trimmed in heavy gold fringe that would put Mrs. Ellsbridge's portieres to shame. The niche held two chairs and a round table that overlooked the stage. At the center of the table was a chimneyed lamp giving off a soft glow that made the space seem at once private and public. Here, they might be seen but not heard.

He held her chair for her as she sat and settled her skirts. Across the auditorium, Lorna could see other couples taking their places in the boxes and it relaxed her. Other people were having a night out, as well. Surely that meant that nothing could be so wrong with this. The last of her nerves fled. A waiter came, bringing a first course of grapes, bread and cheese on a wooden board. "What would you like to drink, Mr. Carrington?"

Jack Carrington glanced in her direction with a conspirator's smile. "Shall we have champagne to celebrate tonight?"

"Oh, no, I don't drink alcohol." Lorna shook her head. "Water or cider will do just fine."

He furrowed his brow in a playful cajole. "Not even a glass on special occasions? Surely, there's some flexibility with your rules."

"Not even on special occasions," Lorna insisted firmly

with a smile before she turned directly to the waiter. "Cider please."

"For me, as well." Carrington gave her a nod. "We will have two prime rib dinners, unless you'd prefer something else?" he asked her. "Prime rib is the specialty here."

"Prime rib sounds wonderful." Lorna favored him with another smile, appreciating how attentive he was to her preferences. He'd picked up right away on her desire to want to make her own decisions.

The waiter left and they turned their attentions to the hors d'oeuvres. Lorna picked up the conversation. "I think you have me at a disadvantage, Mr. Carrington. You've had the benefit of reading my profile and the letter from Mrs. Elliott, but I know nothing of you. Tell me, what brought you to Woods River and how long have you been here?"

He chuckled. "First, call me Jack. Mr. Carrington is my father. It's much too formal for me. You'll find that we don't see the need to stand on ceremony overmuch out here. Second, as to how long we've been here, you might say the Carringtons are the founders of Woods River. We bought the land and came out here to survey it. Once we were assured of the viability of the mine, we began bringing in miners. We sponsored a wagon train and sent an agent back East to recruit for us. That's how we got the Kittredges."

Jack paused as the waiter brought their ciders. He took a swallow before continuing. "I want to do more than mining, though. I want to build something larger— something that will outlast me. I don't just want a boom-town here that will bust and be forgotten in another ten years. I want something that will endure. We're just starting to put down that first layer, bringing in basic services like Cleveland's bank, the dry goods, the church and school. These are immediate services a community needs to anchor itself. Once people feel they can really invest in this town—start families, put down roots—we can work on a second, less essential layer, perhaps more specialized stores and entertainments so that they'll spend their money here instead of taking it to Sonoma," he explained, his plans displaying the ambition Jesse had talked about.

Lorna listened intently, interested and intrigued. "How do you know the town will last, though? What happens if the gold runs out? A town needs income to survive."

Jack nodded, appreciating the question. "You're right, I don't *know* it will last. But I think it will. Right now the mine is producing well, and the potential for further development of the mine is high. Besides, I hope that as the town continues to grow, it will outgrow the dependence on the mine to sustain it. I just need the mine to fund the town long enough for us to diversify and bring in other income generating businesses. That way, when the mine does play out, we'll be able to let it go without feeling the loss." He leaned forward, warming to his subject, his eyes sparking. "For instance, I am in negotiations with a developer who wants to purchase some land here to build a resort spa, a place where people can come to heal and get away from the bad air and all the noise and mess of the rest of the world. With all the clean mountain air here, it's a perfect location."

"It's a long way for people to come," Lorna pointed

out, a little doubtful. "I love the idea but I don't see it truly catching on. There are such spas already back East, closer to home in the Adirondacks and the Catskills. Sick people are not likely to be able to spend months on a ship or suffer the rigors of wagon trains."

"Not today, you're right." Jack beamed and his enthusiasm was infectious. She liked that he didn't seem to be intimidated or angered by her questions. Some men disliked women asserting their own opinions.

"But the world will not always be as it is," Jack continued. "England is already awash in railroads, as is the East Coast. It won't be long before someone builds a railroad that connects both coasts. Just imagine that, Lorna!" he was so excited, she couldn't be upset about the use of her first name without asking her permission first. "Picture what it could do for travel time. What takes months now could be accomplished in a matter of days and in relative comfort." He touched a finger to his temple. "Mark my words, Lorna. It will happen in our lifetime."

"You are quite the visionary. I am impressed," she admitted. She had known ambitious men back in Massachusetts, but none of their dreams had been on so grand a scale. She supposed that was why he had come to California—there was so much room for big dreams out here. All the same, she worried that he was getting a little ahead of himself. "But still, how can you be sure of all this? You could lose everything if you're wrong."

More than that, others could lose everything they had, too. People like the Putnams would lose their store if something happened to Woods River, if the town went bust. She thought about Jesse Kittredge's words, that Jack Carrington's ambition risked the lives of others.

"That's why it's called speculation." Jack flashed her a smile as their prime rib dinners were set down before them, the smell of rich, hot meat filling their niche. "Everyone in boomtowns knows the risks." He arched a slim, dark brow as she cut into her meat. "Even you. You only think risk appalls you. But it doesn't, or you'd have remained in your safe, staid life back East. The risk excites you, it's why you're here. Same as myself." His eyes twinkled. "It's one of the things you and I have in common. We both want to build something. There's so much I want to do for this community. So many plans to help it grow and thrive."

Put that way, the ambition Jesse Kittredge had warned against didn't seem so sinful. Instead, it appeared almost virtuous. Surely there was nothing wrong in wanting to give back to the community by providing it with growth opportunities and a stability to outlast the gold in the mine. Of course, she wasn't sure what that would mean for the miners—but if the mine played out, they'd have to find something else, anyway, wouldn't they? If the town expanded into other trades, at least the families that had settled here would be able to stay and find other work, even if the mining opportunities came to an end.

"Is the prime rib to your liking?" Jack inquired.

"It's the best thing I've eaten in months," Lorna freely admitted.

"I'm glad you're enjoying it. Food, meals, the little things in life are meant to be enjoyed." He flashed her another of his smiles, clean and white and dashing. He certainly did not skimp on those smiles. "Life is hard out here and there's no denying it's rough, but we do have our little luxuries, and I think we've earned the right to enjoy them. We must take our pleasures where and when we can. How is school going?"

Lorna looked up from her potatoes, seeing an opportunity to air her concerns. "School is going well for those who attend. It is those who are not there that I am worried about. Only eight students have come, and I know there are more children in the area than that. I was anticipating twenty-five. The students who *do* come are primarily the shopkeepers' children." She explained how she'd visited the encampment and how positively the mothers had responded, which left her even more confused as to why the miners' children—with very few exceptions—hadn't come.

Jack furrowed his brow in sympathy. "Not everyone values education. It's like the old saying, you can lead a horse to water but you can't make it drink. These families see putting their sons to work in the mine as a means of increasing their incomes. And their daughters are often needed to help with the housework. They don't see any financial benefit to school."

She thought about Jasper Kinney's decision to work instead of attend school. "But surely, at twelve years old, boys should not be working. They should have a chance to attend school."

"Give it a month or so. Perhaps the younger kids will come when the weather changes and being indoors holds more appeal than running around outside all day." Jack gave a patient chuckle when she frowned. "I know you mean well, Lorna, but you mustn't take it to heart if the families decide not to send their children to you. They do have a choice. We can't make it for them. No one forced Jasper Kinney. He chose to go to work."

"Perhaps if his father's wages were increased he and other boys wouldn't feel the need to start so young," Lorna pressed. There were similar issues in Massachusetts, too—the constant debate over child labor laws and adequate wages to live on.

"Ah, dessert," Jack exclaimed as the waiter returned bearing slices of apple pie served with a healthy serving of cream. "My favorite." He beamed at Lorna. "Best crust in town." He gestured with his fork toward the stage. "The show is about to start." And with that, the discussion of wage equity was tabled.

The show was a delightful half hour hodgepodge of comedic skits and musical acts and even a juggler that made Lorna laugh. "You're pleased," Jack said when the show ended. "And perhaps a little bit surprised, I think." He gave one of his easy, warm chuckles. "Although I should be wounded that you thought I'd take you somewhere that would not be enjoyable for a lady of your standing. I hold you in high esteem and would never place you in a situation you might find uncomfortable." He held her chair for her as she rose. "I will tell you that if you had your doubts about the appropriateness of the entertainment, you're not quite wrong. The Golden Nugget's dancing girls will be back on stage in an hour. Hudson runs a clean show during the dinner hours, though, so businessmen can take their wives out for an evening."

He guided her downstairs and out into the street, where the nightlife had indeed picked up. Despite being an evening in the middle of the workweek, the street was crowded with miners. It was a reminder that the population of Woods River was still predominantly male, and single males at that. She was glad for Jack's firm arm to hold on to as they navigated the street, making their way to the quieter end where the church steeple rose into the sunset. She'd not seen Woods River's entertainment district up close at night. She understood better now why Jesse Kittredge had been adamant she not be out unescorted.

"You need more women in town," she told Jack as they reached the church. "Women will settle down the rowdy element. Families will follow and that is what will help Woods River become a more permanent fixture people will invest in." That was Grace Elliott's belief, anyway. Domestic feminism would tame California.

Jack seemed to give the idea some thought. "I've been thinking the same. Perhaps I should send a second wagon train, this time for brides." He smiled at her. "Quality women like you, though. Intelligent women who want to make a difference." He paused suddenly, patting his coat pocket. "I almost forgot. I have letters for you." He pulled out a slim packet tied with twine as they turned toward her cottage.

"Two of them!" Lorna turned the packet over, looking at the handwriting: the letters were from her mother and Theo. "Why, it's almost like Christmas to have mail."

She was still looking at them when Jack gave a grunt. "Looks like you have company." She followed his gaze to her cottage, where Jesse Kittredge leaned against her gate, his battered hat pulled down over his eyes.

A sense of dread swept through her like the time her mother had caught her taking an extra slice of cake before dinner. *I've done nothing wrong,* she reminded herself. She'd only gone to dinner in plain sight of others with a perfectly respectable man who held a high standing in town. She hadn't been sneaking off or consorting with anyone inappropriate. If he didn't like it, that was his problem, not hers.

Yet, she couldn't shake the feeling that she'd somehow disappointed him and in doing so, she'd disappointed herself. What had been an exciting evening now became a guilty pleasure.

"I hope Kittredge hasn't been making a nuisance of himself," Jack murmured. "I can have a word with him if he has."

"No, of course not," she was quick to answer. Jack was Mr. Kittredge's boss. She didn't want to be the cause of any trouble there—or at least any more trouble than there already was between the two men. She did not understand the reasons for it, but it was clear that the tensions between the two ran deep.

"Well, just be careful. I can see you have a kind heart and a soft spot for children. Kittredge's children are charming, and I can already see that you like them. I wouldn't want Kittredge to use that against you. No doubt, he's looking for help with them." Jack gave a sigh. "I feel for the man, I do, his wife dying like that, but he's a hard man. Not easy to like, although he knows mining with the best of them."

They approached the gate and Jack raised his voice. "Good evening, Kittredge. What brings you out?"

Jesse pushed off the gate in a fluid movement, standing at his full height. "Just making sure Miss Alderly gets home safely and at a decent hour." He had an inch or two on Jack, Lorna noted.

"And she has, as you can see." Jack smiled but his usual bonhomie did not accompany it. Behind the shining teeth, she could see that his jaw was tense. "I was unaware Miss Alderly had a keeper."

"She shouldn't need one," Jesse replied. "Unfortunately, not everyone demonstrates good sense. You should know better, Carrington, than to take her out and on a school night, too. It's inconsiderate of her time and her reputation." Jesse's tone stopped just short of a snarl. "What do you think people will say about tonight?" Lorna wondered how many men in town dared to talk to Jack Carrington that way. But she supposed that not every man in town was the best ore finder this side of San Francisco.

Jack gave a patient, condescending smile. "They'll say I was being polite, giving our newest citizen the welcome she deserves and showing off the town besides."

The two men glared at each other. Lorna fought the urge to intervene. She knew that to interfere would mean taking sides, something she was loath to do. She hoped Jack was right and there'd be no aspersions cast on her for the outing tonight. But she did not want to set herself against Jesse. His actions might be heavy-handed, but it was clear to her that his motives came from a place of genuine concern.

What she could do, though, was separate the two men, since neither of them showed any inclination of being the first to leave her gate. "Mr. Carrington, thank you for a lovely evening of good food and good company. I can take it from here. I have a few things to discuss with Mr. Kittredge about the cottage," she improvised sweetly.

Jack made her a small bow, a knowing smile on his lips that said he was perfectly aware of what she was up to, but that he was gentleman enough to let her have her way…at a cost. "Sunday dinner, then, Lorna. We must have you up to the Hill." He named the price of his dismissal.

"Until Sunday. I will look forward to it." She sent him off down the street with a smile. But he turned back after a few steps.

"Kittredge, I'll want to see you tomorrow morning, early. We need to discuss the proposal for the new shaft. Come a half hour before the shift starts and don't be late." Lorna's heart sank. She'd not meant for Jesse to pay, too.

Chapter Nine

How devious that man was! Jesse gave a short nod to acknowledge the summons. The man was exacting his piece of hide in retribution for him having shown up here and interrupted his evening with the lady who had, apparently, caught his attention. Carrington had extracted a price from Miss Alderly, as well…or maybe not.

"*Will* you look forward to it? Sunday at the Hill?" he asked as soon as Carrington had turned the corner and was out of sight. It did occur to him that she might not mind going up to the Hill. She and Carrington had looked cozy coming down the street this evening, her arm tucked through his. They'd been talking in earnest, and then he'd given her something that had lit her entire face up. More than that, they looked as if they belonged together, he in his suit and she in her fancy blue dress.

She opened the latch on her gate and the skirts of that fancy dress gave a feminine rustle as she moved through. "I won't mind, too much. It must be done. Part of making the rounds as a newcomer." She gave an elegant shrug that emphasized her delicate collarbones. Jesse cleared his throat and looked away.

"I am sorry that he's punishing you, though," she said sincerely.

"It was my choice not to keep my mouth shut," Jesse said with a shrug. He knew better, but he'd done it anyway. "For that matter, perhaps I should not have come but I wanted to be sure you were alright. As for my meeting with him tomorrow—it's just a half hour early. It's nothing. Is there really something wrong with the cottage?" He stifled a yawn. He wasn't in the mood to fix anything tonight, but he would if there was a real issue.

"The door squeaks, but it just needs oil and I can see to it."

"I'll take care of it tomorrow after work. It's my job. Good night, Miss Alderly."

"Mr. Kittredge, nothing untoward happened this evening. We ate supper in plain sight of a dozen other couples. We drank only cider. The show was perfectly respectable."

"You don't owe me an explanation, Miss Alderly. Why are you telling me this?" he asked gruffly. This kind of talk made him uncomfortable. He didn't need Miss Alderly thinking she owed him any favors *or* explanations.

"Because you were right. The main part of town is a bit rough later in the day and I should not be out alone in it. I shouldn't have been so dismissive of your concerns. What I am trying to say, Mr. Kittredge, is thank you for looking out for me."

"It's getting late and we both need to be up early.

Good night, Miss Alderly." He said it more firmly this time. Jesse gave a brief touch to his hat brim and made his way back to his cottage three doors down. Never mind that his departure might have been abrupt, that it might have bordered on rude, and it had definitely not acknowledged her kind gratitude. He had no business lingering outside with a woman all dressed up for an evening. It wasn't good for the senses—the pretty dress, the soft smell of roses, the way she could smile with a gentle concern that reached her blue eyes.

It was no wonder the kids were mad for her. She was all they talked about from the moment he came home at night to the moment they went to bed—and when they got up in the morning, they'd just start jabbering about her again. Even Adam liked going to school enough to have set aside his disappointment in not being able to work the mines this year. That was all to the good if Miss Alderly could keep his boy out of the shafts for the time being—but he knew better than to think the reprieve would last long.

Miss Lorna Alderly was a dream, and the wisp of a dream at that. She'd be gone within the year. He didn't want the kids to count on her too much. She wasn't made for the places he lived in, places like Woods River. She was made for Boston, for a man like Carrington who could give her all the comforts a woman like her deserved. Well, not a man exactly like Carrington, unethical cad that he was. But a man with money. Surely, not every man with money was like Carrington.

Perhaps it's you who should be cautioned about getting attached. The warning whispered on the early autumn night breeze. *Maybe it's not just the children who like her. Well, hold on there now,* he chastised his inner voice. "Like" was a pretty strong word. He was *concerned* for Miss Alderly, that was all. Any decent man would be. She was pretty, untried, full of ideals and she had an inflated sense of what she could accomplish here. She was in over her head, and he had a feeling he'd have to be the one to dive in and save her when she finally realized it.

Because that's who you are, Jesse. You have a soft spot for a damsel in distress. That was Evie talking now, her voice chiding and fond all at once in that way only she could manage. He closed his eyes, and the evening breeze caressed his cheek, soft like a woman's hand, and for a moment she was there with him again. Evie. He breathed her name. His body hurt. His heart hurt.

He might have a soft spot for damsels in distress, but it didn't change the fact that he hadn't been able to save Evie when she'd needed him the most. God had not listened to him then.

I'm not that man anymore, Evie. Maybe I never was. Maybe you just saw what you wanted to see, believed what you wanted to believe of me. You always looked for the good in everyone, whether it was there or not.

He opened his eyes and she left him. It was time to go inside and see the children tucked in, time to set aside thoughts of a schoolteacher in a blue dress and a past he couldn't change no matter how badly he wished he could.

The day started badly and didn't get much better. That was how days that began with a meeting with Jack Carrington usually went. Some called Carrington a visionary, but Jesse called him reckless. This latest venture to sink a new shaft in the northwest corner of the mine was further proof of that. Jesse had made the mistake a few months back telling Carrington he thought there was a vein that ran deep but couldn't be reached from current access points. When Carrington had asked him where to tunnel in so that they could access it, he'd suggested the northwest corner as a hypothetical, never thinking the man would take him up on it.

"So, it *can* be done." Carrington sat back in his chair in the mining offices and looked out of the second-story window toward the main entrance to the mine.

"At great expense." Jesse tried to make him see reason. Usually money was the key when it came to persuading Carrington. "We'd have to blast, and blasting means timbering, *a lot* of timbering, to secure the shaft against slides and cave-ins. I don't think you understand just how far down we'd have to go—much deeper than we are right now in the main shaft." That came with other risks, too, beyond the usual concerns. Risks like the heat underground and the lack of good oxygen that allowed men not only to breathe but to be able to think clearly and work hard. Men couldn't work long shifts that far underground. Not without either collapsing or having their judgment so impaired that they were a danger to themselves and to others.

Carrington swiveled his chair around to face him. "You're a mother hen, Kittredge. I tell you what. You take these plans home and you study them. Then, come back here and tell me how you propose we access that vein—either through the northwest corner or by another point." He grinned. "You can't tell me there's gold in there and then tell me we can't get it. That's like telling a man who's been wandering in the desert there's water but he can't drink it. I won't be teased, Kittredge."

He stood up and rolled the plans. "Take a few days to look them over. Think of this as an opportunity for you. I'd make you the lead foreman on the project. It comes with more pay, and if it pans out, you'll be famous. The Kittredge Lode, we'll call it. I am handing you a promotion on a golden platter. Just think what you could do with that money. You could build a good house for your family. You could think about supporting a wife. Surely, you want to remarry. It's been two years."

Jesse stiffened and took the plans. He couldn't get out of the office fast enough. How dare Carrington mention such a thing, how dare he even *think* of Evie when he'd been just as responsible for her death and the other deaths as any man alive. "I am not looking to remarry."

"Playing the field, then?" Carrington laughed and clapped him on the shoulder. "You always surprise me, Kittredge. Just when I have you figured out, you have a twist I never saw coming. You really wouldn't consider marriage? Not even if a certain schoolteacher were available?" he asked conspiratorially. "I thought last night might have been an indication of where you were setting your cap. It was certainly an indication of where I'm setting mine, so if I'm trespassing, you'd best be speaking up now. And don't go expecting me to back off all too easily. We don't have many women of her caliber in Woods River."

Jesse felt his jaw tighten. "You're not trespassing, Carrington. I just want to see her treated decently. She's new here. She doesn't know our ways. I'd hate to see her misled."

"So last night was just neighborly concern?" Carrington seemed intent on goading him.

"Watch yourself, Carrington." Jesse tucked the plans under his arm and strode out of the office. His crew was waiting for him. He didn't have time for Carrington's games.

Lorna was waiting for him when he came to fix the squeaky hinge. She wore a green dress today the color of the towering firs that grew in the mountains. The color seemed to suit the afternoon with its hint of coolness hiding beneath the warmer breeze, a reminder that this was a season of transitions, the time between, Evie used to say, neither summer nor yet quite autumn. She'd loved this time of year. But all that mattered to Jesse was that fall was coming and winter would not be far behind—the longest, coldest, harshest of all seasons when one lived high in the mountains. One prepared all year to survive the winter and then hoped it would be enough.

"Do you have an oilcan?" Jesse asked, getting straight to the task at hand. He didn't need to stand around considering the color of her gown. He hadn't noticed women's clothing for years, and he certainly didn't need to start now. And yet, despite his best intentions, Carrington's words from that morning echoed through his mind. *There aren't many women of her caliber in these parts.* His conscience intruded. *Maybe you're noticing her, not the dress.* Or maybe, Carrington was messing with his mind.

"Yes, let me get it." She bustled inside and came back quickly with a little copper oilcan that shone with newness like everything else at the cottage. He'd noticed the changes last night while he waited for her. There were curtains in the two windows now, white lace panels. They wouldn't last long. White got dirty fast in this town. But they did look pretty for now, and domestic. He could imagine how they'd look with a lamp shining through. Evie had always talked of wanting curtains. She said curtains made a proper home, and he'd promised that he'd get them for her one day—when things were a little more secure and they didn't have to watch every penny. It was one more way he'd failed her.

He worked in silence, hoping Miss Alderly would move away and go about her afternoon. There was no reason for her to linger but she did. "Don't you have papers to grade or lessons to plan?" His words came out more gruffly than he'd intended. All of his words seemed to do that these days.

"I am guessing the meeting this morning went poorly." To his frustration, Miss Alderly didn't take the words as a dismissal but a conversational opening. Of course she would, contrary woman that she was.

"Why would you think that?" He grunted as he lifted the door to position the hinge.

"You're grumpier than usual." She gave a smile and a light laugh as she made the critique.

"I'm not grumpy," he said before he could catch himself, remembering her earlier comment that he argued over everything. Did he really do that? Maybe she had a point.

She offered a soft smile. "I am sorry. Do you want to tell me about it? I feel responsible."

There it was. *That* was why she was hovering about the door. She was looking for forgiveness. He shook his head, dripping some oil on the hinge. "It's not your fault. Carrington and I have locked horns before. This morning's meeting was about a plan that was in motion before you even arrived here. We don't quite see eye to eye on it, but he's the boss, so he gets to decide when we hash it out again. It was bound to happen. Won't be the first or last time."

It happened whenever someone stood in Carrington's way of getting what he wanted—whether it was this shaft, or a piece of property that belonged to someone else, or a particular lady that he had his eye on. Carrington didn't take no for an answer from men or from women. That was the evil side of pride, the part of pride that made it a sin.

Lorna—*Miss Alderly*; he really could not afford to think of her any other way—leaned against the door frame and crossed her arms, studying him with her blue gaze. "If you don't like him, why do you stay? Why not leave? Go somewhere else?"

He gave a dry chuckle, making an experimental push of the door. "Where would I go? Another mining camp? They're all full of men like Carrington at the helm. Same story, different place. It doesn't change. Here's as good a place to stay as any. I can't see my way to dragging my kids to someplace new for no good reason." He stopped his work long enough to return her gaze. "Is that what you did? Run away from Concord? Run away from the things you didn't like?" He said it unkindly, hoping to shock her into stopping her prying. "Not everyone has the luxury of running. Even if they did, you can't run away from your problems. They have a habit of following you no matter where you go."

That got a rise out of her. He could see her creamy cheeks flush, but, contrary to his hopes, his accusations did not deter her. "I did not run away, Mr. Kittredge," she said hotly. "I changed the equation. There is a difference."

He gave her a sardonic look. "I beg your pardon?" There she went using highfalutin expressions just to confuse him. She had to realize that he had no idea what they meant.

"There were no opportunities for me back East. Teaching positions for women were hard to come by. I had to find a place that offered more for me, so I came out West. I changed my circumstances in order to change my chances." She explained it so optimistically but so naively. Did she really think it was so easy? That everyone could just choose their paths in life and everything would work itself out? That it was really possible for people to do whatever they wanted? How wondrous to inhabit such a world. He didn't think there'd ever been a time when he'd lived in such a place.

"Not everyone has the ability to make such changes." Jesse went back to work, finishing his task. "There is no such thing as 'more' for me. I'm a miner. I need a mine to work. Without a mine I'm nothing. I have no opportunity. If a mine doesn't produce, I can't provide for my family."

"Is that why you came out West? To provide for the family?" My, she was a tenacious woman. She'd just plunged straight through his gruffness. Most of the town had given up talking to him by now, except his crew. And even with them, the conversations were strictly about work. They didn't talk about personal things, at least not with him. But still, why not tell her? Why not set the record straight and teach her that not everyone lived in her fairy-tale world?

He squatted down to work on the second hinge. Getting the words out would be easier if he didn't have to look into those beautiful, guileless blue eyes. "The coal mine I was at started laying off men. I could tell that I only had a month or two left before I'd be let go, as well. The company that owned the mine couldn't afford to keep it open. I didn't know what I'd do."

"That must have been awful," she said, her voice full of sympathy.

He shrugged, never really sure how to respond to sympathy, especially when it was expressed with so much sincerity. It was easiest just to ignore it and continue on with his story. "Carrington's agent showed up, talking about the gold rush in camp. We all knew about it. But who could go to California? The expense was enormous enough for one man, but for a family of four it was beyond anything we could possibly manage to afford. We talked about it. We thought briefly of me going on ahead by myself and then sending money back for…" He choked on the words. "For Evie and the children." He did not speak her name out loud often. Her name was his alone. "But I would not consider going without them, knowing it would be years before I saw them again." Neither could he fathom the idea of having them make the rigorous journey without him there to protect them. Turned out, even with him there, he still hadn't been able to protect them.

He wiped surreptitiously at his eyes with the bandana from around his neck, pretending the moisture troubling him was sweat. "But then Carrington's agent shared that he was offering the chance to work off our passage over time. He was putting together a wagon train of miners and craftsmen willing to mine and establish a town outside of Sonoma. Sonoma meant nothing to us at the time. It seemed as good a place to go as any. Better than most, since we could travel there without having to come up with the money and be sure of having a guaranteed job and a guaranteed wage at the end of the journey. It minimized the risk for us."

Lorna nodded. "Sounds like a good opportunity. Everything you wanted. Work, wages, a chance to keep the family together."

"Sounded too good to be true, actually. That should have been my first warning." Jesse grunted and rose. "That should do it." He gave the door another experimental swing, nodding in satisfaction when it swung easily without making any noise. "When things and people seem to be too good to be true, Miss Alderly, they absolutely are. Opportunities always come with a cost. The only difference is whether you know about that cost going in." In his situation, Carrington had not been entirely open about the costs until it was too late.

But was that fair? Even if he'd known more about what he was getting into, Jesse wasn't entirely sure it would have mattered. The situation back East had been so desperate, and he hadn't been able to come up with any other option to provide for his family. Perhaps he would have come West anyway, taken the chance anyway, trusting in faith and hard work to see them through.

She gave him a shrewd look. "What cost was that for you, Mr. Kittredge?"

"I can't leave. Carrington owns me lock, stock and barrel until my family's debt for passage is paid. There was a clause in the contract that requires us to work off our passage over the years. For me, that's four passages—more money than I may ever be able to earn." Even though Evie was dead, he was still paying on her debt. "Between the amount of my salary that I spend on housing, food, clothing and basic supplies, I'll never have enough to cancel out the debt. But I do have a roof over my family's head, food in their bellies and shoes on their feet." Which was more than some could say. He knew he was lucky, but it wasn't enough. "*That* is what 'opportunity' got me." He returned her stare and their gazes locked in challenge.

What would she say to that? Would she come back with some naive platitude or some reasoning that he was better off than others? That he should be grateful for small graces? That God had a plan for him? That this was where God wanted him? He'd believed all of that once upon a time. He and Evie had prayed for direction in making the decision to come West. He'd thought God had offered him guidance. He and Evie both had felt a sense of surety that they were on the right path, in accordance with God's plan. But looking at how things turned out, he wasn't sure he'd heard God's voice at all. Maybe he'd merely done what he wanted to do.

Faith was a convenient cover for justifying selfishness sometimes.

To her credit, Miss Alderly did not respond with any of the trite adages he'd heard so many times. Nor did she fall back on pity or the easy, meaningless words, "I'm sorry." What did those words mean? She didn't cause this to happen. How could she be sorry? Instead, she was silent—but it was a silence so full of compassion for his situation that he felt warmed by it, in spite of himself.

Charlotte came down the little walk. "Pa, will you be home for dinner?" For a moment the late afternoon sun caught her hair and his heart caught. She looked so much like her mother. Except for her eyes—they were all his. She'd probably be a handful in a few years. Both the kids had inherited his stubbornness.

"Yes, I'll be home shortly."

"There's plenty of time." Charlotte smiled and he sensed she was up to something as she turned her attentions to the teacher. "I thought I might get your recipe for biscuits, Miss Alderly." Her eyes drifted to the windows. "I absolutely adore the new curtains you've hung. They make everything look more homely."

"They make for more laundry," Jesse reminded his daughter sharply. He didn't want her to get any ideas. It was bad enough she was using phrases like "absolutely adore" and a whole slew of other expressions she clearly had learned at school. Well, words were free. Curtains were not. They were not spending money on curtains, not when every extra cent he could scrape together went either to offsetting what he owed Carrington or to investing in his little place in the hills, his one hope of setting up independently. He needed to get back up there. He hadn't had time in weeks.

Miss Alderly smiled kindly, sincerely, at Charlotte. "I'd be glad to share it with you. Shall I write it down and bring it over?"

Charlotte beamed. "I was hoping you might show me how to make them and I could practice my penmanship by writing it down as you go. I was thinking about what you said at school about recipes being a good way to practice reading and penmanship. Women can't share recipes very effectively if they can't write them clearly and also be able to read them later." Charlotte turned to him, explaining, "Malcolm Kinney said girls didn't need school as much as boys did and I said that wasn't true, and then Miss Alderly said everyone needs to know how to read and write. That settled Malcolm down good."

Jesse looked between his daughter and Miss Alderly, feeling uncomfortable. "I don't want you arguing at school, Lotte."

"That's not the point, Pa." Lotte put her hands on her hips and fixed him with a stare he recognized too easily. "The point is that women are equal to men and they have to stand up for themselves and help men realize that. Isn't that right, Miss Alderly?"

"Absolutely, Lotte." She was smiling broadly and proudly while Jesse's gut twisted. "Why don't you come in and sit at the table while I whip up a batch of biscuits. I have paper and a pencil for you to write with." Then she glanced in his direction, as an afterthought. "If that's alright with you, Mr. Kittredge?"

"It's fine." What could he say? But it was not fine.

This was exactly what he *hadn't* wanted to happen, this cultivated woman from the East putting radical ideas into Lotte's head about learning, about life, about what Lotte should expect from that life. Miss Alderly was filling his daughter's heart with dreams that would never come true. And in the end, life would only disappoint her all the more because she wouldn't be prepared for it.

Chapter Ten

He was not prepared for what greeted him when he returned an hour later. After finishing with Miss Alderly's door, Jesse had gone to the river to cool off mentally as well as physically and feel more like himself again. Because whomever it was that he'd been earlier was most definitely *not* himself. Under normal circumstances, he never would have divulged what felt like his life story to Miss Alderly while he worked on the hinges.

Even after a long swim that had helped settle him, he still wasn't sure why he'd shared so much with her. Had it simply been to make a point? In hindsight it seemed like quite a lot to tell her just to do that. He'd like to put that error in judgment behind him, but found he couldn't, not when the person he'd disclosed everything to was in his cottage. Cooking at his stove.

"What is this?" Jesse tried to ask the question amiably as he hung his hat on the peg beside the door.

Lotte looked up from her work setting the table. "We decided to make the biscuits here instead to go with supper. I hope you don't mind the change." Jesse glanced at the table and saw four dishes set out. Apparently Miss Alderly would be staying to share the meal. There seemed to be no escaping her today. She was either in his head or in his cottage. Or both.

He was just calculating how the effort would set him back on flour when Miss Alderly turned from the stove, a white apron tied about her green dress. A strand of hair had come loose from her chignon and curled softly at her jaw from the heat of baking. "I brought the ingredients. Consider it my contribution to dinner," she said as if she'd read his mind.

Adam came in from running an errand and grinned. "Miss Alderly, you're here for dinner. That's grand." Grand? What sort of man said "grand"? Jesse groused silently. But he knew. A cultivated man. An educated man. A man unlike himself. Already, his kids had more learning that he'd ever had. It would be petty to begrudge them that, to hold them back simply because he felt left behind, but he couldn't deny, in his heart of hearts, that he did feel left behind. They would outpace him. What would they think of their Pa when they realized it? Jesse squatted down on the floor and unrolled the plans Carrington had sent home. "Adam, come look at these with me before dinner. Tell me what you think." He treasured the look on Adam's face, the way it shone with pride over being consulted by his father, being asked for his opinion. He still looked up to Jesse. How much longer would that last?

He was aware of the occasional glances Miss Alderly threw their way as she and Lotte worked on dinner. He was aware, too, of the glances he threw in return, of covertly watching Miss Alderly with Lotte. He'd not realized how hungry Lotte was for female companionship, how hard it must be for Lotte to muddle through growing up without her mother—hard in a way that was different than it was for him or for Adam. Even as he explained the project to Adam and listened to Adam read the plans aloud and discuss the details, his ear was drawn to the quiet words and laughter from the other side of the cottage. These were the sounds of home, he realized, sounds that had been absent for a long time. Perhaps Lotte wasn't the only one who was hungry for domesticity.

Lotte called them to the table, proudly bearing a plate of hot biscuits. "I made them myself, with a little… What was the word?" She glanced behind her as Miss Alderly brought the pot with the stew.

"Supervision," Miss Alderly supplied, taking her place on the bench. No, not *her* place. Wording it like that made it sound as if Miss Alderly was a regular fixture at the cottage. He could not permit that to ever become the case for several reasons. "Shall we say the blessing?" Miss Alderly smiled and the children bowed their heads. Then, Miss Alderly bowed hers and Adam said the evening prayer.

The evening meal was filled with the children's chatter over school and Charlotte's excitement over having been inside Miss Alderly's cottage at last. She talked nonstop about the "lovely" (no doubt another expression learned from the exquisite Miss Alderly), items inside, from the checked tablecloth to the lamps with their glass chimneys and the vase of flowers. Miss Alderly was a good dinner guest. She did her part keeping up the conversation, sharing how well the children were doing at school and asking them questions about what they liked learning the most.

But Jesse felt apart from the conversation, almost as if he were an outsider in his own family. His children could read, they could write. He was embarrassed to admit that he could do neither.

In his work, he had confidence in his mining skills and experience, to the point where even when he toiled alongside men who had more education, he never felt inferior. But it was different here, with his children, as they showed so much eagerness to learn about things that were entirely outside of his scope of understanding. They felt as if they were miles away, living in a world of learning that he had never entered. He was feeling the distance keenly tonight.

And yet, when he looked about the table, he felt something else, as well. There was a sense of rightness, completeness in watching the children with her. Or was that sense of rightness really just a reminder of what used to be?

Be careful with us, Lorna Alderly. Our hearts are broken and vulnerable, and you are new and shiny. We have little experience with such things. We are drawn in like moths to your flame. We cannot resist.

Did she realize how charming she was? How that smile drew people in, made them feel as if they were the center of the universe? That what they had to say was the most important thing in the world? It was exactly the way someone should feel when they spoke: listened to, appreciated, validated. He did not want to be charmed and yet he was, against his will. Jesse liked to think he was being charmed on his children's behalf.

But he knew better. This woman was working her way under his skin whether he wanted her to or not. Perhaps he should caution her. It was the only defense he could think of. Nothing good could come of this.

Something wasn't right. Lorna sensed it. Beneath the laughter and warm conversation that flowed somewhat boisterously around the table, something or someone was "off." The more discussion veered toward school and what the children were learning, the more obvious it became that the person who was "off" was Jesse. *Jesse?*

The intimacy of his first name brought her thoughts up short. It was the first time she'd thought of him exclusively by his first name. Not Mr. Kittredge or Jesse Kittredge, but simply Jesse. It felt somehow intimate, personal. She wondered if she should allow such familiarity even in the privacy of her own head. Familiarity could be dangerous that way, a slippery slope. Perhaps, she was over thinking it. It was only natural to think of him as Jesse, perhaps it was nothing more than an outgrowth of Jack's insistence of using first names and the informality of the West.

She tried it out again in her mind, 'Jesse.' The name suited him. It was a strong name. The name of a hardworking man. Jesse in the Bible was a sheep breeder, a farmer, a salt of the earth man, not unlike this man who worked hard in the mines by day and sat at the head of his table each night, providing for his children.

Tonight, though, that hardworking man was distracted. He smiled at something Adam was explaining from school and offered a compliment to his son, but it was done absently, as if his thoughts were elsewhere. Was he thinking about the difficulties of the day? The discussion with Carrington? From just the little she knew of him, it was easy to see he was a man who carried much on his shoulders: responsibility for his job, his men, his family. A lot of people were counting on him. Her included.

She didn't like the idea of adding to his worries or responsibilities, but whether she'd meant to or not, she had. Who took care of him these days? Who eased his worries? Her father had many responsibilities, and she knew he worried over each of the boys at the school, over his family, over his community. But he had her mother, and she was a great source of support for him, a sounding board for his ideas and worries, a comforter when things went wrong or the worries became too difficult to carry.

"Pa, tell us a story," Charlotte begged as the meal finished. "Pa always tells us a story after dinner" she explained to Lorna, "I want to hear the story about Gideon and the drinking men. That's one of my favorites."

Jesse shook his head. "Maybe not tonight, Lotte, since we have company."

Lotte looked disappointed and ready to argue the point. "Miss Alderly isn't company any more. She's our friend."

Lorna jumped in to secure the peace. "I don't mind a good story, and I certainly don't want to interrupt a family tradition."

"Well, I can't fight you both," Jesse replied with a wry look in her direction. Lorna could not tell if her intervention had pleased or vexed him. She had hoped to be helpful, but it seemed all she did was vex him even when she tried not to. Then again, from what she had seen so far, it seemed most people vexed Jesse Kittredge. Perhaps she should not take it personally.

Instead of rising to fetch a Bible, Jesse splayed his palms on the table and fixed each of the children with a mock stare as his greeneyed gaze moved around the table. A rare smile took his face, much like the one Lorna had glimpsed the day of her arrival when the children had come to the cottage, not only to welcome her but also to see their father returned.

"Once upon a time, in the land of Israel, there lived a warrior named Gideon. He was a godly man and lived a righteous life. But there came a time when the Midianites crossed the Jordan River and threatened his people. He needed to raise an army, and he did so. But he had one problem—the army he raised was too large. An angel of the Lord came to him, saying the Lord would not grant him victory. Instead, Gideon must reduce his forces by using the following test. He must lead his men to the Spring of Harod and look at how the men drank from the waters."

"I love this part," Lotte whispered to Lorna, wiggling in excitement on the bench beside her. Lorna liked the story, too. Or perhaps it was the storyteller. Jesse's face came alive. Gone was the stoic man who used grunts more often than words to convey what he thought. He looked far younger with a smile on his face and no hat to hide beneath. He was what one might call a born storyteller, knowing just how to embellish a story to draw people in. Across from them, Adam's attention was riveted on his father's every word as if it were the first time he'd heard the story.

"At the springs, some men scooped the water in their hands and brought it to their mouths, lapping it like dogs. Other men knelt at the shore and put their faces down in the water to drink directly from the springs. These men were told to go home. The first group, those who cupped the water, were the men whom Gideon chose for his army because they were the most diligent, not neglecting their duty for personal delight."

The words caught Lorna's attention. These were not the exact words from the story in Judges, although she supposed the intent was not incorrect. He'd not read the story aloud, he'd *told* the story. She wondered if it had been told to him that way or if that was his own interpretation? It made her wonder about other things, like the plans he'd unrolled and shared with Adam, the boy reading the captions and numbers on the plans out loud. She hadn't noticed Jesse reading anything.

Lorna gave a surreptitious glance about the room as Jesse continued with the story, recounting how Gideon and his army of three hundred went on to defeat the Midianites. There were no books, no Bible, in plain sight. Perhaps it was not surprising. Family Bibles were treasures that kept family histories after all. In such rough conditions as a mining camp, a family Bible would be kept safe. The lack of books was not uncommon, either. She'd not seen any books when she'd visited the encampment. Those families did not boast a single literate member.

A thought began to take root in her mind, overriding an earlier assumption. She knew it would not be an easy subject to broach. Jesse had his pride. She would have to approach the topic delicately. But if she was right, it would explain the sense of something being "off" during dinner as they discussed school, *and* she could do something about it, if Jesse would allow it.

Lotte gave a contented sigh and leaned against her. "I like that story so much, especially the part about drinking the water."

"I like the part about how the army defeats the Midianites just by confusing them," Adam said thoughtfully. "What a sight it must have been to see 'camels without number, as the sand by the sea side for multitude.'" He sighed wistfully. "I'd like to see the sea someday and maybe sail across it to Egypt and see camels for myself." Lorna had quickly learned that geography was Adam's favorite subject. He pored over the maps she unrolled for class, asking an endless stream of questions about faraway places. It delighted her to have such an enthusiastic student, but the idea seemed to displease Jesse.

He rose from the table in an abrupt movement. "It's getting late and there's dishes to do while I walk Miss Alderly home."

She barely had time to grab her basket before he had her ushered out the door and into the purple-skied evening. "It's alright if your son dreams of going to Egypt," Lorna began.

"Is it? Do you not see the harm of those dreams, Miss Alderly?" The stoic, taciturn mask of the Jesse Kittredge she saw so often was back now; the smiling storyteller was erased so completely that it was as if he'd never existed.

"No, I do not," she answered honestly. "Your son is bright. Yes, his reading level is not quite what one would hope for a twelve-year-old, but he is eager and quick. He is closing that gap every day. His mind is a sponge, wanting and waiting to be filled—as is your daughter's. I'm proud to have them as my students—and proud to help them explore the subjects that best catch and hold their attention. Adam's interest in far-off places can stimulate his interest in reading. I have books to give him about the places he finds so fascinating. There's one called *A Thousand and One Nights* that I'm excited to share with him. It's a collection of stories from the East. It's a way to enhance his reading and connect him to the geography and cultures of that part of the world, all through folktales."

They reached her gate. Jesse stopped and planted himself in front of her, arms crossed over the breadth of his chest. "What for, Miss Alderly? Miners do not have need of folktales from far-off places. Those stories will be useless to him, other than to tell them around campfires, maybe."

"Adam may not choose to be a miner," Lorna replied, unsure what was so upsetting to him.

"Oh, he gets to *choose*, does he? In whose world? I thought I made that clear today. Not everyone gets a choice. Not everyone is like you."

"But don't you think he could be? Isn't that the point of school?" She almost said "to better oneself," but she feared that Jesse would take offense at that. She said instead in a gentle tone, "To give oneself choices?" They'd had such a pleasant evening, she didn't want it ending this way, with a quarrel.

His green eyes blazed. "No, I don't think so. I love my children, Miss Alderly, and I want them to have things in their lives that bring them joy—but I don't want that joy tied to unrealistic ideas. The bigger their dreams, the more hurt they'll be when those dreams don't come true. Be careful with them. They like you. You don't think you'll hurt them and perhaps you won't mean to, but you will. You will leave here, and when you do, you will take all their dreams with you. Don't give them false hope."

"I can help them change their lives, if you will let me." Lorna stood her ground with a quiet voice. "And I can help you, too." That stalled his tirade for a moment, long enough for her to say, "Would you step inside with me for just a minute?"

Once inside, she retrieved her Bible from beside her bed. She opened it to Judges 7:12. "I enjoyed the story about Gideon very much tonight. I had never heard it told quite like that before. Could you show me the part where the moral of how Gideon selects his men is discussed?" She handed the Bible to him, aware of the hardness in his eyes. He was on the defensive now, as she'd suspected he would be. It was why she'd wanted to do this inside, where it was just the two of them. She had no wish to subject him to prying eyes. It would be difficult enough for him to admit to a weakness or a flaw just to her.

"It's right there. Surely you can see it for yourself," he bluffed.

"No, it's not," she said firmly. Lorna lit the lamp on the table and took the Bible from him. She read out loud. "'And the Lord said unto Gideon, by the three hundred men that lapped will I save you, and deliver the Midianites into thine hand: and let all the other people go every man unto his place.' That's it. There's nothing there about why Gideon chose those men over the others." She softly closed the Bible and set it aside, facing Jesse with a fixed stare. "Can you read?" She preferred to put it to him as a question rather than an accusation.

"A lot of people in Woods River can't read, Miss Alderly." He returned her stare evenly, his features blank and wooden.

"I am not interested in them at the moment. Just you. I asked you a question, and I'm hoping for a direct answer, given that I believe you to be an honest man." Honest enough to care how Jack Carrington treated her, even though that caring put him at risk. She was counting on that honesty now. "There is no wrong answer to this question, only an honest one. Can you read?"

His jaw tightened. "No, I cannot, as you no doubt have surmised from your *keen* observations." But it was obvious that he had done a remarkable job of faking it, relying on what little learning Adam had to make his way up the ranks to crew chief. She could see that pattern now. "I can write my name, but that's all." It would be a thin enough wall to hide his illiteracy behind, though. He could sign a paycheck. He could sign a contract. But of course, the downside of hiding his illiteracy was that he couldn't *read* what was in that contract. And he'd paid for that. Oh, how he'd paid. And he was still paying.

She thought about the contract he'd signed to come out West with Carrington's wagon train. Had Jesse not realized what he was signing? What he was promising? Jesse would not want her pity. She could not pity him. But it did make her angry that he'd been taken advantage of to the extent that now his life was not his own.

* * *

"I would like to teach you," she offered.

He gave a harsh chuckle, dismissing the idea. "I'm too old to be one of your students."

"I disagree. No one is ever too old to learn, especially to learn to read. We could work for a short time in the evenings after supper while the children do their own homework. Think what an example you'd be setting for them, how encouraging it would be for their own studies to see their Pa valuing his own education," she argued gently. "It would be private. No one need know." Was he worried that his crew might find out and laugh at him? Would he understand such laughter was just a defense on their part? Part of their own insecurities? "Give me three lessons as a trial, and if you feel there is no value to them we can stop."

He was still for a long while, his silence filling the room as surely as his bulk. Jesse Kittredge was a big man, a fact made more obvious in the small space of her cottage. As the silence stretched out, she felt her heart sink and she became certain that he would refuse. Men could be so stubborn, could let pride get in the way of common sense.

"Alright, then," he said, to her elated shock. "Three lessons."

"Wonderful. We'll start tomorrow evening." Lorna smiled, and something soft and warm flickered between them for the briefest of moments. She'd call it progress. This was what she'd come West to do, to help people access the world in new ways through the doorway of education.

That night she added a thank-you to her prayers.

Thank you for this little miracle, Lord, for opening Jesse Kittredge's heart just a smidgen. There's so much more of it to open, but all in good time. Jesse Kittredge was proving to be a very complex man, but she hadn't come West to *avoid* challenges. *Please Lord, if it's not too much to ask, as always, open the hearts and minds of the other miners. Let them send their children to school.* This had been her prayer each night since the first day of school, but thus far, the miners' children had not come.

Perhaps Jack was right and she just needed to wait until the weather changed. She didn't want to wait that long. She could hear her mother's voice in her head reminding her that God's time was not always our time. Despite her love of education, that was a lesson she had always struggled to master. Whatever the trick was to learning patience, she'd not learned it yet.

Chapter Eleven

She'd tricked him. Apparently, teaching him to read also involved teaching him to write. That was the first trick she'd played on him when she'd neglected to mention that. The second trick was that the value of the lessons wasn't necessarily limited to the content of them, as he'd assumed.

Jesse had thought it would be easy to say no after the required lessons were completed. After all, who wanted to be confined to a table in a stuffy cottage after working underground all day? But the value of the lessons was part of the second trick. She hadn't told him learning could take place out-of-doors. Instead of limiting him to a table and slate, she talked him into long evening walks in the forests on the outskirts of town, a prospect that did not take much persuasion.

He was an active man, not made for sitting, and he loved being outdoors in the beautiful scenery that surrounded the town. Days underground made him that much hungrier for the clean air and the elevated climes of the mountain fir forests. Perhaps Miss Alderly knew that. Maybe she knew, too, just how hard it was to refuse a lesson that gave him a reason to be out-of-doors in the crisp autumn evenings and in good company. That was a value he'd not looked for and it was uncomfortably addicting—a benefit that was not so easily given up.

Miss Alderly, it turned out, was an excellent listener—nodding her head, asking occasional questions, but never taking the conversation away or steering it in a different direction until he was ready. She had a way of using the conversation to weave in her lessons so fluidly and naturally that the lesson didn't seem like one at all. It felt like just another part of the conversation, with each of them sharing the knowledge that they had. When she would ask a question—constantly curious about the wonders of nature that differed so dramatically from what she'd known back East—he would identify a seed, or a flower, or the tracks of an animal. Then she would respond by spelling the word for him.

If he talked of timber, she'd stop to spell *fir, timber, spruce, trunk, lumber* and more in the dirt with a stick before passing the stick to him and having him copy the words beside hers. It turned out, as well, that he surprised himself. He *could* learn. The mysteries of the written word were far less mysterious when presented by Miss Alderly. What he was able to grasp and remember astonished him.

"Once you know the sounds the letters make," she told him with one of her soft smiles, "you can puzzle out almost anything."

He believed her. He told himself it was because he saw the proof of it with his own eyes, watching his stick write words in the dirt, realizing he could open a Bible and recognize a few words. Not enough yet to read anything out loud, but simple words like *the, and* and *then* appeared before his eyes like old friends, unlocking what had seemed mysterious and incomprehensible before.

Which was why three lessons became five, five became a week, a week became two weeks, and the times between the seasons slipped away with September, until the leaves began to turn, and fall was upon them in all its splendor.

"We have beautiful autumns in Concord," Lorna said as they strolled beside an isolated bend in the river outside of town. The evening was clear and crisp, the sun not down yet. But it would be soon. Last week, they'd started doing their lessons before supper instead of after, out of respect for the changing season and decreasing daylight during the evening hours. Soon, weather would mean lessons moving inside more permanently. She lifted her face to the sky and smiled. "But these colors are magnificent. I did not expect so many leaves. Fir and spruce are evergreens."

Jesse grinned. Was he smiling more these days or was that only his imagination? He *felt* like he was smiling more. Maybe that was all that mattered. "The California mountains have their leafy trees, too." He pointed to a few by the river bed. "There's quaking aspens, ash, white alder. It's not just evergreens up here."

She cocked her head in that way of hers when she was studying something. Right now that something was him. "I must say, it's been a pleasant surprise to see that a miner knows so much about trees. Mining sometimes seems 'against' nature."

Jesse bent down and picked up a flat rock from the exposed river bed and skipped it on the river. "It can be—and in many places it is. Mining digs into the land, takes from the land, blows up the land, dumps its residue into the waters if it's not done right. For some, mining is a war—man against the earth, battling nature for its treasures." He skipped another rock. "Some believe that it's their right, that God gave them dominion over the earth to take what they'd like from nature without giving anything back, without trying to keep things in balance."

"But you don't think that?" She stooped to pick up her own rock to skip, but her rock fell with a sad plop into the river.

Jesse shook his head. "I think to have dominion over something means to be not just a user or a taker but a caretaker. I owe this earth my living whether I am a farmer or a miner. If I respect the earth, it will respect me." He thought about the gold nugget he'd found at his secret place up in the hills, and the gold he'd panned from the creek up there. Gold he could not spend without Carrington and others getting suspicious about where he found it. That gold was his hope. Someday, he'd stake a claim, pay off his debt to Carrington and be free. "A man has to work in harmony with the earth." Lorna was staring at him, something he couldn't name shining in her gaze. He skipped another stone. "Are you surprised that a man who can't read has such thoughts?"

"No, I'm not surprised at all. Not being able to read doesn't mean you're not able to think. I'm not surprised," she said staunchly. "But I *am* impressed. Perhaps more people should think as you do." She tried to skip another rock and failed. "How do you do that? Your rocks skip two or three times but mine just sink."

"It's all in the wrist." Jesse flicked another stone. "Although selecting the right rock helps, too." He bent down and picked one up. "Try this one. The flatter the surface of the stone, the better." He chose another for himself. "Now, copy me. Cock your wrist like this." He demonstrated. "No, like this," he said, modeling the movement once again, but she still couldn't get the angle right. Without thinking, he stepped behind her and took her hand in his, his hand guiding hers into position. "We want to use a sidearm throw." He moved her arm through the motion and the stone released, hopping twice on the river before sinking…before Jesse realized what he'd done. He dropped her arm and stepped back. What had he been thinking? Or maybe he'd not been thinking at all. That was dangerous for a man. That was when a man did things he'd regret.

"Did you see that? I did it!" Lorna's glee was infectious.

"*You* did it?" Jesse laughed, too, unable to resist the urge to tease her. "I'd like to think I had a little something to do with it."

"You're an excellent teacher," Lorna acceded with a happy smile.

"As are you." At the words, the glee in her expression turned to something more serious. For a moment, Jesse regretted it, but the weather was changing and that meant other things would, too, things they needed to talk about before they got back to town.

"You are a good pupil, Mr. Kittredge. It takes bravery to do what you've done," she responded with equal solemnity.

"It would be alright if you called me Jesse. After all this time, it seems more appropriate than Mr. Kittredge." Had she really only been here six weeks? It seemed she'd been here much longer. She'd become a part of his world in that time.

"Thank you. It would be a privilege. I would be pleased if you called me Lorna when we're together." She gave an uncertain smile. Maybe she was also affected by the solemn turn their conversation had taken.

Jesse cleared his throat. "I think that's something else we should discuss. I'm not sure how much longer we can continue the lessons."

Her face changed, the last of the glee of a few moments ago vanishing completely. "We can't stop now. You're doing so well." She hesitated before adding, "I thought you liked the lessons."

"I do," he assured her. "But things are changing. The weather for one. We would have to meet indoors." He could see that she understood what he meant. They wouldn't have the privacy of the woods, the distance from town, where they could meet away from prying eyes that might comment on the amount of time they spent together. "I'm not sure Jack Carrington would approve of the schoolteacher spending so much time with a single man. I do apologize for speaking so bluntly."

In fact, he *knew* Carrington would not approve. Carrington had made that much clear the day after Jesse had found the two of them returning from their supper together. Carrington had all but warned him off, and he had gone on to stake his claim in other ways since then. Sunday afternoons had become Carrington's territory. Lorna dined at the Hill after church every week, although she made a good show of rotating where she sat for the services so that she could spend time with all the families in the community.

Sometimes she sat with other families of school children, other times with ladies from the auxiliary, and only sometimes did she sit with Carrington or with him, much to his children's disappointment. They'd prefer she sit with them every Sunday, but Jesse had explained how she couldn't show such favoritism, how she needed to share her time with others. His children had been disappointed, but they'd understood. Carrington, on the other hand, was far less patient when it came to sharing Lorna's time and attention.

He had also taken to walking her home from school a few days a week when his business brought him into town, knowing full well Jesse's shift at the mines prohibited him from doing that.

You're not in competition with him, his inner voice whispered. *You told him you weren't interested in her, not like that, not like how he means it. Why do you care?* Because he didn't want Carrington to win her. Carrington had been clear about his intentions. He meant to woo and claim her—though Jesse had a feeling that the man might be surprised there. Lorna Alderly was not for claiming. She made her own decisions. Did Carrington realize that? Or would Lorna decide the mine owner was right for her? The thought sat poorly with Jesse but it was not his place to have that discussion.

"No apology needed." Lorna smiled absolution. "I appreciate your consideration. But surely we can con-

tinue with lessons a few nights a week without drawing undue notice. We can at least try. I wouldn't want
to lose the progress we've made. I can't imagine anyone
having a complaint about anything untoward happening
with two children present and sitting at the very table
where we'll be working. For the days we'll miss, I can
leave assignments for you to complete so that you may
continue to practice."

They began the walk back toward town, and he
turned the conversation to the other topic on his mind.
"I appreciate the offer, but I just don't know how much
time I'll have. Carrington is eager to start some prelim-
inary work on his new project before the snow sets in.
It'll mean longer hours at the mine."

"So, you've decided it's safe?" Lorna slid him a side-
ways glance, her fair brows knitting. "The last I heard
you were opposed to the project."

"I still am," Jesse admitted, familiar chagrin rising
as he thought of all the times he'd tried to convince
Carrington to change his mind—and how he'd failed
every time. "However, he insisted that I provide him
with a plan, so I submitted the safest plan I could come
up with. I had hoped the exorbitant costs associated
with it would deter him, but that was not the case." Jesse's hope now was that the snows would be early, early
enough to postpone Carrington's plans until spring. "If
the project is delayed until the spring thaw, though who
knows what might happen? Something better might
come along to distract him."

"We must add it to our prayers, then." Lorna tossed
him a smile and kicked at a pile of leaves, scattering them.

"Add it? What else do you pray for?" Jesse dared the

personal question, finding himself curious. Lorna Alderly was a woman of faith. She'd made that clear from the beginning. To know her was to know that about her, not because she was showy or demonstrative with it, but because she so clearly carried that faith with her everywhere she went, letting it guide every decision she made. Part of him envied her that easy faith. It drew him even as part of him rebelled, screaming reminders in his mind that faith had failed him when he'd needed it most.

"I pray for my family back home. I pray for guidance so that I might serve my students in the ways they need. I pray for the children here in Woods River, especially the miners' children. I pray that with the change in the weather they will come to school and see the opportunities it provides them." She fixed him with one of her penetrating blue-eyed stares. "Do you pray, Jesse?"

It was the first time he'd heard his name on her lips and it nearly stopped him in his tracks. When was the last time a woman had spoken his name? Had it happened at all since Evie had died? He had the feeling that it had not. *You haven't allowed it until now,* his conscience reminded him. But there had been no one to speak it. He did not associate with the women available at the dance hall. Friendship with women outside of marriage was often too tricky of a business to manage. And yet the sound of his name on Lorna's lips represented the sum of his loneliness, the reminder of all he'd lost when he'd lost Evie, not the least of which was someone to talk to, the comfort of sharing, of being listened to without judgment. Would Lorna Alderly judge him by his answer now?.

What a powerful question she'd asked him: Do you

pray? Yet there was no covert condemnation beneath those words, no suggestion that there was a wrong answer that would render judgment. And so he gave her the truth in quiet tones beneath the quaking aspens.

"I used to, but I don't anymore. Not since my wife died."

After weeks of taciturn conversation, Jesse Kittredge had dropped a bevy of conversational threads to follow up on. Which to pick? The wife she was so curious about or the personal revelation about the state of his faith? For a moment Lorna felt like one of the gray squirrels that lived in the trees, faced with a plethora of nuts to choose from, knowing it could only carry so many home to its nest. Perhaps she should pick neither. Jesse was a man who valued his privacy. Not just his physical privacy, but his emotional privacy, as well. Maybe pressing him too hard now would just make him clam up and prevent him from opening up to her in the future.

"Why did you stop praying?" Lorna asked quietly, carefully. This was an important but delicate conversation, and she sent a silent prayer heavenward for guidance. *Give me the right words, Lord. Help this man open himself.*

"Because God wasn't listening. I decided to stop making the mistake of thinking he was." No one would ever fault Jesse Kittredge for not being forthright. Ah, so the wound was threefold for him. He'd felt not only ignored but that his trust had been betrayed, as well as his judgment.

They crested the little rise that dropped into the far

end of town where their cottages were located. From here, they could see Woods River laid out before them: muddy, and haphazard, weather-beaten in places, scrappy and new in others. It looked particularly shabby after the splendors of the trees by the river. "Not much to look at, is it." Jesse halted and stared down at the little panorama, his voice quiet. "I moved my family across the country for this. For *this*, Lorna, all because I thought God was guiding my hand, guiding my choice."

She could hear the anger in his voice and dared to push a little further. "How do you know He wasn't?"

"How do I know?" He shot her an incredulous look. "What sort of God would call this the Promised Land? What sort of God would have a man lead his family here to live in indebtedness to another?"

"The Bible is full of such men. Look at Joseph, at Jacob," she countered quietly. "You are not alone." Jacob had been tricked into working twice as long as his original contract in order to be granted Rachel's hand in marriage, a trick not unlike, perhaps, the situation with Jesse's contract with Carrington, although Lorna kept those thoughts to herself for the present. "As for the Promised Land, don't you think Moses had those same thoughts? That the Israelites had the same thoughts, wandering for forty years in the wilderness and thinking they would have been better off if they'd stayed in Egypt? That there was no point to any of it?"

She paused, then decided her words might carry more weight if she made them more personal. "I have doubts, too, sometimes. I look at my students and wonder if it's worth it for eight children. I wonder why the other children don't come or if they'll ever come. I read my letters from home and I wonder if they're really a comfort or a reminder of all I've given up."

She thought of that first letter from Theo, bursting with all of the incredible things he was doing in Boston at his uncle's emporium. She hadn't wanted that life, had chosen to leave it behind—but she had to admit that, while reading his letter, she'd felt some stirrings of regret. "What I do here doesn't compare with what Theo is doing at home. You are not the only one with doubts."

"But you pray anyway." Jesse finished the thought for her.

"Yes, I pray anyway. Maybe it wouldn't hurt to try again? God loves a good prodigal." She smiled and, moved by the sense of a genuine connection, she reached for his hand and held it for a long moment.

It was a rough hand, calloused and scarred from years of work, but an honest hand with a firm grip. She'd meant to be the one offering comfort, but she found in that grip there was strength on offer for her, as well. She'd not expected that and it touched her to her toes. To know she was cared for, even for just a moment, moved her inexplicably.

She spoke briskly to push the confusing feeling away. "We'd best go down. I promised Charlotte I'd help her with supper tonight. We're trying a new fish soup. Adam was going to catch some after school."

"I'll look forward to trying it. Biscuits would not go amiss if there's time." Jesse favored her with a rare smile as they returned to the real world, hands and thoughts to themselves once more.

Chapter Twelve

Jesse had actually been enjoying himself as he escorted Lorna about town on an afternoon of errands after school. He had a rare afternoon off and the weather was fine. In fact, everything was fine until he caught sight of Jack Carrington striding down the street towards them. It meant the town council meeting had ended early. Too bad Carrington had already spied them. It was too late to duck into a shop and pretend they hadn't noticed him.

"Good day, Miss Alderly," Carrington tipped his hat to Lorna. "Afternoon, Kittredge. I didn't think shopping was part of the handyman's duties." He laughed at his joke and Jesse offered a stiff smile in return. Carrington had better watch himself. There was only so long Jesse was willing to stand there and let Carrington attempt to belittle him in front of Lorna with reminders of who was the subordinate here, all perhaps in an attempt to advance Carrington's own case with her.

Carrington made a back and forth gesture with his hand. "This looks very cozy, the two of you together."

Jesse didn't care for the insinuation. But it was Lorna who smoothed things over.

She offered one of her wide smiles. "If you gentlemen would excuse me, I'll step inside and place my orders." Her departure should have been Carrington's cue to take his own leave. But to Jesse's disappointment Carrington chose to stay and talk in the street, a sly smirk on his face.

"Now that it's just us men, tell me what's really going on here, Kittredge? Are you trying to steal a march on the rest of us poor fellows? You say you're not and then every time I turn around the two of you are together." He gave a shrug. "You play a deep game if you think you can entice the lovely Miss Alderly. She could have her pick of the town, if you take my meaning."

Jesse did take his meaning. It was one he thought of too often. She could have Jack Carrington and all of the material wealth that came with him. Why wouldn't a woman want all that? No one in town could offer more, certainly not a miner like himself with his two children, his debt, and hiscottage. Of course, that was not news to Jesse. He'd long known he wasn't husband material. That was fine. He wasn't aspiring to be. So why did Carrington's insinuations raise his hackles? "I think you should be careful what you imply, Carrington," he said gruffly.

"Me be careful?" Carrington chuckled. "You're the one reaching above himself if you aspire to her. Then again, you've always been the audacious one."

"You used to appreciate my audacity." Jesse took the opportunity to direct the conversation away from Lorna.

Carrington grinned. "Well, yes I did. I haven't forgotten what you've done for me, Kittredge. It was your mining knowledge that found the last big lode. You've made me a rich man." But that was in the past. Jesse knew what Carrington was also thinking: that these days that audacity was turned against him more often than not. Jesse was the one who questioned him at every turn about safety measures, about working conditions and wages. Most recently, Jesse had demonstrated extreme reluctance about sinking the new shaft. He'd dragged his feet discussing those plans. That had not gone over well with Carrington. He'd been livid.He didn't like the idea that a man who *owed* him so much money had so much leverage in turn.

Carrington nodded towards the store Lorna had disappeared into. "Does she know you're nothing more than an indentured servant? Of course, you could change that if the new shaft project goes well. With that money you could pay off your debt to me."

Jesse fought the urge to cringe. He hated any reminder of that debt and Carrington knew it. "Your plan isn't safe. I looked over your plans, I made the suggestions you asked for but no matter how much gold is down there, I won't sign off on it."

Carrington shrugged. "We'll see. I hope that Miss Alderly sees what's in front of her. You've already lost one wife to the West. I'd hate for Miss Alderly to suffer because you've overreached yourself."

It was time to set Carrington straight if he insisted on this line of conversation. "It's not like that. There is nothing between us. I will not tell you again. You misread the situation. I am escorting her because the streets aren't safe for a woman to shop alone," Jesse growled, fully aware that he was clearing the way for Carrington to continue his pursuit of Lorna. But if that was what they both wanted, it wasn't for him to stand in their way. He knew what a catch Carrington would be for Lorna. She could live in luxury on the Hill and be a rich man's wife, wanting for nothing. Such opportunities were rare.

Lorna emerged from the store with Mayor North, the two of them chatting easily. North was glad to see Carrington. "Shall we stop at the Nugget, catch dinner and then the show?" It was enough to tempt Carrington. The pair made their farewells and Jesse was glad to have Lorna to himself once more.

Lorna handed him her packages. "What did the two of you talk about? It looked fairly intense when I came out."

"The new shaft," Jesse began and decided to be entirely honest. "And you," he added. He paused, not wanting to overstep himself and then opted to take the risk. "I don't mean to pry, but I would like to offer some advice. Whatever your intentions are with Carrington is your business, but you'd best make those intentions clear to him." It was good advice that he should take himself. Why did the idea of Lorna possibly having intentions with Carrington leave him feeling let down when he had no desire or ability to re-marry? He told himself it was because he knew what Carrington was really like. But he suspected there might be something more to it. Not that he could anything about that if there was something more. Carrington was right. He had nothing to offer a woman like Lorna Alderly.

* * *

Lorna's thoughts were still on the afternoon a few hours later when she returned to her cottage after supper and lit the lamps. It was only half past seven but it was fully dark outside. She had learned to be frugal with her lamp oil, which meant that she would have to work quickly to finish all her tasks for the night. She had letters to write and a few last-minute decisions to make about lessons tomorrow.

Dinner had turned out well. The fish soup had been tasty, the biscuits fluffy, the company good. Tonight, Jesse had told one of the Samson stories, entrancing the children with the life of a Nazirite. She'd found herself intrigued by the similarities between Jesse and Samson: the long hair and the refusal to take alcohol. He had not told the other part of the story, the part about Delilah. Lorna smiled to herself as she set out her writing supplies. Jesse told a lot of stories from the book of Judges.

She wondered what his fascination with that part of the Old Testament was. Perhaps he didn't realize it? She would have to ask him. For a man who no longer prayed and who was just beginning to read, he was well versed in the Bible. At one point, he must have been a man of great faith.

Lorna sat at the table and took out her letter. It was already five pages long, but there was more to add. If it took months for a letter to reach Concord, she wanted to make it worth everyone's while.

She'd started the letter last week. She looked back over what she'd already committed to paper: descriptions of the lessons she'd taught at school, an account of what the reverend had preached about on Sunday.

There was a small paragraph about dinner at the Hill and a rapturous sentence about Mrs. Carrington's bathtub, which she had generously insisted Lorna use when she visited. It was, in fact, the chief attraction that kept Lorna going back for Sunday afternoons. Lorna added a little note in the margin there. *I hope it is not selfish to crave a hot bath once a week in a real tub. I prefer to think such a luxury is warranted if cleanliness is indeed next to godliness.* She hoped that would make her mother smile. Her brothers would think it a great lark that baths were at a premium in the West. They despised them.

The rest of the letter was taken up with news of the Kittredges—what she'd taken to dinner, what stories Jesse had told, the progress Jesse was making with his reading lessons, a squirrel she and Jesse had seen on a walk. Jesse, Jesse, Jesse.

She'd not realized she'd written so much about him and there was still more to write. She wanted to tell her mother about their walk today, about the colors of the leaves and the things he'd shared and the way he'd shared them. But she would not tell her mother about how they'd skipped rocks at the river, how he'd come up behind her, how he'd taken her hand, the way she'd felt at the strength and gentleness of his touch.

He'd been her very own Samson in those moments. No, she would keep that singular memory to herself. It belonged just to her. She wasn't even sure what it meant or that it had to mean anything. She and Jesse were neighbors and she felt as if they were starting to be friends—real friends who told each other the thoughts they carried deep inside. He'd endeavored to offer her advice today. She appreciated that, it was sweet of him to be concerned for her. It would be nice to have a friend like that here. Certainly, she was friends with the ladies on the auxiliary committee and with the wives of the shopkeepers, but she'd yet to feel a sense of true, genuine closeness with them. She could not imagine confiding in them like she'd confided in Jesse.

She definitely did not talk with Jack the way she talked with Jesse. Her conversations with Jack were always about the town, about the school, about his work. Quite a lot of their conversations were about him and what he was doing. She didn't mind. Jack Carrington was dashing, witty, educated, solicitous—interesting, even—but their conversations were unmistakably one-sided and didn't warrant near the letter space that Jesse did. Perhaps that was proof enough that she ought to take Jesse's advice and be clear with Jack on her intentions, which did not include marriage. She was not looking to be Mrs. Jack Carrington.

Lorna finished the letter and took another sheet. She needed to write to Theo, as well. She would enclose this note with her letter to the family, and they would see to delivering it for her.

Note. The realization brought her up short. Once, she would have had so much to write to Theo. The letters she'd written on board ship and mailed from their ports of call when they'd put in for supplies had been lengthy missives. She'd spent days writing them, and when she hadn't been writing, she'd been storing away thoughts and impressions to share when she next had her pen in her hand. Back then, though, she'd had little else to do all day on board the ship but write or think about writing. Now, she was busy with students, school every day, writing lesson plans at night, visiting families and Jesse's lessons. She didn't have time to write epically long letters.

But in truth, even if she did have that time, she wasn't sure what she would feel comfortable saying to him. She used to believe she could tell Theo anything and be confident that he would understand and empathize with her, but things were different now.

She looked down at the lines she'd written. It had started well enough. She'd made responses to the things he'd mentioned in his last letter and asked a few questions about things he was doing at the store. She responded with what she hoped was appropriate excitement over his descriptions of the social events he'd attended. She pulled out his last letter to make sure she hadn't forgotten something.

He'd written rather extensively about one supper at a Mr. Gladstone's home, sharing everything he'd eaten and that he'd sat beside Mr. Gladstone's pleasant daughter, Edith, who'd worn a dress of water-green silk. How astute, Lorna had thought at the time, of Theo to pay so much attention to Edith's apparel. Such attentiveness would no doubt serve him well in his work at the emporium. Lady customers appreciated being assisted by someone who paid attention to the details.

Edith had made a few more appearances in the letter along with the reference that Theo thought Edith and Lorna would get along well. *Edith is charming,* Theo had written. *She's read everything and you would love her wit. She believes as you do women should have their own voices in this world. I believe wholeheart-*

edly the two of you would be bosom friends if you were ever to meet...

Lorna sat back, smoothing out the pages of Theo's letter and seeing it anew through the lens of this afternoon and her own letter to her mother, full of Jesse Kittredge—and the people of Woods River, but mostly Jesse. She and Theo were growing apart. Would her stories about people he didn't know and would never meet mean anything to him? Probably very little, just as his stories about Boston and his life there meant less to her than he might have imagined. They mattered, of course, because he mattered to her. What was important to him was important to her; that was how friendship worked. But if he had not been present in the stories, the news he shared would not have held her attention at all.

What *did* hold her attention, however, was how often Theo had mentioned Edith Gladstone. Why had she not noticed it before? Perhaps because when she had first read the letter, it was before she and Jesse had skipped stones, before she and Jesse had talked about prayer beneath the scarlet aspens, before Jesse had confessed to her that God had betrayed him. Her new awareness of Jesse seemed to increase her awareness of similar feelings between others, as well.

Did Theo feel about Edith the way she felt about Jesse? Close? Together? As if they were sharing something deep but intangible, something that existed only between them? If so, she ought to be happy for her friend.

She'd not forgotten the way Theo had looked that last day in Concord under the church elm when they'd said goodbye. She'd grieved over the way she had hurt her friend. But apparently, Theo had recovered from the disappointment and he'd moved on.

Well, why shouldn't he? It had been six months since she'd left. She didn't want to think of him moping around Boston. Yet, she could not ignore the hurt that took up residence in her belly. Their friendship was changing and part of her mourned it. But also, she recognized that she'd moved on, too. Boston and Concord seemed like a dream; even the ship and Mrs. Grace Elliott seemed like something shadowy and half remembered. Woods River was her reality now. On that note, she closed her letter to Theo and set it aside. Time to work on tomorrow's lessons, always with the hope that tomorrow would be the day the miners' children would show up.

They didn't show up the next day or the next. Friday arrived with one more week gone without the miners' children in school. Lorna erased the chalkboard Friday afternoon, trying to focus instead on the successes of the week. Her eight students were making enormous strides. Adam was nearly reading at his grade level, an extraordinary accomplishment considering how far he'd had to come. The Putnam girl's spelling was improving alongside her reading. The North boys, who had only been able to add and subtract when they'd begun the school year, now knew their timetables up through sevens. She was pleased with all of them, but Lorna supposed she was greedy. She wanted these successes for all the children in Woods River.

"Lorna, you're still here. Good. I was afraid I had missed you." Jack Carrington strode into the classroom, dressed in a pressed dark suit, his white, wide smile in evidence on his handsome face, his dark hair neatly combed back and pomaded into submission. He might have stepped off the streets of San Francisco or Boston with all that sartorial attention to detail.

She smiled to hide her own disappointment that it was him instead of…someone else…come to walk her home, no doubt. "I am still here. I didn't want to leave a mess for Monday morning."

"Of course, of course. You are so conscientious, Lorna. The town council has just met, and we are wondering if you might be able to join us for some school business? We're just next door in the sanctuary."

"Absolutely. Let me get my things." Lorna understood it wasn't really a question. A knot tied itself in her stomach. She hoped the sudden summons didn't forebode trouble. "Is there a problem, Jack?" she asked as they made their way to the meeting.

"Not at all," Jack assured her, and she felt the knot of worry ease somewhat in her belly—though it didn't disappear entirely. "We have some questions but it has nothing to do with you." That didn't sound good and the knot tightened again.

The gentlemen were all polite, rising from their seats to greet her and thank her for her time. She complimented them on their children, sharing a positive comment about each of her students. "Please, sit, Miss Alderly." Mayor North gestured to an empty chair. "We are interested in an update on the great experiment of our little school."

Oh, was that all? That was easy enough. Lorna regaled them for fifteen minutes about the things they were learning, from reading to geography and history. "Their progress is astounding, owing in part to the small class size. It is possible to focus on each child individually to their benefit." She glanced in Jack's direction. "It has also been helpful to have the support of your supplies. The chalkboard, the primers and the maps help more than you know."

"Splendid," Mr. Putnam said when she finished. "Listening to you talk makes me want to go back to school myself."

"You are welcome to visit any day, Mr. Putnam." Lorna smiled, feeling as if she'd worried for nothing. But she was not out of the woods of the Woods River's ad hoc school board yet.

It was Parker Hudson, the only member with no children enrolled at the school, who spoke up. "You are doing a credible job, Miss Alderly. But attendance is a concern. It is concerning that we have invested in all of this for just eight students when there are several more children who should be there but are not."

"Seventeen," she supplied, overcome with earnestness as the opportunity presented itself to share her greatest point of concern. "There are seventeenmore children, Mr. Hudson, in the mining encampment who are of school age. I am so glad you brought that up. I have discussed the matter with Mr. Carrington, and I am aware that some of the older children might feel compelled to work for a wage instead of attend school. I was thinking that if wages for family men could be raised, it might take away the need those children feel to start working at such a young age, freeing those children up to attend school after all."

The men exchanged looks between them that she couldn't read. Mayor North arched a brow that designated Jack the group's spokesperson. Jack cleared his throat. "Miss Alderly and I did speak of such an option." He gave her a friendly look and for a moment hope flared. Had Jack taken her suggestion? "I did raise wages last month right after you and I discussed the idea.". "I am sorry you haven't seen an improvement in attendance."

"She managed a smile. "I must thank you, Mr. Carrington for trying my suggestion. I truly thought it would work. Indeed, I am mystified as to why it did not." Something felt off here, to Lorna. I will redouble my efforts to find other ways to reach them and convince them of the benefits of education." She addressed the others. "Mr. Carrington shared that perhaps the miners' children would come when the weather changed and they realize the school offers them a chance to be somewhere warm all day. I will go visit the families again and renew my invitation." But if extra wages hadn't swayed them, she wasn't sure a hot fire would. She was feeling extremely pessimistic at the moment and suspicious as if she were missing something. Everything didn't quite add up. People had seemed open to school in the beginning. What had changed?

The board nodded their heads. "You are welcome to try, Miss Alderly, but don't get your hopes up. Miners are illiterate. They don't always appreciate the importance of an education," Mr. Putnam said, echoing Jack's earlier sentiment. "They simply don't see the need for it, and change is hard. Education will potentially change things for them, for their children."

"Change for good," Lorna protested, "and it's not all just the classics," she argued politely, remembering Jesse's earlier comments. "We learn practical material like how to add accounts and figure interest."

"Parents won't thank you for showing them up in front of their children, Miss Alderly," Mr. Putnam explained patiently. "How do you think they'll feel once their children know more than they do? There will be resentment all around."

Or there might be success. Children might teach their parents to read and raise them up, too. That was the greatest hope, that children would teach their families. But Lorna kept that opinion to herself, sensing that might be too much for the board to hear at present. There would be another time, a better time for that argument. "I will try, nonetheless. Surely, one would think resentment would be outweighed by empowering one's child to do better than themselves." Lorna rose, sensing the interview was at an end.

"We are sorry, too. We want you to know that." Mayor North rose with her. "When we hired a teacher, we truly thought there would be greater interest. We'll run the school through the year until June, of course, and honor the contract regardless of how many students you have. However, if we can't get enrollment up, we'll have to revisit whether or not our community can support a school next year."

Lorna froze. "What are you saying, Mayor North?"

"I am saying, Miss Alderly, that at the end of the year, if we don't have the numbers, the school will not continue. The Carringtons have pledged to pay your way back home, if that happens. You needn't worry about being stranded here."

Jack stepped to her side, a reassuring hand at the small of her back. "Who knows what the future holds, Miss Alderly. If that were to happen, you might find another role to play in our community that would convince you to stay. But gentlemen, June is nine months away. Let's not be too hasty or worry Miss Alderly unduly."

"Of course. My apologies if the news upsets you, Miss Alderly." Mayor North tried to make amends.

Lorna gathered herself. "What of your sons' educations? The boys are quite bright. Will you leave them without any schooling?"

North shifted on his feet. "If they're bright enough, Miss Alderly, as you say, my wife and I have discussed sending them to a boarding school in St. Louis. There is also a school in San Francisco that is new but has a good reputation."

She nodded. "Well, June is a long way off. We'll discuss this again, I am sure." She hoped she sounded more confident than she felt. Was it just a few nights ago she'd felt as if this place had become her home? And now she was about to lose it, to be given her marching orders in June. Unless…unless…she got the miners' children to come.

"Shall I walk you home, Lorna?" Jack asked once they were outside.

"No, thank you. I would like some time to think over everything that was discussed." She left Jack and headed home. But when she reached her little gate, she walked on, her feet knowing where she wanted to go. She wanted Jesse. If anyone would have ideas about convincing the miners, it would be him.

Chapter Thirteen

What did she think *he* could do about her problem? Lorna had asked to speak with him outside after dinner. In truth, that should have been his second hint that something was bothering her. His first should have been realizing something was off during dinner, but he'd been too busy enjoying the stew and biscuits and rambunctious conversation at the table. That's what he got for being distracted. They'd gone out back to the little patch of garden at the rear of the Kittredge cottage, and Lorna had given full vent to her frustration. He could listen, and he had been listening for the last twenty minutes as Lorna recounted her conversation with the town council. But beyond listening and commiserating, what more he could offer her?

"So that's it. I either get enrollment up to a level worth sustaining or I pack my bags and go home at the end of the year." Lorna threw up her hands. "Perhaps I can convince the school board that quality is of equal merit as quantity, that it's worth it to invest in even just eight students." But from her tone, it didn't seem that Lorna felt there was much possibility that direction.

"I am sorry to hear the news," Jesse said at last. "You've traveled a long way, and I know how committed you are to your work. But, now that you know, you could spend the year sending out inquiries for other posts in the area. Maybe Mrs. Elliott could help you find another if you don't want to travel back home."

Her blue eyes flared. Somehow he'd said the wrong thing. "And just give up?" She started pacing again. At this rate, she was going to wear a path in the fallow garden. Nothing had been planted there since Evie had died.

"We can't make students materialize out of thin air." Jesse crossed his arms and leaned against the house wall.

"That's the point. We shouldn't need to. The students are there. The schoolroom should be full—it *would* be if the students eligible would simply show up," Lorna said fiercely. Her tenacity was admirable, but Jesse didn't want to see that determination wasted on a lost cause. "We just need to figure out how to get them there."

We. Such a small word and yet so powerful. When had this become a "we" problem? Or, when had they become "we"? He'd not been a "we" for a long time. He wasn't sure how he felt about that. Yes, he had responsibility for his children and for his crew. But to be a "we" with Lorna would be different. He was a caretaker for his children and his crew. He looked out for them. Lorna would want more than caretaking. She'd want to be a partner, an equal. He studied her in the falling dark, her slim, elegant silhouette outlined in the fading daylight, her elegance at odds with the muddy, overgrown garden patch. She was made for symmetry and order, not for chaos and its uncertain jagged edges. Yet here she was, and she was putting everything she had into staying. Maybe there was something he could give her, after all. Understanding. He could show her what she was up against.

"Do you want me to go with you tomorrow?" It would mean he wouldn't have the whole day up at his secret place—but he didn't regret making the offer.

Especially when it seemed to cheer her. "Would you? Perhaps they'll listen to you. Thank you, Jesse. We can go at noon after the auxiliary meeting." She smiled for the first time that evening and Jesse thought losing a half day of work in the hills was a fair compromise, even though he was sure she wouldn't be smiling this time tomorrow. The visit wouldn't change their minds.

Jesse met her at the church shortly after noon the next day, feeling conspicuous as the ladies filed down the steps with their considering gazes. These were the women who aspired to ape Mrs. Hamish Carrington in fashion and lifestyle, the town women like Ellie Putnam and Catherine North. He touched his hat politely. "Good day, Mrs. Putnam, Mrs. North."

"Mr. Kittredge, it's good to see you. You haven't been into the store for a while." Mrs. Putnam smiled knowingly as Lorna joined him. "Perhaps Miss Alderly should bring you by to see some of the new things we've gotten for winter. I am sure your children need new clothes."

He gave her a nod. "Perhaps," he offered noncommittally. "Shall we be off, Miss Alderly?" He was eager to be away from the ladies and their speculations. He didn't have to be a mind reader to know what they were thinking. *Was there something between him and Miss Alderly? Or was his presence at her side purely for business?* Small towns would read an entire history in the smallest of events if given the chance. It was the same everywhere. It had been that way in the coal town in Appalachia. The whole town had known that he and Evie were courting almost before they'd even begun. Back then, he hadn't minded. He'd wanted the whole world to know he loved her. But this wasn't like that. He didn't know what "this" was with Miss Alderly. It had somehow become something more than his obligation to the new schoolteacher. Whatever it was, it needed to be handled with care and discretion so that no one was hurt by false assumptions or misunderstandings.

"You fit in with them," Jesse said as they began the walk to the encampment. It required them to pass through the center of town, which was crowded on a Saturday afternoon, and Jesse was glad he was with her. A lone woman would have been subject to catcalls and inappropriate overtures. A few men from his crew called out to him as they passed.

He did not miss the knowing look Lorna slid him. "Is that your way of saying that I don't fit in at the encampment?" It was exactly what he wanted to warn her of.

"It's a compliment." He tried for a tactical retreat now that the words were out. "The ladies of the auxiliary like you. You are a good addition to their circle. What sort of events do you all have planned?" He moved her around a pile of manure.

"We are planning an autumn box lunch social for the third Saturday of October to raise money for Christmas food boxes." The event was just two weeks away.

"Christmas already?" He liked too much the way her face lit up. *Don't you dare care about such things, Jesse. You are helping her, that's all. Don't get invested like this. You know she won't stay, that she can't stay. And even if she did, what could she ever be to you? Could she replace Evie? No, nothing and no one ever could.*

"We have to plan ahead because everything must be ordered in, and we have the weather to consider. Wagons can't get through if the snows are too deep. Best to get supplies in as soon as possible. Mr. Putnam will handle the ordering."

"Spoken like a true Woods River citizen," Jesse said thoughtfully. She might look like the woman he'd picked up in Sonoma, but she was definitely adjusting her perspective and fitting in here. He'd not have guessed that. Well, fitting in with a certain crowd, he amended, as if the qualifier could be used to protect himself from liking her too much. From missing her too much when she left.

They approached the encampment and Lorna smoothed her dark blue skirts. "I wore my plainest dress." He knew what she meant. He could hear the unspoken words: *I tried. I am doing my best to be approachable.*

He nodded. "I'll be there with you." For whatever that was worth. He hoped, for her sake, it would be worth a little something.

At the tents and shelters, the visits took on a pattern. Lorna would greet the women and the men who were home. The men knew Jesse and he shook hands with them. But wherever they went, the reception was the same. "No, thank you. Our son needs to work." Or, "What does our daughter need any learning for? She's already thirteen, too old for school. She'll be married soon anyway."

To her credit, Lorna did not shy away from the argument. "Perhaps that's all the more reason she should come to school," Lorna answered Mrs. Davis smoothly, while holding Mrs. Davis's youngest on her lap, a three-month-old babe. "She'll have children of her own someday, and she'll want to be able to teach them the basics. It is often a woman's responsibility to educate the children as part of running the household." As if the tarp in the wilderness beside a cook fire and river could be termed a "household." Jesse wondered how Mrs. Davis, who couldn't read a single word, would take that comment. "A year of education could teach your daughter quite a bit," Lorna pressed in her gentle way.

"But who would help with the children?" Mrs. Davis referenced the other six, in various ages between the thirteen-year-old and the three-month-old. How old was Mrs. Davis? Thirty perhaps? She looked forty. But Jesse knew her husband, Alan. He worked on Kinney's crew. He was in his early thirties and supporting a family of eight on wages less than Jesse's. How did he do it?

Just a glance around was enough to answer that question. He did it by cutting everything that wasn't essential—and some of the things that *were* essential, too. He was living under a canopy, his kids running barefoot. A family could survive like that in the summer, but what would they do when winter came? This area didn't see the heaviest of the snow but it did see some and temperatures definitely dropped. Shoes would require a visit to the company store and perhaps buying on credit if they couldn't get them at Putnam's.

Jesse thought about the contract and the transportation fee. He knew what it had cost for a family for four. It would be double that for Davis's family. Davis would never be out from under that obligation—if they survived long enough to even try.

"Perhaps you could spare her for half a day? She could come home at lunch. We do reading and math in the mornings and that would be most useful for her." Lorna had a ready answer for everything. "Would you please consider sending her and letting her decide?"

They left the Davises and moved on to the next family and the next, Lorna politely accepting the families' noncommittal responses. "It's like they're afraid of something," she mused as they walked down the way a bit to the next cluster of households. "I feel as if they're holding back, that these reasons are just excuses. Is it me, Jesse? Are they afraid of me? Are they afraid of education? I must try harder."

She did try harder at the Everts', who had an actual tent. She sat outside at the trestle table with Mr. and Mrs. Evert, their ten- and eleven-year-old boys running nearby. Jesse listened to her make the same arguments, that any education was better than no education. But the Everts remained stoic.

At last, Lorna gave up the mask of politeness. "I know you've been given an increase in your wages, Mr. Evert. Mr. Carrington has offered family men with school-age boys a bonus so that the families needn't feel they must choose between giving their boys an education and making ends meet. So, forgive me if I don't understand why you continue to not send them."

Jesse watched something flicker in Mr. Evert's eyes. The man was not used to being addressed directly by a woman or argued with by one, either. "That's not how the money was explained to us, Miss Alderly. Carrington did not attach any stipulation to the money. It's simply a raise. The money does not require the children to attend." His boys, Jesse knew, both worked as lamplighters in the mine shafts, carrying lanterns to the darker places, helping to light the tunnels. The raise this fall hadn't just been for one person in that family but for all three, if the boys didn't go to school. They weren't the only family who saw the raise that way. If increased wages were good for one worker in the family, then increased wages for two more people in the family was even better.

Lorna crossed her arms for a thoughtful moment. "And you work, as well, Mrs. Evert?"

"Yes, she does," Mr. Evert answered for his wife. "She takes in laundry."

"All four of you are working, bringing in a wage." Lorna did not waiver under the censure of Mr. Evert's glinting stare. Something akin to pride swelled in Jesse even as he wished she'd proceed with caution. "Are you saving money? Putting something aside? Does all four of you working get you ahead? Are you making progress on your debt to Carrington?" she said boldly. "How long have you been here?"

"Two years. We came on the same wagon train as

Kittredge. They picked us up in Independence. What's your point, Miss Alderly?"

Lorna reached into her basket and pulled out a tablet of paper and pencil. She wrote a series of numbers on the tablet. "Here's my point. Mr. Carrington charged you five hundred dollars to transport your family of four. One hundred and fifty dollars for you and your wife, and then one hundred dollars for each of your sons. This was part of your contract with him. You are to work this off over time."

"And I can pay as I like, a little extra some months, or a little less other months, depending on my need. It's a very flexible arrangement." Mr. Evert was getting defensive.

"Flexible—but calculated at ten percent interest. Do you know how to calculate interest, Mr. Evert? Fifty dollars is ten percent of five hundred. Every month there's a balance on your account, and then ten percent of that sum is added to that balance." Jesse watched Lorna's pencil fly across the paper. "If I owed a debt of five hundred dollars and I paid ten dollars a month on it, I might think that I would have it paid off in fifty months, a little over four years. That doesn't sound that bad. But, that's not how it works. Only about seven of those dollars actually goes toward the five hundred I originally owed. The other three dollars goes toward the interest. So every ten months, instead of bringing the total down by a hundred dollars, I'm only bringing it down by seventy. That means it will really take a third more time to pay off the fee and the five hundred dollars will actually cost me seven hundred. And that's only if I really am paying ten dollars every month—never missing a month, never paying in less when times are lean."

Jesse wished someone had explained that to him before he and Evie had left Appalachia. It might have made a difference. "It's how all of our contracts were written up," Jesse offered, thinking to soften the blow for Evert. He could see the man doing another kind of math, the math of mortality. Miners didn't have long lives. If Evert was already thirty, with eight to ten years to go on the fee to Carrington, the man would be forty before he could claim all of his wages free and clear.

"We only make seventy dollars a week with all of us working, and there's the rent to consider and the cost of food. Prices here are expensive," Mrs. Evert put in, speaking up for the first time. Jesse knew she was thinking about all the months where they weren't able to pay ten dollars. She was, no doubt, realizing that paying off the total might take them more like fourteen years. Shortly, she'd realize how important the autumn raise had been for the whole family, how they couldn't pass on the boys making that money, too.

Evert was defiant. "That can't be right. What sort of benefit does Carrington get out of having people owe him money that can't be paid back?"

"He doesn't make money off of us, Evert," Jesse offered. "He makes money off what we take out of the mine." He was only just now starting to understand how much money their work produced. Certainly enough that the man could afford to hire wagon trains of workers and front their transportation expenses. Of course, wages were somewhat minimal. It was really only the initial cost of bringing everyone to California that would truly set him back. "And we can't leave. He's guaranteed a work force." There were other things they couldn't do, too, like protest. Carrington held all the money and the debt—and that meant he held all the power, too. They had no leverage.

Evert shook his head. "I didn't know."

"Actually, you *did* know. We all knew. It's in our contracts. Carrington hid nothing from us. We signed of our own free will," Jesse reminded Evert. "I couldn't read my contract, though," Jesse admitted. "I imagine you couldn't, either. We relied entirely on what the agent told us. It sounded pretty good. We pay as we go for the transportation fee—a fee none of us could have afforded on our own, ever—we have a guaranteed salary, seven dollars a day. I know just how enticing that sounded. We pay a little out of that every month and keep the rest of our wages. Interest meant nothing to us. We chose the opportunity." He could see Evert was distraught and overwhelmed. He'd ease it for the man if he could. There was nothing more to be done but bear the burden.

"I can see this is somewhat dire news." Lorna brought the conversation back around to her original point. "This is why school matters for your sons, now. They should be able to read their contracts, to have a full understanding of the commitments they are making. Perhaps more education could mean they might also have more opportunities so that they don't feel trapped."

"So they can be hoity-toity gentlemen, looking down on their old man?" Evert growled.

"Now, hold on, Evert. She did not say that," Jesse cut in. "You feed your family, and you keep them as well as you can. No one should ever have cause to look down on that." Jesse paused, then added, "I am sending Adam to school. I don't want him in the mines when he's thirty wondering if his boss will care enough for his safety to spend the money on proper timbering, or if he'll be able to come out of his shift and go home to his family. I don't want him to feel hopeless. I can't change things for me. I've accepted that. But I don't get to decide that for my son." He felt Lorna's eyes on him, warm and perhaps surprised after their discussion about foreign folktales.

Evert rose. "We'll talk it over. Thank you for your directness, Kittredge. Miss Alderly. I'll talk with some of the others, as well, and see what I can do." It was the best they were going to get today and Jesse hoped it would be a start. He also hoped that start wouldn't raise trouble with Carrington. Hopefully he'd forestalled that by pointing out that Carrington hadn't done anything wrong with the contracts. They weren't generous, certainly, but they weren't unfair, either.

He'd hated having to defend Carrington, but neither could he honestly paint Carrington as a swindler. Carrington had hidden nothing. It had been there for anyone to read, only people hadn't read, hadn't understood what they were signing, committing to. Carrington had kept his hands clean…mostly. But there was also no denying Carrington had an agenda and miners' children in school was not part of that agenda.

Carrington would never come out and say it; he preferred more covert methods of making his disapproval evident. That way, nothing could be traced back to him directly. It was not how Jesse liked to do business. But it wasn't as if he had any choice. Not while he labored under the weight of a contract, too.

Chapter Fourteen

"I would like to see where you work," Lorna mentioned as they made their way through town on the return from the encampment. Jesse hesitated. The request had caught him off guard. "I've been in a mining town for two months and I have yet to see the actual mine."

"That's because it's on the outskirts of town. It's a bit of a walk." Jesse nodded to a man he knew on the street, and Lorna had the impression he was trying to ignore answering.

"You walk there and back every day. I am sure I can handle it," Lorna argued. "I want to see it, Jesse. Is it true what you said to Evert about the timbering? Is the mine not safe?" Jesse had been quietly fierce at the end and impressively so. For a few moments, he'd worn his heart on his sleeve, his love for his children evident in his argument—an argument Lorna hoped would resonate with Evert as a father. Perhaps Jesse's plea would reach them in ways her arguments couldn't.

She understood better today the gap between her and the miners. It wasn't only that she came from a different background, a different life, it was that she was a young, unmarried woman with no children, no family of her own—no responsibility to anyone but herself. What could she possibly know about their struggles? But Jesse was like them. He had a family.

Lorna hoped it would be enough to convince some of them at least. That would be an improvement. And if she could just convince a few, perhaps things could grow from there. Big things came from little seeds. She'd seen a spark of interest in Susannah Davis's eye before her mother had sent her off to watch the other children. The girl was willing. It was just the mother. *Please God, move Mrs. Davis's heart.* Lorna sent up the simple prayer as she and Jesse turned left at the church. But perhaps it wasn't Mrs. Davis's heart that needed moving, so she added, *And Mr. Davis's, just in case.*

"You're an exasperating woman, Lorna Alderly." Jesse blew out a heavy sigh. "Are you never content?" He was only half teasing.

"How can I be content when there is justice to be done?" She shot him a look that matched his half teasing, half serious response. "Before I left Boston, there was a movement to support compulsory education in the state of Massachusetts. My family hopes that it will become law, that all children will be required to attend school. That way, every child will have a chance to open up their world because they *are* educated."

"This is not Massachusetts, Lorna," Jesse cautioned. "California is not a seat of revolutionary fervor, social, political or otherwise."

She slid him a saucy smile. "I disagree. I think it is—or at least, it certainly could be. A woman has more opportunity in California than she does in Boston if she is brave enough to take it. I think California needs to begin as it means to go on." They left the row of cottages behind them, heading out beyond the town. She hid a smile. He was taking her to the mine.

She'd not been this direction yet. There were more tents, more encampments. These seemed to be lived in by single men instead of families. They were in far worse condition. But there was also a long row of large, neat cottages with gardens and whitewashed fences. "Who lives here?" Lorna asked.

"Carrington's foremen. He likes them to live close to the mine in case he needs them quickly," Jesse explained.

"Are they married? Do they have families? I'd like to meet them."

"You cannot start a revolution here." Jesse's hand briefly touched her arm. She wasn't sure if it was to emphasize his warning or to simply guide her over the terrain. Perhaps both.

"I don't want to start a revolution. I just want to ask questions." She smiled sweetly, but Jesse narrowed his gaze to convey his doubt that that would be the end of it. She didn't know why he was so suspicious—she had no intention of starting trouble. Though that would, of course, depend on the answers she got.

They turned a corner and the timbered entrance of the mine came into view, built into the side of a hill. A sign above it read The Carrington Trend, and the place was bustling. It was like turning the corner into a whole new world. The mine was a little town of its own. There were tracks laid that ran into the mine and out, moving carts of ore to the surface to wagons that would carry it to the refinery. "It's busy," Lorna commented as some men called out to Jesse.

"Mining never sleeps. I'm just glad that my crew is fortunate to work days. Plus, we have Sundays off and one Saturday a month. There are crews that work all night, crews that work on Sunday," Jesse explained. "But we were one of the first here, so we have what you might call 'seniority.'"

Lorna looked about her, noting the men and the amount of young boys, boys younger than twelve, younger than Adam. "What do the children do? Surely, they don't wield a pickax?"

Jesse shook his head. "No, the younger boys carry lanterns to the darker places in the mine so that the miners have light. I won't take you inside, so don't even ask. But if you were to go inside, you'd find a corridor that you'd follow back deep into the hillside. There are tunnels—stopes, we call them—that branch off the main corridor. Tunnel One, Tunnel Two and so on. There are eight tunnels on the main level so far."

"Main level?" Lorna inquired, shading her eyes to get a better look at the mine entrance and the towering hillside.

"There are ladders down to the second and third levels, nearly thirty feet below ground. The arrangement is the same on each level—a corridor with branching tunnels. It's like a rabbit warren down there."

It would also be hot and airless, Lorna surmised, although she didn't say it out loud. "Men work that far underground? Do the lantern boys go down that far, too?" Jesse nodded and Lorna felt her anger start to simmer at the idea that boys traded an education for this. Yes, they brought in a wage, but the danger they must face! And by choosing to work instead of learn, they lost the chance to gain the skills for any other kind of profession.

"What level and tunnel do you work on?" She didn't like imagining Jesse working in that hillside, shut up inside all day. The landscape suddenly seemed menacing and evil. Everything in the vicinity of the mine was stark and gray. There were none of the vibrant fall colors or towering evergreens.

"My crew works Tunnel Thirteen on the main level, the newest tunnel Carrington has opened up."

"Because you're the best?" Lorna commented. "Seems like if you're the best you should have the tunnel closest to the front where there's more…air."

Jesse shrugged. "I am pleased to not be working on level three. I take my blessings where I can get them." She slanted a dubious look his direction to say, "What blessings?" He gave her a strong look. "I don't expect you to understand, Lorna. I'm a crew chief, so while Evert makes seven dollars a day, I make nine. I work in the main shaft. I get Sundays off so that I can take my children to church and I work during the day so that my children are not unattended at night. Nearly every man, excepting the foremen and Carrington himself, would trade places with me in an instant. To them, I am someone to be envied." He jerked his head toward the road back to town. "C'mon, let's get back. There's nothing more to see here."

It took Lorna most of the walk to get a grip on her anger. She was having trouble assembling her thoughts into coherent words with all she'd learned and seen today. This morning, she'd thought only to go and visit families, to convince them to send their children to school, but the day had become so much more, a revelation of the corruption in Woods River. "You didn't answer my question earlier, Jesse. Are the mines not safe?"

Jesse gave a harsh chuckle. "What is safe? Mines can never be completely safe, Lorna. The very air in them is full of dust, and most of the dust is made up of mineral particles. It's very hard on the lungs over time. Then there's the risk of a cave-in if the hillside cannot support being dug out. That's where timbering comes in. Ideally, enough poles are put in to stabilize the roof and hold up the hillside, but timbering is expensive and it takes time. Time is money to men like Carrington. Time spent timbering is time and manpower not spent extracting gold."

"But men lost is expensive, too," Lorna argued.

"Men are replaceable. Time is not. There are plenty of men looking for work now that the initial excitement of the Gold Rush has settled," Jesse explained. They'd veered down to the river to the place where they'd skipped the stones. "Early in the Rush, there weren't these underground hard-rock mines. There was just gold in the waters, waiting to be plucked out. Men stood in the rivers with tin pans and pulled nuggets practically out of thin air." Lorna nodded, smiling at the excitement that had crept into Jesse's voice. She'd read those stories, too.

"Those were real stories, Lorna. There were still men trying to do that—panning for gold and placer mining, mining streambed deposits for gold—when we arrived.

Carrington was one of the first to get in on underground mining and he did it at the right time. The gold that was in rivers was just the tip of the iceberg. The real rich deposits lay beneath the earth and can only be reached by underground mining. Underground mining takes money and a larger effort than a single ordinary man can take on by himself. But Carrington had a fortune to lever and with it, he's made himself another fortune or two."

"At the expense of other men. I think his methods must be questioned." Lorna threw a rock into the river. It felt good to let out some of her anger with the physical act. It wasn't just Jack Carrington that she was angry at. She was angry with Jesse, too, but for different reasons. "You knew the miners' children wouldn't come. Why didn't you tell me? Warn me?"

Jesse gave her a solemn gaze. "Would you have listened?"

She threw another rock and gave him a wry glance. "I suppose I deserve that. I'm not going to say you're wrong."

"You're a fixer, Lorna. You see a problem and you want to solve it. Like my reading lessons. I'm glad for them and I'm grateful to you for goading me into it. But you cannot fix every problem, Lorna. And you need to be careful. Do not challenge Carrington. He has all the power, all the money."

"But you have all the labor. He needs his miners to show up for work. He can't make money without you."

"How long would we last without our wages? Carrington has the only operation in town—and he could probably get us blackballed from any mine in the area if we tried to just leave and go somewhere else. We can't afford to outwait him. His fortune runs deeper than ours, and when we come back he can reduce our wages in retaliation. Where would that leave men like Evert who are barely making ends meet even now? Already mining wages are falling. Four years ago, a miner might be lucky to make ten dollars a day at some places, and now, the most he can hope for is to make seven out here."

"Seven dollars a day for risking his life." Lorna shook her head, another worrying idea creeping in. "Jesse, have you ever been in an accident at a mine?" she asked softly. His face changed and he gave a slow nod.

"There was a bad one at the mine in Appalachia right before I left. Four men were killed and a whole tunnel was lost due to poor timbering. At the time, I thought it was the sign I'd been praying for that I should take the offer to come to California. I felt if I stayed, it would only be a matter of time before such an accident happened to me. The owners were closing the mine eventually. They were not interested in investing in safety measures knowing the end was near. There'd be no return on their investment."

"Do you worry about it happening here?"

"I don't worry *if* it will happen because it *will* happen here. It is inevitable if you mine something long enough. It's just a matter of when."

She wanted to ask how he managed the courage to go to work every day but she knew what he'd say. Because his children depended on him, because he could do nothing else. He had no other choices.

In tacit agreement, they turned from the river and walked back to the row of cottages in silence. Lorna's mind was too full to talk. Never had she encountered a situation firsthand where exploitation was so nakedly obvious. Something must be done, starting with asking questions. And she *would* ask them of Jack, tomorrow at Sunday dinner.

Jesse saw her to the gate of her cottage. "Thank you. I didn't realize I'd be asking you to give up your only Saturday," she said quietly. "I appreciate you coming all the more for it." She paused and then, because she wouldn't see him again until Monday night for lessons, she said, "You will be safe, won't you?" She suddenly couldn't bear the thought of Jesse going to work in that dark mine, couldn't bear the idea of him going in and not coming out.

She felt rather than saw his hand reach for hers in the folds of her skirts. "I can say that I'll be careful. And you be careful, too, Lorna. Mines are not the only dangers in these parts." He gave her a tight smile, but she couldn't miss the worry in his eyes. Worry for her more than for himself, because that was the kind of man he was. But she'd not been raised to stand idly by while others suffered and she had the power to do something about it. That was the kind of woman *she* was.

Until now, going to the Hill on Sundays had been like a little oasis—a sanctuary of comfort and serenity outside of the toils of her daily routine. After yesterday, Lorna had revised her thinking on that. There could be no comfort or serenity when the cost of it was paid by the broken backs of others. That new thought reshaped the lens through which she saw every luxury— the imported Irish linen tablecloth with its expensive cutwork, the china from England, the crystal from Paris, the exquisite cuts of meat and fresh vegetables grown in a garden for the exclusive use of the Hill. Until yesterday, she'd wondered why the Hill had been built a distance from town, but after seeing the mine, Lorna finally understood.

The mine was unbeautiful. It was dirty and it dirtied the landscape around it. Residents of the Hill did not want to look out its white curtained windows and be reminded that mining polluted water and landscapes, and men's lungs.

By the time Jack was ready to drive her home, Lorna understood that she would have to give it up—the meals and the bathtub, too. Her conscience demanded nothing less, and it saddened her. She'd come to look forward to Mrs. Carrington's bathing room, and she'd come to think of the Hill as a piece of civilization amidst the wilderness. But as her father was fond of reminding them, ugly was not compelling. Ugly would not persuade someone to compromise their ethic. It was far harder to give up beautiful things than ugly things.

"Jack, may I ask you something?" She felt some trepidation as she began what could be a difficult conversation—although she hoped that Jack would surprise her.

There was a flash of his smile. "Anything at all. Do you want to know my secrets?" he teased.

She smiled back, a little weakly. "The miners you brought here by wagon train signed contracts they couldn't read. Did you know that? Many of them had no idea how interest worked or that they'd end up paying more than the stipulated amount. Some of these men have a debt that will outlast their working years." She watched Jack for his reaction, wondering if he'd argue with her or perhaps even be angry.

"I think that's unfortunate," he said at last. "It was not the intention of those contracts to trap anyone. The terms were offered freely and stated plainly within the document. No one was compelled to sign. It's a big decision to come out West. People leave a lot behind. They've got to want it." He gave her a small, private smile. "As you know firsthand, Lorna."

"But they can't repay you. Surely you know that and *knew* that when the contracts were drawn up. Those contracts set them up for a lifetime of what constitutes indentured servitude." That was the part that bothered her the most, that these contracts were designed for the men to fail in their bid for financial freedom.

"My father handles the contracts. I do the legwork," Jack reminded her. "But I assure you, no one held a gun to their heads." He furrowed his handsome brow. "Is this what's been bothering you all day? You seemed 'off' at dinner, and I thought it was just lingering upset over the school board news."

"You're not wrong. I *am* still upset over the news. But the two issues are tied together. The miners are so far into debt that everyone in the family who can work must work. It's not just the contract money, Jack, it's the prices at the stores, and it's food and it's rent. Their wages aren't keeping up with the cost of living out here, particularly when you account for their need to pay off their contract debts." By contrast, Jack's family lived far better than many people in Concord, her family included. She knew what her parents would say about Jack's wealth: those with fortunes ought to share them.

"If those children don't get an education, they will be no better off than their parents and will be unable to make different choices or live different lives."

It dawned on Lorna as she said the words out loud that perhaps Jack was less bothered by that reality than she was. He might even *prefer* that reality. An illiterate workforce was in his thrall for as long as he needed it. One that could fend for itself—and had the wherewithal to negotiate on contracts—was less useful to the Carringtons.

Jack tooled the buggy down the row of cottages and parked it before her gate. "I shall speak to my father about your concerns, Lorna. You've a good heart and I want you to be happy. Your happiness is important to me. I hope you know that." His protestations made the butterflies flutter in her stomach, especially when he looked at her like that, with the full attention of his blue eyes.

How many women in Woods River or even San Francisco would welcome attention from this man? Was she one of them? She was not naive. Jack's interest and his invitations to Sunday dinner exceeded his civic duty. These continued invitations signaled a different sort of interest, and her acceptance of them signaled something on her part, as well. If she did not return that interest, she had no business misleading him. So *did* she return the interest? She wasn't certain, but she had a feeling she'd need to decide that very soon.

Chapter Fifteen

The two weeks leading up to the autumn box lunch social passed in a series of gains and setbacks that had Lorna reeling, alternatingy from the thrill of small successes to the little heartbreaks of disappointments. One success was that Susannah Davis came to school. Sometimes. She only came part of the week and even then only stayed for half a day. But it was a start. Lorna made certain to take special care with the girl on the days that she did come. Every minute, every hour with that one needed to count. Although, Lorna was certain the town council wasn't going to count Susannah as an increase in enrollment.

Enrollment was the epitome of "small gains." Including Susannah, Lorna did have three new students: one of the Evert boys and a girl from one of the other families she'd visited. While that was exciting, three—or really two and a half—students wasn't much to show for an afternoon's worth of work, especially when there were still so many children who weren't coming. It was definitely a victory mixed with disappointment.

She could only hope it signified a start and that as the weather grew colder and rumor of the warm stove in the classroom spread, parents might send their children for no other reason than that they could be warm for most of the day. At this point, she didn't care what the motivation was as long as they came. She reminded herself constantly that where she started with the school didn't matter as much as where she ended the year. She had to be patient. She had to be diligent with her prayers. They'd been answered so far. Susannah was here, after all. Lorna had time; the children would come. God had a plan. He had not sent her here only to send her home in June.

The other disappointment was realizing that Jesse wouldn't be at the box lunch social. He'd be at work at the mine, having already had his one monthly Saturday off. Knowing he wouldn't be there dimmed some of her excitement over the social occasion. She supposed she'd been counting on him to help her "work the crowd" during the social, to use it as an opportunity to offer yet another pitch to parents to send their children to the school. But apparently, she'd be on her own.

Lorna finished packing her basket for the social and stepped back from her table to give a final, critical look. She'd baked all day yesterday, making fresh bread she then cut into thick slices and layered with ham for sandwiches. There was lemonade in a jar, and Nazareth cookies for dessert. There were also a few extras, like the remainder of the loaf and a dozen extra cookies for whoever purchased her basket to take home. She thought that feature might enhance the appeal of her basket. She'd also stitched a set of blue-checked cloth napkins. Truth be told, she'd stitched them with Charlotte in mind. Charlotte had admired the cloth on her table, and Lorna knew Jesse would never allow her to simply give the girl something. But if he'd bid on a basket with the napkins in it, he could hardly give them back. Unfortunately, that wasn't going to happen today.

Lorna bit her lip, rethinking the basket. No one else would appreciate those blue-checked napkins like Charlotte. She had an inspiration. She swapped out the napkins for a nice piece of white linen trimmed in lace instead that she had brought from Concord but had yet to use. She had some Nazareth cookies left over, too. Perhaps after the social, she'd stop by the Kittredges and make some excuse to leave the cookies wrapped in the napkins. That prospect made her feel better. Lorna slipped the basket over her arm and set out for the social, already looking forward to it being over after weeks of waiting for it to begin.

The social hall attached to the church was decked out in festive autumn colors. Seeing it this afternoon, after a morning of decorating before she'd gone home to collect her basket and change, was a chance to view it afresh. The sight restored some of Lorna's lost excitement over the event. Vases arranged with beautiful multicolored leaves were set in the center of white-clothed tables, brightening the hall. One table along the far wall already had baskets on it, each basket adding its own sense of decoration. For people who ate most of their meals under a tent or standing up, Lorna thought the hall would be a treat, a nice change of pace.

"Miss Alderly! You're here. You look splendid. That

is the perfect autumn gown." Mrs. Putnam bustled forward from the basket table. "Come put your basket over here." She lifted the lace-trimmed cloth and peeked inside. "This is lovely, and homemade, too." She gave Lorna a sly look. "Some man is going to smell that bread and see those cookies and want to snap you right up." Her eyes twinkled. "Perhaps you have a young man in mind?"

"I just want to help raise money for the Christmas baskets, Mrs. Putnam," Lorna assured the older woman, feeling a little dismayed when it was clear that Mrs. Putnam didn't believe her.

In the end, Jack bought her basket for an unnecessarily exorbitant fee after a brief, good-natured bidding war with Parker Hudson that earned a round of applause and smiles of approval from the little crowd. Hudson didn't seem to mind losing too badly and went on to win the bid for a basket offered by Mrs. Putnam's oldest daughter, Deborah, who worked in the store.

"You are a woman of many talents." Jack beamed at Lorna as she laid out the contents of their lunch at a table. It would apparently just be the two of them at this table, even though it could easily seat six. It seemed that was the way of things, though. Most couples had retired to their own tables, and there was plenty of space, given that there were only about thirty people present, which had surprised and disappointed her. Joseph Knight and his wife, Anna, passed their table. Anna flashed an approving smile at the sight of her with Jack.

"I thought there'd be more people." Lorna took her seat across from Jack and poured them each a jar of lemonade.

Jack made a quick survey of the room and shrugged. "This is the usual collection. All the merchants are here, along with the reverend and his wife." He made a nod of approval. "This seems about right." He gave her a considering look. "Who else did you think would come?" He gave her a smile of realization. "Ah, you thought the miners would be here, that this was an event for the whole town. In its own way, it is. The proceeds raised here benefit those who are not in attendance." He leaned in and lowered his voice. "Lorna, the miners could not afford to bid on the lunches. If they were to come, it would be an embarrassment to them, a damage to their pride. No one wants to be reminded of what they can't afford."

She rather thought Jesse would say the same thing, but somehow it would make more sense and sound less condescending coming from him. Hearing it from Jack made it sound pompous instead of considerate. Jack surprised her by taking her hand. "I have news, Lorna." His eyes were twinkling with secrets.

"You've talked to your father about the contracts?" she asked hopefully.

He chuckled and her hopes fell. "No, not yet. He's been busy. It's something else, something bigger," he teased.

"What could be bigger than helping the citizens of one's community?" Lorna couldn't resist the little prod. This could be a problem easily fixed with a little debt forgiveness. It would take nothing more than the stroke of a pen—and similar problems could be prevented going forward if these miners' children were sent to school and given the tools to take charge of their futures.

Jack either didn't understand the prod or chose to ignore it. "The California State Senate." He grinned.

That *was* big news and it was intriguing in its own right. "The senate? Do you mean to stand for election?"

"Yes. Elections are next fall but you know how these things are, campaigns must plan ahead. I need to begin to get all my ducks in a row now if I want to succeed." He ran his thumb over the back of her hand in a gentle motion. "A strong candidate needs a strong woman at his side, a woman who is lovely, educated, cultivated and has a heart for important causes." He held her gaze. "I wonder where I might find such a woman?" he said in soft, teasing tones that implied that woman might very well be sitting right here.

She gently extricated her hand from his, a tremor that was part excitement and part anxiety rippling through her. Did she want to be that woman? A senator's wife could do a lot of good. The prospect was not without some appeal, but was it the right choice? "You need a wife who doesn't have a career."

"I think a senator's wife makes her husband's career her own. It's a demanding position, after all," Jack corrected, apparently seeing nothing wrong with the idea that a woman should give up her own aspirations in order to embrace her husband's. Would he think the same thing if he were asked to give up his mining ambitions in order to grow the school? But she knew the answer to that already, didn't she? He couldn't even make time to speak to his father about the injustice of the miners' contracts. That spoke to where his priorities were—and where they were likely to remain. A man could not serve both God and mammon.

Around them, people were finishing their lunches. Lorna took the opportunity to pack up the remnants of their basket, hoping to avoid any further conversation that might require a commitment from her. "I hope your mother likes the piece of linen." She folded the cloth and tucked it into the basket. "There's extra bread and cookies." Although, she'd not included those things with Jack Carrington in mind. She'd thought perhaps a miner might bid on the basket, and she'd wanted to make it worth his money by giving him food that would provide him with more than one meal.

Jack rose, as well. "This was a lovely way to spend the afternoon. I so seldom have you to myself these days. Will you come to the Hill tomorrow? We missed you last week."

Lorna's hands paused in their task. "I can't, Jack. My conscience demands it. You know how I feel."

"And you know how I feel, as well. I think your conscience is admirable, but your sacrifice accomplishes nothing but to deny yourself some small luxuries. Do you think any of the miners know or care about what you've done?"

"*I* know, Jack. That matters, too." She smiled and excused herself, hopefully without giving Jack any sense of how much their talk had discomfited her.

She'd never missed her mother so much as she did walking back to her cottage, her mind whirling. Her mother would help her sort through Jack's barely-veiled intentions and make sense of them. She knew what Jack was hinting at: marriage. And she knew what it could mean for her. She could be a senator's wife with social status and a fortune at her disposal to use for her causes.

She could imagine writing those lines to Theo and taking a little petty pride from it. He could have Edith Gladstone, shipping heiress. She would have a senator for a husband. They could both compliment themselves on how well they'd done. But such a triumph would be small and short-lived.

She had no doubts Jack would win his election. He had a fortune to throw at a campaign and he had the ambition to go after the votes through whatever means were necessary. That's what worried her.

Jack would use her heart for charity and justice as a shield for his own less committed social agenda. He appreciated charity when it benefitted him, like it had today. He'd paid twenty dollars for her box. The money would go a long way for Christmas baskets, but it had also gone a long way in communicating other messages to her and to others. To her, it was an announcement of his intentions, that he meant to pursue her actively now. To the other people present, it was a public declaration of those intentions—and also perhaps a reminder of how much power he held and how much more he might wield.

Even if Jesse had come, there would have been little he could have done about it. Jesse didn't have twenty dollars to throw away on a box lunch. She thought of the Evert family and their seventy dollars a week, which had to cover rent and food for four and a never-ending loan. Perhaps it *was* best that the miners weren't present. To see such a flagrant show of money would have angered them.

Are you really considering Jack Carrington? The little voice in her head whispered the all-important question. *Is that what all this worry is about? You worry about his ethics and his character because you are actively considering his proposal*? Well, that was one way to burn something down to its most important core. Did she care about Carrington's behaviors because she was indeed considering yoking herself to the Carrington name?

What sort of marriage might she have with Jack once one looked past the money and the busyness that would characterize their lives? They would have to move to Sacramento for part of the year when the legislature was in session. She would have her charitable projects, and she would also be expected to manage his dinners and host his entertainments. It would be a full-time job, especially on top of establishing and moving households twice a year.

Jack would have his meetings and his politics. When would they see each other? She would be on his arm at events but would she really have a husband in the sense that mattered to her? One where he would be a true partner in her life, sharing in her sorrows and joys, supporting her dreams, cherishing her company? When would there be evenings like the ones her parents shared after the children were abed for the night and the dinner dishes cleared away? Would Jack be capable of changing his ways? Did she want to give up her teaching in exchange for marriage?

Thinking of it on a purely practical level, she could see that there would be clear benefits to saying yes. Marriage might offer her a way to do more for her causes. She'd have access to the whole state as a senator's wife.

But that was not a reason to marry. Marriage was not a political transaction, it was a gift from God, the foundations upon which a family was built. Could she really see that sort of spiritual familylife with Jack? Life with Jack would be materially comfortable perhaps but what would there be beyond that? For her there had to be more. When she did manage to think of marriage, she didn't picture it with Jack, but with someone else. Someone, who told Bible stories after dinner, whose love for his children overrode all else, and unfortunately, who had no intentions of marrying again.

Jesse had not expected to see Lorna Saturday night after working all day in the mine. Tunnel Thirteen was proving to be problematic, the earth unwilling to give up the gold he knew was there. He was very afraid they were going to have to blast. He was tired and sore and wanted nothing more than the privacy of his home in which to lick his proverbial wounds. He might have worked all day, but Lorna had not been far from his thoughts.

At noon when he'd sat down to his own meager lunch with his men in the tunnels, he'd thought of Lorna at the social. Had she worn her blue dress or her green one? Or did she have a dress he hadn't seen yet that she saved for extra special occasions? What had she put in her basket? Had she baked some of her fluffy biscuits? Who had bought her basket? He thought he knew the answer to that, and it riled him. Whoever bought a basket got more than just the basket's contents. They got the privilege of the basket preparer's company for the duration of the meal.

It was that last bit that was stirring his gut up this evening as he muddled through a lesson Lorna had left for him. He did not like imagining Lorna with Jack Carrington. He liked even less exploring the reasons for those feelings. He liked her; he cared about her. Just as a friend, he told himself. He would never love again. It hurt too much.

I never asked that of you, Jesse, Evie's voice scolded him. *I never asked you to spend your life alone.*

No, it wasn't Evie's memory that kept him from love, from a second marriage. It was his own guilty conscience, his own fear of failing again as a man, as a husband. He'd made a bad decision and Evie had died because of it. How could he take that risk again? How could he ask another woman to take that risk? It was safer alone, even if it was lonelier.

It was also easier to cling to the memory of Evie, to cling to the past, than it was to take a leap of faith into the future. It was the very opposite of what Lorna Alderly had done. She had leaped into the unknown with both feet in coming West. Her courage was admirable. *You didn't used to think that. You found her actions foolhardy and naive when she first arrived.* That was before he knew her, though.

When the knock came, he groaned as he pushed up from the table to go answer the door. The children looked up from their reading, faces alight with the excitement of an unexpected visitor.

"What's this?" Jesse looked warily at the cloth-wrapped package Lorna held out.

"I brought you some Nazareth cookies." Lorna gave a tremulous smile—the one that said she was trying too hard. But why? What had truly prompted this unexpected visit? "I hope you don't mind. I wanted to talk." Nothing a woman ever said boded well when it started with those four words. Jesse looked up and down the street as he ushered her in. He had the distinct impression she'd brought trouble along with the cookies.

Chapter Sixteen

Senator. Well, that explained why Carrington was so keen to marry. It would be rather difficult for him to convince people he was an upstanding businessman if he was a single man with a reputation for the dance halls. Jesse squatted down amid the weeds of the old garden and pulled a few. He and Lorna had come out back once the children were settled with a pitcher of milk and the cookies at the table. He pulled at another patch of weeds and then another. He thought better when his hands were busy, and there was much to think about—not only what Lorna shared but the reason why she was sharing it. A reason she had not yet stated.

He brushed his hands against his work pants. "May I ask why you're telling me this? Is there something you expect me to do? I can't make your mind up for you." The words came out more roughly than he intended. In truth, the news upset him more than he cared to admit. He suspected this was her way of telling him she was going to marry Carrington. Reading lessons would be over. Suppers and after dinner Bible stories sitting around the table would be over, too. She could not be Jack Carrington's wife and also be Jesse Kittredge's friend. This brief burst of happiness would come to a close.

Happiness. It was the first time he'd used the word in relation to himself in years and definitely the first time he'd used that word to describe being with Lorna. There was truly no other word for it. Lorna Alderly made him happy, made his children happy. But he'd known it would end. He just hadn't known when or how. He thought he'd have more time. But that had been foolish of him. He should have learned his lesson the first time.

"Carrington can offer you a lot of opportunities," Jesse said tersely, tearing at the weeds. If his gruffness was off-putting, Lorna gave no sign of it. She was perhaps the one person who didn't find it intimidating. Usually, people gave up talking with him after a while. It had been an effective tool for establishing his privacy after Evie died and a valuable defense ever since. Not so with Lorna.

She squatted beside him and joined in the weed pulling. "You'll get your dress dirty," he warned. It was a nice dress, too, as all of hers were, this one a russet wool the color of autumn leaves.

"If I do, it will wash." She pulled at a few clumps before picking up the conversation. "Maybe I'm not looking for the kinds of opportunities Carrington offers."

"Money, security, a position from which you can use that money to work for the changes you want to see in the world?" Why was he arguing *for* Carrington? Jesse scolded himself.

"Those are good reasons to go into business with

someone, or to join a charity group, but are those reasons to *marry*? I think marriage belongs to a higher plane than such worldly considerations. Does not the Song of Solomon suggest that all one's earthly possessions cannot purchase such love as that which ought to lie between a husband and a wife?" She sat back on her heels and gave him a long look. "You, of all people, cannot tell me otherwise. You loved your wife beyond reason."

"And she died because of that love. Love, even the kind you describe, wasn't enough to save her." Jesse stood and strode away from her. "It couldn't put food on the table, or buy medicine for the sick, or build a house." He could feel the old anger rising as he said the words, revisiting the old feelings and arguments he'd carried with him since the day he'd put Evie in the ground. "The Song of Solomon was written by a rich man, Lorna, who had every advantage, who could afford to promote the merits of that love. The rest of us make do with an imitation of that, and those that don't end up disappointed. So, maybe you should think about that before you turn down Jack Carrington. He can give you the imitation."

"And prayer? Is that for only the rich, too?" Lorna prompted.

"Seems like it—at least if you want your prayers to be answered. God helps those who help themselves. Those who have the *means* to help themselves. I prayed for medicine, for a cure for my Evie, for a doctor to come and save her...and I got nothing." The unfairness of it, the heartrending injustice, swept through him, the old memories leaving him trembling with anger and despair. "But two hours after she passed, a doctor arrived from Sonoma and saved Nellie Putnam, a woman whose husband had money and resources. Two hours!" He howled in anger, his hurt coming in fast and furious words. "God could not have given the doctor a faster horse? Could not have moved the man to pack his bag faster? God answered John Putnam's prayer but couldn't answer mine. But John Putnam is a rich man."

He turned to face Lorna, not bothering to hide his anger and his grief. "Two hours and my Evie would have been among the living." Suddenly it was too much here in the muddy, overgrown garden, the one Evie had loved so much, had tended so carefully, taking such pride in the vegetables she'd managed to grow for the family. *We'll have greens, Jesse. Our children will be healthy. This is wonderful weather for a little bit of farming.*

His voice cracked when he spoke again. "She thought this place was the Promised Land, and it killed her. I brought her here. *I* killed her." This was why he never talked about it, never talked about her, because it would break him anew and he had to be strong. He couldn't afford to break. Inside, he could feel his soul shattering, cracking once more like a mine shaft collapsing in on itself, the hillside hollowed out, unable to support itself any longer.

He fell to his knees, giant sobs ripping themselves free from his body. But he was not alone. Lorna was there kneeling beside him in the mud, her arms about him, holding him close, rocking him, her soft voice urgent and soothing at his ear—not with requests to stop his sobs, but to let them out, to let them have their moment at last. And because she would be there to keep vigil with him, he did.

For the first time in two years, Jesse wept for his wife, for all that he'd lost, all that he had loved. And for the first time in two years, he wasn't alone. Beneath the grief that poured out of him, there was something else rising up to take its place, something that brought with it a sense of peace and rightness. Even after the storm of sobs had passed, even after he'd regained control of his emotions, he clung to her, unwilling to let go lest he lose the connection.

"It was dysentery," he said at last, drawing a deep, shuddering breath. "We had only been here a few months and facilities were not what they should have been. Everything is chaos when a town or camp is in the early stages of its development. It was every man and family for himself. Carrington was more concerned about the mine than he was about living conditions. The water was fouled." Jesse swallowed hard against the memory of it. "It was eventually traced to inappropriate management at the mine."

Carrington had known the runoff was not being managed properly, that it put the newborn settlement at risk, and he'd dragged his feet on taking the necessary steps to correct it, not wanting to be burdened with the expense. It was only when the falling performance of the miners started to seriously impact the daily yields that he finally accepted something needed to be done.

He felt the press of Lorna's hand in his. "You don't have to tell me, Jesse. You don't owe me," she said softly.

"I want to tell you." He stood and helped her up from

the dirt. "Come and sit? There used to be a bench out here. I made it." Jesse found the bench lying on its side amid the overgrowth. He righted it and brushed off the dirt. "It's a little worse for wear...but it should still take our weight."

They sat and, out of natural reflex, he found himself taking her hand again, wanting to reestablish the connection. "Disease doesn't care about a person's social status. Dysentery struck men, women, children, those better off and those of us newly-come and just trying to survive. We'd just moved into the cottage a few months earlier." Jesse gave a little smile at that memory. "Even when it was brand new, the cottage didn't look much better than it does now, but Evie was excited. I'd been named a crew chief and Carrington wanted his crew chiefs to have something more than a canvas roof over their heads." He kicked a clump of dirt. "It was spring, and Evie put the garden in right away. The garden was just showing its first sprouts when dysentery hit. We boiled our water, we took precautions, but it was too late for Evie. Somehow, the children and I managed to escape it. I'll never understand why." She squeezed his hand and he took strength from it.

"She went fast after that." He met her eyes as he said the words, letting her see the pain he'd buried for so long, the pain he showed to no one, not even his children. "I prayed by her bedside. I did everything I could—cold cloths for the fever, liquids to keep her hydrated—but nothing helped. Others were sick. We asked Carrington to send a man for a doctor but it wasn't until people like the Putnams took ill that he finally listened. When Evie got worse, I thought if I went to the church to pray, God might hear me better. The reverend was there, along with John Putnam, who was praying for Nellie. We all prayed together." In those moments he'd felt sure God would deliver Evie. He'd had all the faith in the world. *Ask and you shall receive.*

But God had only saved one of their wives and His answer had been swift. "I'd only left for a half hour, but when I got back the children were sobbing beside the bed and Evie was gone." Tears swam afresh in his eyes as he said the guilty words aloud. "I wasn't even there to help her pass, to be a witness to her last breath, to tell her one more time I loved her." Even if she'd been too delirious to hear him, to even know, he knew, and he *would* know for the rest of his days that he'd failed her in her last moments. To her credit, Lorna said nothing, not giving voice to the useless platitudes he'd heard too many times in the early days following Evie's death: that this was God's plan, that there must be a reason for it, that this too shall pass. He didn't want it to pass.

"You loved her very much," Lorna said quietly into the stillness of the new evening.

"And that love meant so very little in the end, as did my prayers." They'd come full circle, back to the start of the conversation. "I made her promises the night before. She was awake and lucid, the way people often are right before they die. Only, I thought it was a sign she was getting better. I think she knew, though."

He'd relived those moments a thousand times since then. "She made me promise her some things." He slanted a brief smile at Lorna. "She made me promise to send the children to school if I could. Adam had a little schooling in Appalachia. Charlotte had been too young. Evie and I never went to school. Evie had picked up a little learning on her own and taught Charlotte as much as she could at home in the mornings, but it wasn't much."

He looked out over the little scrap of land. "She would hate seeing the garden like this. But I didn't have the heart or the time to replant it." They'd harvested Evie's vegetables that summer—it had seemed like a fitting tribute. But after that, he'd just let nature take over.

"In the spring, maybe Charlotte and I can set it to rights."

"Don't, Lorna. Don't make promises you can't keep." She might be Mrs. Carrington by spring. Perhaps she should be. His story was a cautionary tale as much as it was anything else.

Lorna nodded. "I won't marry him, Jesse. I don't think I can. You and Evie, my parents, had marriages that embodied the three purposes of matrimony—companionship, passion and purpose. Perhaps Jack can offer purpose, but it's not the purpose the Apostle Paul spoke of in Ecclesiastes."

"What if it's all one can have? Perhaps those other things could follow in time." It appeared his cautionary tale hadn't gotten through to her—not with the right lesson, anyway.

"I will wait and hope for better."

"Better than Jack Carrington? Don't wait too long. Future senators with fortunes to their names don't come around too often."

"You would see me wed to an unscrupulous man? That seems odd considering you don't like him very much. And I thought…" She paused. "Well, I thought that you liked me at least a little. Would you really wish your friend married to a man who puts himself first and his people second?"

"Perhaps I only wish to see you safe, to see that you have the opportunities to espouse your causes as you wish. Maybe I just want to help you see your choice clearly. Carrington does have limits to what he can offer, but perhaps 'some' is all we have the right to expect. Have you ever considered that you might want too much from a man, from marriage?"

"No, Jesse. I never have and I won't start now. I turned down Theo Todd in Concord for those same reasons. He could not offer me all three." She did not elucidate on which of the three this other man had lacked, leaving Jesse to guess. It wouldn't be companionship, since he'd heard her speak of the man with a great deal of fondness, and he doubted it was purpose, which only left passion. Lorna Alderly drove a hard bargain.

She rose and dusted at her skirt. Jesse hoped the gown wasn't ruined beyond repair. "Will you be alright?" she asked, a light hand on his sleeve in a gesture of comfort.

"I will be. Thank you. I didn't mean…" He had no words. Neither of them had come out to the garden with any expectation the conversation would take the direction it had.

"I'm glad you did. I will treasure everything you shared. And Jesse? It did help." They held one another's gaze for a long moment. "I'll look in and say goodnight to the children before I go. May I sit with you in church tomorrow?"

"The children would like that, but only if you think

it wise?" Jesse felt in his gut such a choice would be courting trouble.

She offered one of her smiles. "It will be no different than any other Sunday. I haven't sat with the Kittredges for a few weeks." But, Jesse thought, that was before Jack Carrington had spent twenty dollars on a lunch box and all but proposed. He hoped there would not be repercussions. Rejecting a rich man's affections could wreak havoc with one's reputation.

Chapter Seventeen

The rumors reached her by Monday. Lorna had not recognized the early signs. She'd thought her students were merely excited to talk about the box lunch social. Since most of her students were children of families that were involved in the event, their chatter over the event seemed entirely natural. Katie Putnam reported in great detail on the lunch between her sister, Deborah, and Parker Hudson, even though Katie hadn't been present. "Of course, Mr. Carrington bought our dear Miss Alderly's box," Katie said when she finished talking about her sister's success.

Katie meant it kindly, but Lorna saw Adam frown and shift in his seat as if the subject made him uncomfortable. "I was thrilled anyone bought my box since I'm new." Lorna laughed it off, trying to make it seem as if Jack had merely shown good manners and done her a favor in a friendly way.

"He didn't just buy it, he paid twenty dollars for it," Eliza Cleveland put in, impressed as any banker's daughter would be, Lorna supposed.

"Well, Mr. Hudson was making it difficult for him," Lorna tried to explain. "The two of them had a fun, high-spirited competition. I think they were getting worried they'd be left without a lunch. My box was one of the last to be auctioned off, after all." Lorna attempted to frame her words in a way that would make the sum Jack had paid seem unimportant.

That seemed to satisfy the class enough to use the twenty dollars as a springboard to a math lesson. That should have been the end of it. And it might have been if those comments had merely been prompted by childish curiosity. But her students weren't the only ones interested.

Mrs. Putnam inquired about it when Lorna went to the dry goods store to pick up an order on Tuesday. Oh, she didn't ask directly—Nellie Putnam had more savvy than that. She asked instead, "Were you surprised when Mr. Carrington bought your box? He is quite a catch," she added with a wink and a sly, womanly smile as she looped an arm through Lorna's and pulled her over to the shelves holding bolts of fabric. "We got some lovely new prints in the other day, and we'll be placing one more order that should get here before the snow makes travel difficult. Keep that in mind in case you want to order any material…for something special, perhaps?" It took Lorna a moment to realize the woman meant fabric for a wedding gown. When she did realize, she blushed furiously.

"It was just a lunch, Mrs. Putnam."

"Well, it was a very expensive ham sandwich, then," Nellie teased good-naturedly, her own cheeks pink with excitement. Lorna thought for a moment about the story

Jesse had told her, how this woman had nearly died during the dysentery outbreak. She looked the picture of health now. One would never have guessed she'd once been at death's door.

"It was for a good cause and the man had to eat." Lorna offered the woman a friendly smile and moved off to collect her order, hoping that she would now be done with the topic for good.

By Friday, however, Jack's attentions had been commented on to her several more times. It was with some hesitation that she stopped by the bank after school to deposit her paycheck. It was her second paycheck. Though it was small, there was a certain thrill to seeing the money go into her account, where it joined the rest of the funds left to her by her great-aunt.

Meredith Cleveland, Eliza's mother, waited on her personally. Lorna rather liked the idea of a women's teller, another female whom women could conduct their transactions with, although Lorna suspected Meredith Cleveland wasn't all that busy most days. Only the shopkeepers' wives would be by to make deposits. Still, having the female teller did validate the idea that at least here in California, any woman who aspired to it might have her own account.

"Thanks to you, we had our most profitable box social yet." Meredith's eyes twinkled. "I imagine you won't be making paycheck deposits for much longer, at least not under this name." She touched Lorna's arm. "There's no need to play coy about it. Mr. Carrington made his intentions quite obvious. You needn't pretend." She sighed. "Aren't you the lucky one? Handsome men with fortunes are a rare find."

"I think people are setting the cart before the horse," Lorna hedged, trying to mitigate Meredith's speculations as she'd done with others all week. But her curiosity was getting the better of her. This was more than people excitedly talking over a weekend event. That sort of talk should have lost its interesting edge within a few days. This had gone on for days. "Might I ask, Mrs. Cleveland, who did you hear all of this from? Surely, you haven't gleaned it from a simple bid at an auction."

Mrs. Cleveland leaned forward across the teller's box, her voice low. "Why, my dear, I heard it straight from Jack's mother herself. Mrs. Carrington was in to make a deposit and she said quite plainly that she expected to have a wedding to plan in the near future. She's hoping for a date in early spring when the wildflowers are in bloom. But not too early, since so much will have to be brought in by wagonload." Mrs. Cleveland gave a knowing smile. "How daring of you to try to throw us off the scent, sitting with the Kittredges last Sunday. I wasn't fooled but a few others were confused by it. If you want my advice, I'd be careful there."

"Careful? How? I'm not sure I know what you mean." Lorna gave Mrs. Cleveland a sharp glance, her stomach tightening with worry. The last time she'd gotten Jesse involved with Jack, Jesse had paid for it.

Mrs. Cleveland had the good grace to look abashed. She lowered her voice even further. "I know you're a decent woman, Miss Alderly, but to some it might look as if you're keeping company with more than one man. That can't be what a schoolteacher wants. Women have to be so careful even in places like Woods River if they want to keep their reputations intact."

If anyone needed to be careful it was Jack, who'd told his mother things that had not been decided upon between them. And Mrs. Carrington should be more careful, as well, before going out and telling the whole town they were as good as engaged. Lorna checked her balance, pocketed a portion of the money for household expenses and thanked Mrs. Cleveland before managing to walk out of the bank without giving the impression anything was wrong. Making a spectacle of herself in public simply would not do. But on the inside she was seething.

God grant me patience. She needed patience *and* tolerance *and* understanding, when what she really wanted to do was march out to the mine, stomp up to the mining office and call Jack Carrington to account for what he'd done.

That's not fair, her conscience reminded her. *You don't know that he did anything malicious. It might have been nothing more than a conversation with his mother that caused her to get overly excited. You know how that is. Weddings excite mothers.*

Her own mother had been thrilled at the prospect of her marrying Theo. She must curb her initial anger. She couldn't allow it to rob her of reason. No, flying off the handle was not the way this situation needed to be handled. So, then…what *was* the right approach?

While confronting Jack might not be the most productive way of handling the situation, she could take steps to disabuse people of the idea that she was… How did Mrs. Cleveland put it? Seeing two men at once. The idea would almost be laughable if she didn't know her own mind so well.

She had to admit, it wasn't entirely untrue to say that she had been keeping company with two different men—although the motives behind it were entirely pure. She considered both Jack and Jesse to be her friends. But she might need to take a step back from those friendships—at least until the talk died down. She was expected at the Kittredges tonight, but she would cancel and eat alone. It must be done, although the thought left her feeling deflated. She'd not realized how much she'd counted on being there, on not being alone.

She'd just turned down the street to the cottage row and steeled her resolve to cancel when she spotted Charlotte at her gate. "Lotte, can I help you with something?" She smiled at the girl. "Do you need some extra flour for biscuits?" The girl was forever finding reasons to stop by and come inside. She was mesmerized by the things in the cottage. Lorna was usually happy to oblige.

For once, the girl didn't smile back "No flour, Miss Alderly." Charlotte was normally a cheerful child but today she seemed…pensive. Lorna thought Lotte would appreciate that word. She could add it to her vocabulary collection. "I came to remind you about dinner." Lorna didn't quite believe her.

"I don't think I can come tonight, Lotte. I am sorry." She watched as Lotte's face crumpled.

"Are you sure, Miss Alderly? We had everything planned so nicely. I was going to use the new napkins you brought over last Saturday with the cookies, and I used leaves for an arrangement in a jar like the ones you talked about from the social last weekend. It was going to be a pretty table, just like yours. Adam caught some fish. You love Adam's fish," she said hopefully. "And Pa says he has a surprise for us."

Lotte's eyes began to tear up and Lorna felt her resolve wavering. How could she bear to disappoint Charlotte? And really, why should Charlotte be disappointed all because Jack Carrington's mother had fired off her mouth? *But remember, you're the one that will pay for her firing off, you and Jesse.*

"Is this because you're going to marry Mr. Carrington?" Charlotte blurted out.

"Who says I'm going to marry Mr. Carrington?" Lorna felt her newly curbed anger surge again.

"Everyone. Eliza Cleveland and Katie Putnam. Adam says you won't be able to teach school anymore if you marry him, and that you won't be able to come and see us."

"Nothing has been decided, Lotte. But it's complicated and I must be very careful so that no one gets hurt." Perhaps this was a taste of how it would always be with Jack. Jack and his ambition running roughshod over the feelings of others, all for the sake of him getting what he wanted.

Lotte seemed to take heart from her words. She reached shyly for Lorna's hand. "If you need to marry someone, you could always marry my Pa. Adam and I need a ma and I think Pa needs someone, too. We could be a real family again. It already feels like that when you come over."

"I know, I feel that way, too. I will always be grateful for how your family has taken me in and befriended me, Lotte. It is difficult to be among strangers and to be so far from home," Lorna admitted quietly. This child was going to slay her with those words. Only the hardest of hearts could resist such a plea. But she also didn't want to be the sustainer of false hopes. "Your father loved your mother very much. I know he misses her. Sometimes it is hard to love again after a great loss. He might never be ready to bring someone else into his life again like that."

Charlotte thought about that for a moment before nodding sagely. "Well, you could still be *our* ma. Me and Adam. I mean, Adam and I," she corrected herself. "We are ready for a ma if it was you."

"I appreciate the vote of confidence, Lotte." Lorna smiled, her mind made up. She was not going to let Jack Carrington roll over *her* on his way to the California Senate. "Is that invitation for dinner still good?"

Charlotte beamed. "Yes, it is. Dinner will be at half-past six. Will you bring a hostess gift?"

Lorna nodded. "Something special. It will be *my* surprise for all of *you*." She was already running through what she had in the house—enough blackberries for a cobbler, perhaps.

It was the best meal Lorna had eaten in ages, and that included the meal Jack had treated her to at the Golden Nugget. Perhaps it was the bitter realization that it might be the last meal for a while until the rumors blew over, that lent the meal an extra sweetness. Or perhaps that sweetness came from Charlotte's heartfelt desire to be part of a complete family again. It had been there in her words this afternoon. *It feels like a family when you come over.* Lorna knew that hunger, too. She came from a large family and she missed them—but the homesickness hurt a little less when she was here with the Kittredges.

She glanced at Jesse across from her at the table. Did he know how his children felt? That they wanted a mother? That they'd picked up on his loneliness? They wanted someone for him, too. They were not selfish children. But was she the right person? Being a teacher was different than being a mother. Was she really ready to take on that role instantly? It would be quite the transition to go from being a single woman to being a wife and a mother, and to be stepping into roles that had once been filled by another.

Whoa. She reined in her thoughts. Now it was *her* cart that was set before her horses. She was no better than Jack's mother. Marry Jesse? He hadn't even hinted at an interest in that direction. Lorna looked down at her plate and gathered her wits . She'd been caught up in the dinnertime fantasy of family and had let those ideas run away with her.

And yet, it was hard to shake the image of Jesse Kittredge, family man and husband, the haunting sadness and hardness chased from his green eyes at last.

Do you even want to marry anyone? Her conscience prompted. *You came here to liberate women, not to put yourself in chains.*

Well, that was a question for another time. When she looked up, she said, "This was the most delightful meal. Everything was perfect. Charlotte, your table was beautiful." The girl beamed. "And Adam, once again, your fishing skills have not failed us." She set aside her napkin. "Is everyone ready for dessert? I've brought blackberry cobbler." Charlotte clapped her hands in delight and Adam's eyes went wide with anticipation. Even Jesse looked pleased.

"There's no cream," Lorna apologized as she set down a large serving in front of Jesse.

"I like mine plain." He smiled at her. "Cream washes out the tartness of the berries."

"Tell her what you do, Pa, with leftover cobbler in the mornings," Charlotte teased. "It's so silly, Miss Alderly," she warned and then couldn't hold back. "He puts it in a bowl and pours milk over it and mashes it all up. He eats it like porridge."

"Delicious porridge." Jesse laughed, the corners of his eyes crinkling beneath his tan. They ate cobbler, talking and laughing until the last crumb had been eaten off the plates. Then, Jesse pushed back from the table and said, "Now it's time for my surprise. I'm not sure it can top blackberry cobbler, but it might get close." There was laughter in his eyes when his gaze met hers. "Adam, can you fetch the family Bible from the other room?"

Adam returned with a battered book whose leather cover spoke of having seen years of Kittredges. "We brought this from Appalachia. It's traveled across the whole country. It's seen three generations of Kittredges," Jesse explained as Adam set the Bible down in front of him and took his seat. "It's time for tonight's story. I thought we would finish the story of Samson." His gaze met hers once more. "And tonight, I thought instead of telling it, I would read it." It was said so casually, as Jesse opened the Bible to where a frayed silk bookmark held the spot, that it took a moment for Lorna to realize the import of his words. *Read.* Jesse was going to read aloud.

"You're going to read, Pa?" Adam's eyes were as wide as they had been over blackberry cobbler.

"I might not be perfect." He looked at his children, each in turn. "But you can help me if I get stuck." Then he cleared his throat and began, picking up the story with Samson's imprisonment. He read slowly, enunciating each word, but with great inflection to build the drama of the story. Lorna wondered if he'd been practicing in secret and her heart was overwhelmed with joy for him. Even though their lessons had been somewhat curtailed, he had obviously persevered and continued on his own as she'd asked.

The children were enthralled, both with the story and with the sight of their father reading to them, and it brought tears to Lorna's eyes to see their little family quietly celebrating this achievement.

"'And Samson took hold of the two middle pillars upon which the house stood, and on which it was borne up, of the one with his right hand, and of the other with his left. And Samson said, Let me die with the Philistines. And he bowed himself with all his might; and the house fell upon the lords, and upon all the people that were therein. So the dead which he slew at his death were more than they which he slew in his life.'" Jesse finished the story and shut the book, sitting back in his chair. "Here endeth the reading." He smiled and chuckled. "I've always wanted to say that. The traveling minister who came through one Sunday a month in Appalachia would say that at the end of the scripture."

"Well done." Lorna smiled her approval, her throat too clogged with emotion to say any more. She hoped he would know all those words held, all she couldn't say.

"Thank you," Jesse said. "You are the reason I can read the Bible to my children."

"I suppose this means you won't need me to help you with work anymore," Adam spoke up nervously.

"I will still need you, Adam. I will always want your opinion, whether I need you to read plans to me or not. Two heads are better than one," Jesse assured his son. It was the perfect note on which to end the evening but it came with a surprising revelation: she wanted those words for herself. She wanted him to need her. Dare she ever hope for such a thing?

Chapter Eighteen

The note came at the end of the Ladies Auxiliary meeting, most of which had been spent congratulating each other on the splendid outcome of the auction and sending sly looks Lorna's direction whenever anyone made a reference as to the reason why. All Lorna could do was smile and nod. She'd offered her defense all week to anyone who would listen. But no one had. Now, a week later, the town remained convinced a marriage between her and Jack Carrington was simply inevitable, although Mrs. Knight had intrepidly indicated that she hoped Mr. Kittredge didn't take the blow too hard.

Lorna unfolded the note, trying to be discreet, aware that everyone was surreptitiously looking at her. Her hands clenched on the paper, crinkling it at the margins. The town council wanted her to drop by at her earliest convenience. Mrs. Putnam quickly looked away, and Lorna wondered if the ladies had known this would happen—that the council would send for her just as the ladies meeting was wrapping up so she would have no excuse to delay. Given how many of the women had husbands on the council, it seemed highly unlikely that the women were totally unaware.

"I hope it's not bad news?" Mrs. Cleveland asked, but Lorna thought the inquiry was more likely a prompt for information than a question, perhaps even an attempt at a facade of innocent unawareness of what might happen.

"I suppose we'll see," Lorna replied noncommittally. "Ladies, I'll say good day here and see you next week," she said cheerily. But she did not feel cheery or hopeful. She was sure it would be bad news. The last time the council had issued an unscheduled summons, it had been to inform her that her position was likely to be eliminated at the end of the school year if numbers didn't go up. That had been right before everything had started to go wrong. She was going to lose her job and face the prospect of going home unless something changed.

And things have *changed.* As if on cue, some might say. Lorna walked slowly to the sanctuary where the council met, a thought coming to her. Numbers had not been a consideration when the letter had come to Mrs. Elliott inquiring about a teacher. Numbers of students had not figured into any conversation Lorna had had with the town council in the days after her arrival when she was familiarizing herself with the town and with the expectations of her as the schoolteacher. Of course, that was before students hadn't shown up. But surely, the town council wasn't surprised by that? So, to be concerned over numbers seemed to be a relatively new consideration.

Had someone pushed this issue? Had that someone seen something to be gained by suggesting the school could be shut down and she could be sent home? Had that someone thought losing her job might make an offer of marriage more appealing if it became the only way she could stay in California? And of course, there'd no longer be the temptation of wanting to choose her position over a husband.

Lorna drew a deep breath and settled her temper, which had been leaping with her suppositions. Surely, Jack Carrington would not be so devious. But on the other hand…his mother had been quite diligent and efficient in rapidly spreading rumors about her son's intentions to marry her.

The first thing Lorna did when she entered the room was scan the council for Jack, but he was not there. She wasn't sure what to make of that. "Gentlemen, good afternoon. How can I be of service to you? I have new numbers to report," she said, brandishing her confidence like a sword, the increase of three new students her shield. "I am sure once word gets around to the other mining families that our school curriculum is useful and relevant to all occupations and stations, others will come."

Mr. Cleveland gave her a rueful half smile. "I'm afraid, Miss Alderly, that's not the word that is getting around. There are some unfortunate rumors we must discuss this afternoon."

Her heart sank as she sat in a chair before the half circle of councilmen. She felt as if she were in Henry VII's Star Chamber about to be questioned. They'd want to discuss Jack. Was that why he wasn't present? "Where is Mr. Carrington, today?" she asked politely.

"He's occupied with matters at the mine, but he is

aware of this meeting, Miss Alderly. This is not being done behind his back. You needn't worry about that," Mr. Putnam said kindly, misreading her cause for concern.

Joseph Knight began. "It is important that the ladies of this town—particularly those who interact directly with our children—set a high standard for our girls to model by which they can bring up the moral code of our men. One of the things that appealed to us about Mrs. Elliott's organization was the belief that a cultivated woman could help tame a man's wildness by putting forward values of family and home. We expect the wives of our businessmen, and women like yourself, to adhere to that."

"You run a dance hall, Mr. Knight." Lorna couldn't help but cut in. There was an undeniable irony in a man who ran a business that relied on women dancing in short skirts trying to teach a lesson on decorum. "Do your ladies adhere to that standard?"

He cleared his throat. "They are working girls, not ladies, Miss Alderly. They have different standards and they perform a different service for the town. I am sure you don't wish to number among them. As such, we felt it was important to remind you of your place and the high esteem in which a certain population of the community holds you."

"Thank you for the compliment, Mr. Knight." Lorna folded her hands in her lap, the model of propriety. If they wanted to launch a complaint about her conduct, which was above reproach, they would have to do more than insinuate there'd been a breach in her behavior. The men looked uncomfortably at each other.

It was Mr. Cleveland who broke the tense silence. "Mr. Carrington has made it known that he intends to seek your hand, Miss Alderly, and you have given appearances to welcome his attentions while also seeming to welcome the attentions of Mr. Kittredge. You are misleading one of these men."

Lorna gathered her calm. "*I* am misleading one of these men? Are you so sure that I welcome attentions from both of those men? It seems you are quick to blame me for a circumstance not of my making."

Parker Hudson glared smugly at Cleveland. "I told you Kittredge was making a nuisance of himself, using his position as the assignedhandyman to worm his way into Miss Alderly's good graces. That man is hunting a mother for his kids."

"He is doing no such thing!" Lorna burst out. "If anyone is to blame for this debacle, it's Jack Carrington. He has talked out of turn about his plans for marriage without first garnering my consent."

Putnam eyed her with a discerning gaze. "Are you saying you are *not* marrying Jack Carrington?" He eyed her as if she was touched in the head.

"He has not asked me, not directly."

"But when he does, you will say yes, of course." Parker Hudson joined the conversation.

"It is not your business how I answer. A decision to wed should be private, through consultation between the two parties involved, not the whole town." Lorna felt more confident in her position now. "I'm glad we're having this discussion, gentlemen, and I hope you will have a similar discussion with Mr. Carrington about the hazards of airing his personal affairs in public. If he'd kept his business private, we'd not be having this discussion resulting from this false alarm." She rose, but Knight apparently wasn't convinced of the soundness of her argument.

"You say he's not made his intentions clear, but he paid twenty dollars for your lunch box, if you pardon my saying so." There was a collective indrawn breath at the table at the implication.

Lorna fixed him with a hard stare. "I do *not* pardon you, Mr. Knight. After all you just said about the difference between a lady and a working woman, I'm astonished at your allusion suggesting that a *lady* can be bought. Your argument also suggests you may be spending too much time at your dance hall if you think twenty dollars is enough to turn a lady's head when it comes to the sacrament of holy matrimony, a commitment intended to last forever. Good day, gentlemen." She squared her shoulders and marched out of the room, hoping she wouldn't pay too dearly for her rebellion.

It was a shame she'd have to pay at all. A woman should be able to speak her mind and stand up for herself, especially when she was being slandered. *So that Jack Carrington could get what he wanted.* At the moment that seemed to be her. Her earlier thoughts about Jack maneuvering things to his advantage seemed even more plausible now.

That decided it. She'd been patient long enough. It was time to confront Jack and make him answer for what he'd done. He was the only one who could set things to rights. She just needed to be clear with him that his suit would get no further with her.

The afternoon was overcast and there was a cold

wind. Lorna was glad for the warmth of her coat as she made the walk to the mine, a walk that seemed far longer than she remembered from when Jesse had been at her side. She pulled her gloves out of her coat pocket and put them on. That was better. She made a mental note to quietly check on Lotte and Adam's winter clothing situation and make sure they had coats and gloves in good repair and in the right sizes. If needed, she'd find a discreet way to offer those items that wouldn't offend Jesse's pride.

She drew stares as she approached the mine. There were catcalls and whistles, and a few lewd suggestions from men she didn't know. It was a reminder that what she knew of Woods River was indeed limited to town and the mining families. These men—single men— made the mining families look positively aristocratic by comparison. She had a new appreciation for Jesse's insistence on accompanying her during times when she might be exposed to the town's rougher element.

She kept her gaze forward, focused on her destination. It was with some amount of reluctant relief to hear Jack call out from the stairs leading to the mining offices. "Lorna, darling, what are you doing here?"

"I came to talk," she said as he took her arm and escorted her up to the offices. "As you know, the council had words with me today about my so-called conduct." She waited until he shut the door behind her, giving him the privacy for this discussion that he ought to have given her before bandying her name and reputation around town. "However, I think it is your conduct that should be under scrutiny. You've put me in an untenable position, Jack, and I do not think it is by accident."

He gave a broad smile, a smile she'd once been intrigued by, found handsome even, if only in an objective way. At some point, that smile had worn out its welcome. It was a smile she questioned more than she trusted. "What do you mean by that, Lorna?" he said, all silk and flirtation.

"You've insinuated that we will marry when nothing has been decided," Lorna said bluntly.

He laughed. "My mother is anxious for grandchildren. Can you blame her? I think it is she who has said too much too soon, through no fault of my own." He gave a downcast look with his eyes as if remembering something. She thought it felt like acting. "Sunday night, she and I had a moment to talk. I told her about the box social and confessed that my feelings ran rather strongly where you were concerned. I think she might have extrapolated quite a lot from that admission."

"Did she think what you wanted her to think?"

"Lorna! Are you suggesting I manipulated my own mother?" He put on a show of being aghast, making her out to be the villain for hurling such an accusation. Then he softened. "I understand you might be upset with current circumstances, but does it really matter in the end? The only important thing is that you and I marry. We suit well, Lorna, and we'll have a dashing life. I can give you every luxury, every platform for your causes."

"And what can I give you?" She cut in sharply. It had occurred to her that he was, ethically or not, going to great lengths to win her. There must be some reason.

He smiled and kissed her hand. "Your beauty, your grace, your intelligence. You are a cultivated woman,

Lorna, a rare gem in these parts. You will be an asset to a senator. *We* will be assets to one another."

"Shouldn't marriage be more than the curating of assets?" she questioned. "I happen to think it should be. And that is why, on those grounds, I have come here today to tell you that I appreciate the offer but I must refuse. There can be no further pursuit, and I respectfully ask you to set the record straight with the town council now that it is clear we will not be married."

Jack's face hardened. "You would refuse me?" No one had probably refused him for a long time.

"I am sorry, Jack, but it is my firm opinion that we would not suit. I am sorry, too, that this became a public matter when it should not have been." Jack's pride would be wounded a bit in the short term, but he had no one to blame but himself. If he hadn't been so blatant, no one would have realized that he had made an offer—and then been rejected. "Goodbye, Jack."

She made it as far as the first step before Jack was after her, his temper on full display. "Do you think you can walk away from me?" He reached for her arm in a rough grab.

She'd counted on Jack graciously accepting her refusal, on him understanding that whatever was between them was over. But it appeared she had given him too much credit.

"I do not think you understand what walking away from me means," he hissed at her ear. "It means you will go home at the end of this school year, if I cannot arrange it sooner. I will close your school and I will make sure you are unable to find any work in this area again. Once everyone knows you led me on, made me fall in love with you, made me think you'd marry me, they won't want such a shameless piece of baggage teaching school for them. I might even go so far as to blacken Mrs. Grace Elliott's organization, too, telling people what kind of woman they send out West."

"You would not!" Lorna cried. "This is between us. Mrs. Elliott has nothing to do with this. You are black-mailing me."

"I am mad for you, Lorna. I will fight for you," he growled, his grip tightening on her arm. For the first time, she began to genuinely fear for her safety. How would she get out of this? She doubted a scream would serve her. The mine was too noisy—she doubted anyone would be able to hear her. It was a mistake to have come here on his territory where she had no recourse.

"Jack, please," she began, sending up a little prayer in her mind. *Please, Lord, let me find the words to persuade him. Or better yet, send me a little help.*

"Yes, that's a good start. A little begging might work," Jack snarled.

"Is there a problem?" a gravelly voice called up, and Lorna nearly sagged in relief. Jesse. *Thank you, Lord.* She heard the heavy thud of his work boots on the plank stairs. Within moments, he was beside her. "What's going on here?" He split his gaze between her and Jack, his sharp green eyes missing nothing, indicating that the question was for form's sake. His gaze landed on Jack's hand gripping her arm. He *knew* what was up.

Jack's eyes glinted. "Miss Alderly has refused my proposal. I can't understand it, can you?" Lorna felt her cheeks heat. She wanted to wilt with embarrassment, but Jesse was unfazed.

"Maybe she resists on grounds of being coerced. A lady likes to be asked, Carrington."

"One would think a *lady* would realize when she had an opportunity that was too good to turn down," Jack retorted, still glaring at her. "But if you haven't the sense to appreciate the value of a match between us, then in this, *I* will have to be the one to educate *you*. Don't go thinking this is over, Miss Alderly. I am not about to give up."

"I'm not seeing as how you'll have much choice in the matter," Jesse interjected, drawing Jack's attention onto him.

"Oh? And why is that?"

"Because I doubt even you would have the poor taste to pursue a woman who is married to someone else. Or did it never occur to you that the reason for her refusal might be because she has another offer she prefers?"

Jack looked positively lethal. "And what offer might be that be?"

Jesse reached up and took her hand, drawing her away from Jack before he uttered the single word that turned Jack Carrington's face thunderous and set her reeling. "Mine."

It was a good thing Jesse had a tight grip on her hand, as he ushered her down the stairs and past the onlookers that had gathered, or she might have tripped. It was almost impossible to do the simplest of tasks like walk or breathe when her mind was in chaos.

Well, she'd prayed for help, so she couldn't argue there. Nor could she argue with the adage that the Lord worked in mysterious ways. *But now what, Lord? You'll have to show me the way because I have no idea what comes next.* What had Jesse done? She feared it hadn't helped so much as it had made things worse and committed them both to a path neither of them was truly ready to walk.

Chapter Nineteen

What had he done? Jesse took off his hat and pushed his hand through his dusty hair once they reached the curve in the river where they liked to walk. He'd faked a proposal and publicly announced that he and Lorna Alderly intended to marry. Such an announcement would validate the gossip floating around town that Lorna was more than his neighbor and perhaps had been for a while. But that was short-lived drama that would fade once he made "an honest of woman of her." The problem was, what if he didn't? What if Lorna refused him? What would happen to her reputation and her job, then? There were other problems, too, if she said yes.

Either way, his brash words had birthed quite a few complications. But how could he have done otherwise? When he'd come out of the mine and looked up to see her on the stairs with Carrington, the scene had not appeared friendly, even at a distance. His blood had boiled at the sight of Carrington's hand on her with such a look of rage on his face, and Jesse's feet had set their path before he could rethink it.

He hazarded a glance in Lorna's direction. She stood a little apart from him at the river's edge, her back turned to him, her shoulders heaving with emotion—probably more than one emotion. He could imagine her mind must be a mess at the moment, grappling with anger, disbelief, fear, uncertainty. He was responsible for some of that—and he was deserving to be the target of some of that anger, even if he didn't feel he quite deserved all of it. Perhaps the best thing to do would be to give her space to cool down and process all that had happened this week and in the past few hours.

So, he waited. He was a patient man by trade. Gold mining wasn't for the impatient, as he'd tried to tell Carrington time and time again. A man who rushed the mountain was a man who'd find himself buried beneath it. But a patient man worked with the mountain to reveal its treasure, to reap it over time.

Getting to know Lorna Alderly had turned out to be a lot like mining. Drawing quick judgments about her based on first impressions had not done her justice. She had proven to be far more than the sum of her pretty clothes. He had learned that after just a few days. But it had taken time for the real treasure of her to be revealed. He wondered if Carrington even saw her true worth at all or if all he saw was the pretty exterior?

What a shame that would be. Lorna should be with a man who understood her, who appreciated all that she was: stubborn, tenacious, kindhearted, a woman of God with a faith that moved mountains, a woman who never gave up. She hadn't given up on him. Now, he was returning the favor. He wouldn't abandon her to Carrington. But could he be the sort of man who deserved her as her husband? Jesse threw a rock into the river, wishing he could sink his doubts as easily. Still, maybe it wouldn't come to that. Maybe they could find a way out.

Her half boots crunched on the shale of the riverbed. Soon, the November rains would extend the riverbed over the rocks and they'd have to find another place to walk. *They*. A lot of his thoughts these days involved thinking collectively about him and her. That kind of word made him wonder deep down if he actually wanted a way out. Maybe, he'd been looking for a moment like today, a moment in which he felt compelled to declare himself and he'd be able to justify it to himself as a duty of honor later.

"What happened to 'a lady likes to be asked'?" Lorna took up position beside him, calm and in control—even sounding a little amused in a wry, understated way. Gone were the earlier signs of emotional turmoil.

"I'm sure she still likes to be asked but it's not always possible." Jesse handed her a rock to skip. Sometimes it was easier to talk when one's hands were busy. "Especially when that lady confronts a man with his own treachery and threatens him to his face in public. A cornered man is as dangerous as a wounded bear, Lorna."

She slanted him a look. "Hence your proposal."

"I meant Carrington, not me. I was not the cornered man on the staircase," Jesse corrected.

"You're cornered now, though, aren't you?" Lorna moved the conversation swiftly to what mattered most. There was no sense in discussing what she should or should not have done in regard to Carrington. It was too late for those words to matter. "You don't really want to marry me."

"That's not true," he started to argue and then stopped when Lorna began to laugh despite everything.

"You can't help yourself, can you? You simply must argue with everyone even when that someone is trying to help you wiggle out of a situation you don't want to be in. You don't want to marry me, Jesse Kittredge. It's alright to say it."

Jesse found himself laughing, too. "Maybe you're right. Maybe I am too argumentative." Then he sobered. "It's been a good strategy for the last two years when it comes to keeping people at a distance. Agreement brings closeness. I have not wanted to pursue closeness with anyone for a while."

"I know. Maybe that's why I bother you about it," Lorna said quietly, and he reached for her hand. The gesture seemed automatic and natural these days and yet he still marveled at it, at wanting to touch someone, wanting to make human contact again.

"I will marry you," Jesse said succinctly. "My word is good, Lorna. But I worry it's not fair to you. Is there a way out that spares you from marrying a miner?"

"What do you have in mind?" Lorna sighed as if the weight of the afternoon was suddenly too much for even her shoulders. Or was it the prospect of marriage to him that weighed her down? He yearned to take the burden from her.

"Perhaps we settle on an engagement. We can tell everyone we plan to marry in June when school is out, so you can finish the year and give the council time to plan what they want to do with the school program. Then, we can fabricate a reason to break the engagement."

She thought for a long moment, the passage of time

filled with the rushing ripple of the river. "And then what? I go back East? I leave? Or Jack presses his suit again? An engagement that we're already planning to break is just a stalling maneuver."

"It might be enough," Jesse countered. "If Jack is intent on marrying before campaigning begins in earnest, he can't wait until June. Perhaps he'll go to San Francisco and court a lovely girl there, or even go back to St. Louis or New Orleans." He doubted there was enough time for the latter journeys, though, at this point.

She nodded, divining a deeper agenda. "It would be good for Jack to leave, wouldn't it? For us. For the mine. If he went to San Francisco, it would stall opening that new shaft in the northwest corner."

Jesse nodded. "I was hopeful that the upcoming senate race would distract him from that particular project, but instead it seems to have spurred him to act even faster. I won't lie, Lorna, that situation is not good. But that's a topic for another time. Right now, we have to figure this proposal out. Would a long engagement suit you?"

He was surprised when she shook her head. He'd expected her to be relieved. "No, I don't think it would. We're forgetting two very important people in this muddle. The children won't understand, and I can't bear to get their hopes up, to pretend for months that we'll be a family and then to walk out on them. I could not get on a train and simply leave. They would be devastated and so would I." The naked truth of that was on display in her blue eyes and the confession caught at Jesse's heart. How had he managed to find such a woman? He had not even been looking. He was not nearly worthy enough for the goodness of her.

"What do you propose, then?" Jesse tossed his last rock into the river. "You do understand that your choices are limited. You can't choose to not marry at this point, otherwise you will be branded a loose woman who has turned down *two* proposals. You will be sent home." He furrowed his brow as her gaze lit with an idea. .

"You and the children could come with me. If Jack doesn't leave, maybe we could? We'll go to Concord." But even as she said it, Jesse shook his head.

"What would I do there? I couldn't support us, and I won't have your parents thinking I can't take care of my family." How would he ever fit in back there with educated people like her family? Every day she'd be reminded how she'd married beneath herself. Even now, she looked as if she was reconsidering the idea.

"What is it?" Perhaps there was something more worrying her that he didn't know about.

"Moving back east wouldn't be enough. It's not just my own reputation that worries me. If my name is sullied, I'll ruin Mrs. Grace Elliott through association. Jack threatened to bring her down if I refused him, along with threatening to make sure I wouldn't be able to find any work in this area."

Jesse felt her pain. How dare Carrington take everything from her so callously. She'd done nothing to deserve such enmity except refuse him, and Carrington was reacting like the spoiled child he was. All the mine owner knew how to do was take. He was a modern day pillager and plunderer, taking from the earth, taking from people.

"Don't you see, Jesse? I am going to lose the school no matter what happens, unless I recant my refusal and marry Jack. My only hope in staying here, and in protecting Mrs. Elliott's organization's reputation, is through marrying you. A marriage may not save my position, but it will save my reputation and the reputation of a woman I care for, who has been nothing but good to me."

It was Jesse's turn to draw a deep breath. "Despite my fear of being accused of arguing," he began slowly, a bit of a smile fighting through, "I feel I need to point out what a horrible catch I am for a woman like you."

"A woman in trouble?" Lorna interrupted. "I was unaware that beggars could be choosers."

"No, you're not a beggar, Lorna. You're a woman who is more educated than I am, who comes from wealth. You are not meant to be a miner's wife. You've seen those women at the encampment. They look ten years older than they are. They're worn-out. Their lives are hard. I don't want that for you." It would kill him to see her age like that, to see her pretty clothes fade and know he could never think to replace them with anything equal to their quality.

"We'd do better together than that. I have money, Jesse. We can have choices."

He interrupted swiftly, his pride fierce. "I will not be a kept man, Lorna. I will not have anyone say that I married you for your money. This is the problem with us as a couple, can't you see? We are not suited to be together."

Lorna was quiet, studying the river. "That's what marriage is for, though, isn't it, Jesse? To have a lifetime to learn one another? To figure out *how* to rub along together, despite your differences? It wouldn't be realistic to think people married with it all figured out beforehand."

Jesse chuckled. "Is that why you refused your friend Theo? It was too easy? He had it all figured out?"

She smiled. "Quite possibly. He believed he had it figured out for the both of us, and I prefer to have it be the work of a partnership, something that grows over time. Don't you think we could learn to suit, Jesse? We both care for your children. That's something to start with. And we are friends." She gave a light laugh. "We didn't use to be. You didn't like me when you first met me and now here we are."

Yes, here they were, standing at the edge of the river, getting ready to dip their toes in a river of a different sort.

"You offered, Jesse. Don't doubt yourself now." Her blue eyes slanted toward him, a bit of mischief glinting despite the gravity of their situation. "Do you know why you came to my rescue this afternoon? Because I prayed for it. When Jack grabbed my arm and I realized that his anger was more than I was prepared to handle, I prayed. I said, 'Lord, send me help.' And then you were there."

"I came up because I needed to talk with Carrington about a development in the number thirteen shaft." Jesse looked away, uncomfortable with her words. She was a woman of faith and he appreciated that about her, but he was not able to match that faith—not since God had failed him.

"You are welcome to think that. But I know better."

Lorna refused to back down from her belief. "I still have hope for you, Jesse. I pray for you, you know. I pray that God will open your heart again to accept His love. In time, He will." She said it with a certainty that warmed him and very nearly convinced him.

"I am a broken man, Lorna. Surely, that is not the sort of man you want to tie yourself to." It had to be said. He cared for her too much to have her walk into his impromptu proposal blindly or to accept simply out of desperation because she had no other option. "My faith is broken. My heart is broken." There it was, perhaps the one obstacle that was bigger than even his fear over Carrington's retaliation. How could he love both Evie and Lorna? How would such an arrangement ever be fair to Lorna? How could he expect her to share his heart with the woman who'd claimed it first?

Lorna smiled softly. "I was wondering how long it would take you to mention that. You don't have to give her up, Jesse. You love her very much—and it's right that you do. From everything I've heard, it sounds like she was a wonderful woman. I don't expect you to love me in the same way. Have you ever thought that you don't have to choose between us? That you have enough love for both? You don't love one child more than another, do you?"

"No, of course not," Jesse protested the idea. "They are different people. They need different things from me." She smiled and he saw too late that he'd walked neatly into her trap.

"Why should it be any different for Evie and me? She was your first love. You built a life with her, had children with her. You traveled across the country with her. I want you to honor those memories always, Jesse. You and I will make our own memories, we'll build our own life and there will be room for her in that—she'll be part of it. The children deserve to have her there. As do you."

She watched as Jesse's throat muscles worked visibly. "Most women would not be so generous. They would want all of their husband."

"Then they wouldn't understand you. They wouldn't see that to have you, to have all of you, there has to be room for all those you love." Lorna squeezed his hand. "Unless it traps you and makes you unhappy, Jesse, I think seeing the marriage proposal through is the best way forward. But you must speak up now."

Jesse cocked his head, feeling some of his earlier tension leave him. "Perhaps this bodes well if you're worried about trapping me and I'm worried about trapping you." He gave a brief smile. "Lorna, I am a difficult man."

"I know."

"But I promise you this. I will provide you with all that I can. I have a small piece of land, a little mine that I work when I can get up in the hills. It has promise if I can claim it before someone else finds it. One day, it might be a way for us to leave Carrington Mining, but that is a day that is not here yet." Even as he spoke, hearing the words gave him hope that a future beyond this place was possible. "I will always seek to protect you and I will honor my vows to you. But I will require your patience."

That earned him a smile from her. "And I will require yours. I did not come West looking to marry, certainly not so soon. Nor did I expect to inherit an instant family along with a husband," Lorna confessed, and her openness touched him. He'd been so caught up in the immediacy of the situation and his own doubts, he'd not spared much thought yet for hers. "'Love is patient, love is kind,'" she quoted. "We'll be patient with each other, Jesse, and in time, we'll find our way together." She drew a deep breath. "Well, that's settled. Shall we go tell the children?"

Jesse liked the sound of that. The children should be the first to know—aside from Carrington, who he decided didn't count. It would mean so much to Charlotte and Adam, and in truth he wanted to celebrate. He'd had little to celebrate in the last few years. Besides, they should enjoy celebrating while they could—it was bound to be short-lived.

Only a fool would think a marriage would settle things with Jack Carrington. What he couldn't stop, he'd retaliate against. It was only a matter of time before Carrington would make a move. But until then, there was time for joy. The verse from Ecclesiastes floated to him in pieces—a time for joy, a time for all things under Heaven.

Chapter Twenty

"It's time." Jesse turned at the sound of the reverend's voice. The reverend stood at the gate to the little cemetery behind the church, the November sky gray and lowering overhead, a break in the rain that had been present more often than not in the past two weeks since Jesse had proposed.

"Thank you, I'll be right in." Jesse tugged at the lapels of his new suit, a purchase bought in honor of the occasion. The new material felt stiff and foreign. *He* felt stiff and foreign in it, as if he wasn't really himself but someone else. He'd looked like someone else when he'd checked his appearance in the mirror this morning. He'd shaved and pulled his hair back and put on his new clothes. Charlotte and Adam had been impressed with their pa. They had new clothes, too. Adam appeared quite grown-up—and very pleased with himself—in his new suit, and Charlotte had spun around in endless circles, thrilled with the way the skirts of her blue dress billowed out.

He'd not thought new clothes were necessary but

Lorna had insisted that new beginnings required new clothes, and he did feel he owed it to her. If a girl got only one wedding, she had a right to a decent one whether or not it had come about under duress.

"But I do care for her, duress or not," Jesse said aloud to the gravestone carved with two simple words: Evie Kittredge. This was why he was out here while the reverend and the wedding guests were inside. He needed Evie's blessing.

There was a softness in the cold November air, her voice in his head. *You don't have to make excuses, Jesse. You can care for her. It is alright to feel something. It is alright to live, Jesse. You promised me this one last thing. That you would live.*

That had been the hardest promise to keep. He'd not wanted to live, not for a long time. To live meant to feel, meant to love, meant to risk hurt and loss again. But now he had to keep that promise to Evie by trying to embrace life again with Lorna.

Perhaps God has sent you a second chance, Jesse. Of course, Evie would think that. She was a woman of faith like Lorna.

I pray for you, Jesse. That was Lorna's voice now. What powerful words those were. To be prayed for was… comfort. Peace. To know that someone cared.

"Jesse, are you alright?" There was a rustle of skirts behind him. Lorna was there as if his very thoughts had summoned her.

"I thought the groom wasn't allowed to see the bride before the wedding." She certainly made for a stunning sight, though. She stole his breath in a soft blue gown with a skirt of layered tulle flounces and see-through long sleeves that gathered at the wrist. It was high necked with a line of cloth-covered buttons that ran from neck to waist where they met with a slate blue sash. Unlike the new clothes he and the children had purchased, this was a dress she'd already owned—one of the fancy gowns she'd brought from Massachusetts.

Doubts tinged his joy. Would she regret marrying him when she couldn't afford such dresses? He pushed the thought away. He wouldn't think on it today.

"I was worried about you." Lorna picked up her skirts and delicately wound her way through the cemetery to stand beside him. He watched her gaze skim the words on the gravestone. Would she be angry he'd come to see his first wife on his wedding day? Despite her earlier words to the contrary, he worried that perhaps it was wrong to have come here. Perhaps Lorna should have at least one day of her own. But Lorna continued to surprise him.

"I will care for him and for your children as best I can, Evie," she whispered. "From this day forward, I will hold them in my heart and love them as my own. I promise they will remember you, that I will keep your memory alive for them so that you will walk beside them all their days."

They stood in silence then, hands clasped together, each with their own thoughts, heads bowed as they paid their individual homage to Evie Kittredge. "Thank you, Lorna," Jesse said at last. "That was beautiful and exactly what I needed to hear." He looked away and cleared his throat. "I'm not very good with words or feelings, and today I fail on both accounts." He gave a self-deprecating laugh.

"The Egyptians believe that a person dies twice. The first time when the body passes away but the second is when your name is no longer spoken. As long as we're remembered, we live forever in the hearts of those who love us." She squeezed his hand. "Let's go in and begin our life together."

It was not the wedding day Lorna had envisioned for herself, but wasn't that why she'd come West in the first place? Because she'd not wanted a wedding in the First Parish Church wearing her mother's old lace? One should be careful what one wished for. There was nothing reminiscent of a First Parish Church wedding here in Woods River. The guests were people she'd known for three months instead of her whole life, and the gown was just the best dress from her trunks instead of a white silk creation handmade by a renowned modiste in Boston especially for the occasion. There was no quartet to play music to mark her walk down the aisle, there were no satin ribbons or bows affixed to the pews in decoration.

Instead, she focused on what there was, starting with two smiling children who sat in the front pew, beaming at her. Never had she expected to marry and have two children immediately, but she couldn't be more pleased.

There was also the turn of the heads of new friends and acquaintances. The Ladies Auxiliary was out in force for her today as they sat with their husbands dressed in their best in honor of the occasion, and Jesse's crew had the day off to attend. These were men she didn't know, but she would get to know them starting today.

Most of all, there was Jesse waiting at the altar in his new suit with his clean-shaven jaw, his green eyes intent on her every step.

In the moment, it seemed that the sight of him was more than enough. He looked extraordinarily handsome today, the tailoring of his dark suit calling out the breadth of his shoulders and the leanness of his waist. Her soon-to-be husband was built as rock-solid as the mountains he mined. He was her very own Samson, she thought, with his long hair and a muscular build hewn out of years of pickax work. She hoped she'd be worthy of him.

Please Lord, don't let me steal his strength. Do not let me be his Delilah. Let me be a good wife to him. She sent a final prayer.

Jesse's pride was everything and it would be too easy to accidentally trample on it. He was human just like everyone else and just as vulnerable. She'd nearly trampled on that pride down at the river the day they'd discussed Carrington's power in town. She'd not meant to. She'd merely meant to be helpful. It was one of the many things they'd learn to navigate together as husband and wife.

The Ladies Auxiliary had outdone themselves in the social hall where everyone adjourned after the ceremony. The long table that had sported the box lunches a few weeks ago now positively groaned under a fabulous spread of breads and meats and small delicacies, a two-tiered wedding cake standing in its center to the oohs and aahs of the children present. Lorna was not sure who had made it, but she'd have to thank them.

There was a punch bowl, too. A space for gifts wrapped in lengths of calico or plain brown paper had been set aside at one end of the table. Lorna had not expected that. "Every bride needs to start married life with something new to her at least," Mrs. Cleveland whispered as she passed through the receiving line.

A fiddler had been found after the receiving line was complete and dancing ensued, which was yet another festive surprise for Lorna. Lorna danced until she was breathless, reveling in the thrill of being in Jesse's arms and—even more so—reveling in the smile on her new husband's face.

"You're happy today." She smiled up at him as he whirled her about the floor. "This is a pleasant surprise to discover you're a good dancer." She laughed up at him, letting the joy of the day take her. She'd been so careful with her emotions these past two weeks, not daring to indulge in any hopeful fantasy about what their life might be like, what it might be like to be Jesse Kittredge's wife. But today, happiness insisted on breaking loose, no longer contained or restrained. "I want to remember today, forever. I want to remember how you look right now. Most of all, I want to remember how today *feels*, how it feels to be this happy."

He swung her around, stealing a kiss as he did so. That was new. He'd not kissed her before the kiss that was part of the ceremony. But she'd liked the warm press of his mouth.

There was a break in the music and someone announced that it was time to cut the cake. Even the adults were excited for a bite of the rare treat of cake. Together, Lorna and Jesse sliced into the cake to a round of clapping and cheers, placing the first piece on a plate for the reverend. Mrs. Putnam moved in to take over the cake cutting so that Jesse and Lorna could enjoy their own pieces. Lorna had just taken a bite when there was a rustle at the door of the social hall. Jack Carrington had arrived.

"What's he doing here?" Jesse growled, his happy face turning thunderous.

"We invited him. He has every right to come," Lorna reminded him. She'd thought it best to make it clear to the town that she and Jesse bore Jack no ill will. If they were all going to live together, there was no room for family feuds. Besides, Jack had taken the news fairly well in public. She'd thought the matter was settled. The town council had agreed to let her keep teaching until the end of the school year because it was far better to have a married woman teaching than a woman of loose morals. To her way of thinking, it seemed that the unpleasantness had been neatly dealt with. She was disappointed to lose the school in June, but that had become inevitable regardless. At least she could continue to teach Adam and Charlotte at home.

Carrington spied them and made his way through the crowd. "Congratulations." He favored them with one of his broad, easy smiles. He took her hands briefly. "Lorna, what a beautiful bride you are. Happiness becomes you." He turned to Jesse, extending a hand to shake. Jesse took it reluctantly. "You look well. Marriage already agrees with you. I am truly happy for you both. I have a gift for you." He reached into the inner pocket of his suit coat and passed Jesse a long, narrow envelope. "Go ahead, open it."

Jesse unfolded the paper inside and scanned it slowly. Lorna felt a surge of pride as he did so. Whatever was in the envelope, he could read it for himself. Jesse lifted his gaze and met Jack's eyes as he passed the paper to her. "He's giving us a foreman's house."

"Well, you have a wife now, and two growing children." Jack grinned. "You need a bigger house than that little shack of yours." He clapped Jesse on the shoulder as if they were best friends. Anyone looking on would think they were, that whatever rift once existed between them had been mended. "You can't expect Lorna to live in such conditions, man. The four of you in that place will be too crowded for her. Besides, it's your due now that you're one of my lead foremen."

Lorna slid a look at Jesse. He'd mentioned nothing about this new title. Jesse's jaw was tight. "I thought we'd agreed to wait on the northwest corner until spring."

Jack laughed, loud and heartily. "Of course we're not going to wait. By springtime, I'm going to be busy campaigning. I want this under way before I'm called away. You're my man, Jesse. You found me the mine's two biggest veins. If you say there's gold in the northwest corner, then there's gold. We just have to go get it. I know you'll get it for me." He turned to Lorna. "How about that. Your husband gets a promotion, a house and a raise, all on your wedding day. If that's not a good omen to start married life on, I don't know what is." He clapped Jesse on the shoulder one more time. "I'll expect you on the job tomorrow, Foreman Kittredge. We have no time to waste. Besides, your wife will want you out of her hair while she's busy with moving into her new home." He made a short bow. "I do apologize for having to run. I can't stay but I did want to wish you both the best."

"Well?" Lorna hazarded the single word after Jack left. "I think this sounds wonderful. What do you think?" she added, because it was clear that Jesse didn't share that opinion.

His grip on her hand was tight and something moved in his eyes, gone before she could decipher it. Then he smiled—though it wasn't the warm, joyous smile he'd worn before. This one looked strained around the edges. "I think we should get the kids and go up to the new house. They will be thrilled. I can hardly wait to see the look on their faces when they realize they'll have their own rooms."

She held him fast for a moment. "Jesse, everything will be fine. We are going to have a good life together and it's just starting. Good things can happen. You just have to have faith." She wanted that for him more than anything. She would not give up on it or on him.

Thank you, Lord. Lorna sent out a quick prayer, her first as a married woman. *Thank you for this day, thank you for the house, for this man, for a chance to make a home for him. My cup runneth over.*

Chapter Twenty-One

Jesse's temper boiled over as he sat at the mining office's meeting table with the other foremen, listening to Jack Carrington outline the plan for opening up the northwestern portion of the mountain.

"Have you not heeded anything I've shared with you for the last three months? The northwestern corner is unstable. If we mine there, it could very well destabilize the entire mountainside. A cave-in at the new shaft would be the least of our worries. If that hillside goes, it could impact the existing mine, as well, especially Tunnel Thirteen, our highest producing tunnel at this point." Jesse summarized the argument he'd been making for months now, ever since Carrington had sent home the plans in September.

Jack fixed him with a hard stare. "That is speculation only. If we were cautious, nothing would ever get done. What we know is that there's a vein of gold running deep in that northwestern pocket. You yourself have said so. Here's the other thing we know, as you and others had attested to." Jack's gaze swept the table. "The mine isn't producing like it used to. Profits are down. I don't want to cut wages. I don't want to cut jobs. It's bad enough that I'll probably have to shut down some of the older tunnels, like One and Two." He eyed the foreman in charge of those tunnels. "Your men would be out of work if we can't find a place to reassign them."

"That's not a reason to risk the whole mine, Carrington," Jesse argued. He might be framing it as a move to help his workers, but Jesse was well aware that there were other reasons Carrington would take the risk. Senate seats were expensive; campaigns were expensive. Jack was already talking about building a grand new home in Sacramento for the months of the year when the legislature sat.

The foremen on tunnels Five and Six nodded. "Kittredge is right. If it's that risky, we can't ask men to work in such conditions."

"Easy living has made you soft. Since when is mining ever without risk?" Jack countered. He speared the table with another quelling stare. "How do you all like your houses? How do you like your wages? How would your families feel about opening the northwest corner if the refusal to do so came at the cost of *your* jobs and all they provide?"

His gaze rested on Jesse. "I'd expect a little more loyalty out you, Kittredge. You're the one who has benefitted the most lately from the largesse of the Carrington Mining Corporation. How do your children like their new house? How does your new wife like your much-improved salary?"

Jesse met his gaze evenly, refusing to be cowed. "They like it just fine, Carrington, although they wish the house was closer to town, truth be told. The walk to school is a bit longer these days." The house was not nearly as convenient for them as the old cottage was. Still, the house itself was an improvement.

"We're adjourned. It's getting late." Carrington grimaced. "Go home and think about your choices. Kittredge, stay for a moment."

Carrington waited until the meeting room was empty. He leaned a hip against the table. "How's married life?"

"It's only been two weeks, and it's none of your business. It will never be any of your business, just so we're clear."

"Fair enough." Jack held his hands up in a gesture of surrender. "I just mean to be friendly. You've been with me from the start, Kittredge. You're my best man and I need you on this. I can either get your compliance the easy way or the hard way."

Jesse just waited. He'd known that the other shoe was going to drop since the wedding and now it was about to. In some ways, it would be a relief to have Jack's revenge out in the open.

"The easy way is this. I'll wipe out your remaining debt for transportation to California, all of it. I will also offer you a ten percent cut on the gold we find in the northwest corner. You know it's a sure thing—you've never been wrong about where the gold is. Just think what that could do for you. All of it would be free and clear without that debt to pay off."

"And the hard way?" Jesse could practically smell the desperation in the room. Jack Carrington gave away as little money as possible and here he was offering him ten percent? He wasn't doing it for generosity's sake—as always, he was driven by greed. He must be overextended as well as trying to finance a campaign and a new house.

"I'll simply take all you have. I'll take the house. I'll take your job. I will call in the money you owe me. You will have nowhere to go, no way to support your family. I'll wipe out your wife's funds, too. I know she's got a bit in the bank. It will put a dent in those funds to pay your loan. Where will you go? Back East, begging to her family? I don't think they'd find such a son-in-law very appealing."

Jesse gave a harsh laugh. "You're bluffing, Carrington. You fire me and you'll never get the gold out the mountain."

Jack gave a cold smile. "We'll see, won't we? Go home and talk it over with your bride. See what she has to say. I want to be in the new section of the mountain before Christmas. I've got the explosives coming in by wagon. They should be here tomorrow."

"And the timber? When will that arrive?" Jesse replied with equal coldness.

"We may have to use what we have if it doesn't arrive in time." Jack gave another broad grin. "Just think of the celebrations when we announce we've struck gold by the holidays. I was thinking we might name the new shaft Christmas Gold or something like that if you don't want your name on it Perhaps Lorna might like to involve the school children in a naming contest. Well, don't let me keep you."

It wasn't just the shoe that had fallen, it was a whole boot and a heavy one at that. Jesse made the short walk to the new house and stood outside for a long while, unwilling to go in. To go in would mean he'd have to tell Lorna. It would mean that the "honeymoon," such as it was, was over.

What a honeymoon it had been, too. They had not taken a wedding trip of course. There was no money for it and no time. He'd gone straight to work on Monday and so had Lorna. They'd spent Sunday after church moving their things into the new house. Lorna and the children had spent the first week finishing that move, bringing a few last things from her cottage up on their way home from school each day. And each night, the new house looked a little more like a home, *their* home—Lorna and Jesse Kittredge's home.

Through one of the front windows he caught sight of Lorna lighting a lamp and placing it on the dinner table. This was his house now, and secretly he was more pleased about it than he dared to let on. Lorna may have lived in a finer home, but this was the finest house he'd ever had, ever dreamed of.

Lorna's lace curtains were at the front windows, and her three lamps shone throughout the downstairs of the house, sending light out into the gathering dusk. Every night, they were a beacon to him as he finished his shift, showing him the way home.

The foremens' homes came furnished with basics, so there'd been no need to bring furniture up from the cottages. They had a real—to Jesse's mind—dining table now, on which resided Lorna's tablecloth. She and Charlotte set the table every night and made him feel as if he were eating in a restaurant. Upstairs, the children had their own small rooms. Lorna and Charlotte had done up the beds with some of Lorna's colorful quilts.

But it wasn't just the house that had made the last two weeks special. It was the change in his life—seeing his children happy, seeing Charlotte not having to work to take care of a home and meals or Adam working to fish and provide food while he was gone on his shifts. With his new salary, he could afford to buy all the food his family needed. His children were getting the childhood he'd dreamed of for them, one where they could go to school, one where they had a chance to play. *Can you see us, Evie? I've kept your promises, all of them. We're going to be alright. Because of Lorna.*

But because of him, they might lose all that they'd so recently gained. Jack Carrington did not offer threats or rewards idly. Jesse could not let Carrington take away everything he had gained. It would destroy his marriage before it even had a chance to thrive, before they even had a chance to see what they could be together, and it would destroy his pride. He'd already failed his family once, already failed the woman he'd loved. He did not want to fail those he loved a second time.

The front door opened and Lorna came down the steps toward him, an apron about her waist, a smudge of flour on her cheek. A blond curl had escaped from its confines. "What are you doing out here, Jesse? You're a little bit later than usual. Come wash up. Dinner will be ready in a few minutes." She kissed his cheek and wrapped her arms about him.

"You'll get dirty," Jesse cautioned.

"I don't mind. Did you have a meeting after your shift got over?" She smiled up at him and his decision was made. He would not take this from them. No matter what he had to do, he'd preserve this for his family.

"Yes, Carrington thought maybe the schoolchildren might want to think of names for future shafts. He wanted me to tell you."

"That would be a fun, creative project for them." Her smile faded. "That means he's going ahead with the northwestern corner? Will it be alright?"

"It will be." He would make sure of it. Somehow. There was no need to worry her over things that could not be helped. Worrying wouldn't change anything. Carrington's mind was made up. He was going to move forward no matter what Jesse said or did. It seemed the best way to protect his family, his men and the other miners was to move forward with Carrington and do what he could to offset the mine owner's recklessness.

Lorna nodded. "We'll pray on it, Jesse. Between you and the Lord, I'm sure the mine will manage." Jesse hugged his wife tight and wished he had her faith.

The explosives came in on schedule, much to Jesse's dismay. He had hoped for early snow or bad weather to delay things. But he had no such luck. Still, laying explosives took time, and he hoped some other delay might arise as the explosive team worked. But there were no delays, or at least none were countenanced. The calendar turned to December, and the explosives team blasted by day and laid new fuses by night to create a viable corridor for exploration.

Jesse was running out of time. He knew the summons was coming. It was no surprise that he and his team were called up from their shift early, three days before Christmas, by a beaming Jack Carrington dressed in a fur-collared wool coat and top hat. He shared the announcement that his prized team would go into the new shaft tomorrow to see the potential.

"I have envelopes for all of you. A Christmas bonus, you might call it." Jack handed each member a fat envelope that lit up their eyes and for a moment offset the danger of what was being asked of them. Jesse knew better. This was bribery money. He took his envelope grimly and stuffed it in his pocket. The moment he'd been dreading had arrived. He clapped his men on the back as they departed, exhorting them to have a good evening. There was only he and Jack standing in the cold outside the mine entrance now.

Carrington frowned. "You're acting as if this is a death sentence instead of a splendid opportunity. I am going to make you a rich man."

"*If* we can reach the gold. *If* we can get it out. *If* the mountain doesn't bury us alive." Jesse saw no reason to mince words. "You know what you're sending us into, and you know there is every chance we will not come out again."

"If anything happens, I'll take care of Lorna, if that's what you're worried about."

That was precisely what Jesse was worried about. He'd heard the tale of David and Bathsheba too many times. "I'd rather you stay away from her and my children," he said tersely.

He turned for home and wondered if it would be the last time. The mountain's stability was anyone's guess. The explosives team had done minimal timbering. It wasn't their fault; they were just following orders. The shipment of timber he'd been expecting hadn't arrived. Perhaps it had never been ordered. He'd had a few weeks to prepare for this, to put his affairs in order, to think through what must be done in case the mountain went. Because he could write now, he had written a few letters, notes to Charlotte and Adam that he hoped they wouldn't have to read.

Perhaps he was being too morbid. The mountain might not go tomorrow. But even if it didn't, that would just delay the inevitable. If not tomorrow, it would go at some point in the future, and probably the near future at that. It was not the best place to dig. He hoped that this was not an elaborate form of revenge on Carrington's part, a chance to remove him entirely so that the way to Lorna was clear, so that Carrington could swoop in as the hero and redeem himself. But Jesse had little reason to put his faith in the goodness of a man who'd already proven himself to value ambition over safety, personal desires over the needs of others. The time had come to warn Lorna.

He found her in the kitchen, rolling out a pie crust. He stood for a moment in the doorway, watching, memorizing. If the worst happened, he wanted this image with him, wanted it to be the last picture in his mind as life faded—his wife, this woman who'd given him the ability to read, to write, who'd forced him back to life if even only for a short time. What a shame that was, to rediscover the joys of living only to lose them so soon. And yet, he would not trade these weeks with her. It gave him a sense of peace to know that his children would be safe with her. "Lorna," he said.

"You're home early." She smiled, but it faded quickly as she realized the reason for it. She wiped her hands on her apron. "Jack has given the word."

"We go under tomorrow. They put the ladders down the shaft today." He'd watched them go in much like a condemned prisoner might watch a gallows being built. He pulled out his envelope. "Carrington gave all the men a bonus." Bribe money, death money. "Where are Charlotte and Adam?"

"Upstairs, doing homework."

"Good. I want to talk to you." Jesse pulled a stool up to the kitchen table. "I want to tell you some things that might be hard to hear, but I don't want you to argue. I can't have you argue, Lorna. This is not a time to be stubborn. Tomorrow morning, I want you to go to the bank and withdraw all of your money. If anything happens, I don't want to run the risk that Jack will find a way to freeze your account. Can you do that?" Lorna nodded. "Good. Secondly, if the worst happens, I want you to take the children and go back East to your family. Do not stay here. Get out."

She reached for his hand. "You're scaring me, Jesse. What do you think will happen? You said you thought the shaft might be safe enough. But surely, he's not sending you down if it's not reasonably safe?" Disbelief was evident on her face. She simply could not fathom such callousness. He loved that about her.

"I want to believe it will be safe—that Jack is too greedy to risk his enterprise unless he truly believes he can make the new shaft a success—but Jack *is* sending my team into the shaft knowing full well what the risks are."

"All of this for the sake of money," Lorna said quietly. "What foolishness."

Jesse shook his head and gripped her hands. "It's

how Carrington is." He paused. "Will you promise me, Lorna, that if something happens to me that you will go East? Go home to your family with Charlotte and Adam? I know they'll be safe with you. They love you so much."

Tears brimmed in her eyes. "I will promise you because you ask it of me, but I will pray that it is not necessary." A fierce light took her eyes. "Even if you come out alive tomorrow, we cannot stay here and keep you safe. Perhaps you should get out. We can all go back East and if that doesn't suit you, I have money, we can buy your claim and pay off your debt. We can start anew at your mine and have nothing more to do with Carrington Mining."

"One day at a time, Lorna," he cautioned. I don't want to talk about it tonight. I just want to enjoy my family."

Lorna drew a shaky breath. "I'll make something special for dinner."

"Don't worry about that. Everything you make is special." Jesse raised his thumb to brush at the tear sliding down her cheek. "Don't cry, Lorna. Tonight, we will still have joy awhile longer. We'll help each other be brave for the children. I don't want them to know." Lorna nodded and he knew he could count on her. How odd to think that this time tomorrow, he might not be here to see her set the table, to smell her cooking, to hear the chatter of his children around the table. But they would be safe. Lorna would see to it.

It was a beautiful night, with the lamp on the table shining light on his children's faces as he read the story of David and Goliath from the Bible. In the morning, he rose early and left them sleeping. If Lorna was awake, she didn't stir, just as he'd asked. He didn't think he could manage leaving if he had to face her. She would be praying today, and the knowledge that he'd have her prayers gave him the courage he needed to face the day and whatever it might bring.

Chapter Twenty-Two

It was the longest day Lorna could ever remember. Jesse was gone when she got up. He'd wanted it that way, although it broke her heart not to see him off, not to wrap him in a final embrace, not to give him a final blessing. She'd made breakfast for the children, trying to be cheerful as if it were a normal day. They walked to school in the cold December air, frost heavy on the ground, and the children speculating about the chance of snow for Christmas. She prayed the whole time.

Please bring him through safely, Lord. The children need him. I need him. Their marriage was just getting started—surely it wouldn't be over so soon, not when there was so much more for them to learn about each other. *Not when he hasn't come back to you, Lord.*

At school, she couldn't remember what she taught for lessons, only that all of her students were excitable between the twin prospects of school being out for the holidays and the hope of new gold being found. After-ward, she took Adam and Charlotte to the shops to let them look at the store windows decorated for the holidays. They were excited about their first Christmas in the new house, as a family. *Please don't let them be disappointed, Lord,* Lorna prayed as they eyed the striped peppermint sticks in Mr. Putnam's glass candy jars. Surely, it would be too cruel to take their father from them before Christmas after having lost their mother just a few years before.

A horrible thought came to her. *Please don't let that be the reason I've come into their lives, so that I can care for them when both of their birth parents are gone.* Lorna fished a couple pennies out of her pocket and bought the peppermint sticks, as if the treat could ward off tragedy.

On the way out of town, they stopped at the bank and Lorna made the withdrawal just as Jesse had asked. It was nearly four o'clock. Jesse's usual shift would be ending in an hour. That gave her hope. There'd been no word from the mine all day and that day was nearly over. Surely he'd be home soon and safe.

They'd reached Foreman's Row and were nearly home when Lorna heard the sound. At first, it was no more than a pop, a crackle or a grinding. Then there was a clap like a door being shut, but they were outside, no doors in sight. "What's that?" Lorna looked skyward, thinking perhaps it was thunder. But she'd never heard thunder like that before.

Charlotte clutched her hand and Adam went pale. "It's a landslide," he whispered as the rumble grew louder.

Her first thought was for the children. Lorna looked around wildly in those early seconds, expecting to see rock and dirt descending on them, but there was nothing except the eerie sound of the rumble. Then she knew. It was the mine. The sound was coming from the mine.

"Pa!" Adam's eyes met hers in shared realization. She clutched Charlotte's hand and they ran the last of the distance, running straight toward the sound. Later, when she relived those horrifying moments, she would wonder about the wisdom of that decision. There was chaos by the time they reached the row of foremens' houses. People were running all directions, some away from the mine, others running toward it. Everyone was covered in dust and debris, some were bleeding. One man had a gash along his forehead.

"Take Lotte and get in the house," Lorna yelled over the noise to Adam before joining the river of people and pushing her way toward the mine.

It was worse the closer she got to the mine. There were cries for help and no one seemed to be in charge. "What's happened?" Lorna grabbed the arm of one passing man, desperate for news.

"There's trouble in the new shaft. That's all I know." The man moved on. Lorna felt her stomach lurch. This was exactly what Jesse had feared. She pushed on toward the mine entrance, stumbling amid the crowd. If it was the new shaft that was the problem, why was all the chaos here at the old entrance? She spotted Peter Kinney and called out to him.

"Lorna! What are you doing here?" Peter dragged her to the side, out of the chaos of rushing people. "You'll be crushed."

"What's happened? Where's Jesse?" She gasped, choking on the dust. The air was full of it.

Peter passed her a handkerchief and she pressed it

to her mouth and nose. "There's been a cave-in at the northwestern corner and it's triggered a chain reaction in some of the other chambers." Peter coughed.

"Where's Jesse? Where's his crew?" She tried to peer through the dust.

Peter shook his head. "I don't know. I barely got my own crew out. Tunnels Seven through Thirteen are shut down. We might lose the whole mine. There are still men down there. Go home. I'll bring news when I can." He gave her an apologetic look and plunged back into the melee, doing his best to organize some kind of rescue attempt.

Lorna couldn't move. It took a moment to fully process what Peter had told her. The mine was collapsing in on itself. The northwest corner had destabilized the entire structure. Jesse was down there. Trapped. She wouldn't let her mind think anything more than that. No, she wouldn't go home, not to stay. She would go home and gather supplies, and then she would come back and work.

Lorna cleaned cuts, bandaged gashes and offered countless drinks of water throughout the long night. Charlotte and Adam had come with her, eager to help, and she let them, knowing that they would not be able to sit still while their father was missing any more than she could. When he came up out of the shaft, they would want to be there.

Over the course of a few hours, chaos was slowly replaced with order. Lorna helped the Ladies Auxiliary set up a makeshift hospital and Jack arrived to spearhead the recovery. Every time a new group of miners came up the shaft, Lorna's hopes would surge. Surely, this time it would be Jesse. But each time those hopes were dashed. She could not falter. Jesse needed her belief, her prayers, more than ever wherever he was. He *would* come up. He would. She could not doubt it. Because she was praying for it. Because God would not fail her. And yet, that faith was tested as fewer men were brought up each time as the night went on.

By dawn, they'd begun to bring up the bodies, the recovery effort shifting now toward retrieval instead of rescue. She no longer looked with hope but with fear in the pit of her stomach when a new load came up. She did not want to see Jesse's body among the broken, not Jesse with those broad shoulders that had hefted her trunks so effortlessly that first day. Surely, the mountain would not claim him. But the news at sunrise was terrible.

Jack pulled her aside, looking haggard and disheveled. She'd never seen him not looking immaculate before. "Lorna, you need to prepare yourself and the children for the worst. The shaft is blocked. Even if Kittredge and his crew are still alive at the moment, we cannot reach them, we cannot get a rescue crew down there. It will take days for us to dig through the rubble."

"Then you'd best start digging now," Lorna snapped, his words not fully registering. She was tired; it had been a long night. Why was he standing around when there was still work to do?

His hands were at her arms, forcing her to look at him. "Lorna, you're not listening. We'd never reach them in time. Even if they're still alive at this moment, they won't be by the time we get to them, do you hear me?"

This time she did hear him and it stalled her, made it

hard for her to breathe. "So, you won't even try? You'll just give up?" Men could live for days underground if they had supplies and air. Jesse's men would be supplied—Jesse would have seen to it. As long as there was air... She couldn't think of that now, couldn't think of Jesse suffocating in the dark, choking to death. "Fine, I'll go. I will pull every rock out of there with my own two hands if I must." Anger pushed past her weariness. "And I won't stop until I know whether my husband is alive." She tore past him but Jack was hard on her heels.

"Lorna, stop. We can't risk it. If we start digging in there, we could bring the rest of the mountain down and lose what tunnels we have left."

"What are tunnels, Jack, when there are lives at stake?" Lorna cried. But in that moment she knew Jesse had been right about all of it. "You knew this could happen and you sent them in anyway. Jesse told you it wasn't safe and you didn't listen!"."

"I did *not* want this to happen," Jack argued hotly. "I have lost a fortune tonight."

"I may have lost a lot more thanmoney. You were warned. Jesse warned you. How could you show such disregard!" Lorna felt the tears start. She dashed them away with her hand. There was no time for them, not yet. Jesse needed more than tears from her. She spied PeterKinney moving among the stretchers. "Peter," she called out. "Take me to the northwestern shaft. I'm going to get my husband."

They weren't going to get out. Jesse held the lantern up, shining the light about the space left to them. He took in the wreckage. Shale and dirt were piled to the roof and he had no idea how thick the wall of debris was. It was thicker than his arm, though. He'd tried to shove through it to test its strength against his. The wall had won. Early on, they'd tried to simply pull the rocks away. That had been a mistake. It had brought down another dangerous round of debris on their heads.

"Well, boss, we can't go backward, we can't go forward, we can't go through it or over it, so what do you suggest?" one of his men asked.

"We wait and hope they dig us out," Jesse answered with what he hoped sounded like confidence, for the men's sake. In truth, he was worried. Digging them out from the other side had the same risks as digging out from this side. The flame in the lantern flickered. That was another worry. His men knew it, too. Flame needed oxygen to be sustained. Just as men did. They had a decision to make. "We can do one of two things, men. We go down fighting, try to move this rock even though we know the risks of bringing down even more, or we can blow out the lantern, save what air we can and wait for the rescue crew to find us. We should be fine until morning. When it's light out, it will be easier for a rescue crew to dig safely." Not that they'd know it when it was morning. In the dark of the shaft, time was all the same. He knew what he'd choose. Jack Carrington would know by now the shaft was buried. Jack would declare it hopeless and not bother to send a rescue crew.

"What would you do, boss?" someone asked.

"I'd dig."

"Then that's what we'll do."

They didn't talk as they worked. Conversation was a luxury when air was in short supply, although Jesse did offer a few words of encouragement every so often throughout the long night to keep the men's morale up. He thought of Lorna, of the children. He tried to imagine Lorna in the kitchen but couldn't. She wouldn't be there tonight. She would have heard the noise and, knowing her, she would have run toward it. She would be outside now, helping the hurt and haranguing anyone who wasn't literally moving mountains to find him. That thought made him smile. She'd be praying, too. He craned his ears, hoping to hear the sound of her prayers being answered, the sound of digging. But through the long night, no sound of rescue came from the other side.

Jesse lifted rocks until his muscles ached. Sweat ran down his back, and it seemed they got nowhere. There was always more rock. It was hot down there and his breathing was labored, not entirely because of the exertion. It must be nearly morning. They were running out of time and air. Some of his crew slept where they could, taking a break while others lifted rock in their place.

Jesse had not slept, had not stopped. He could not die like this, not when he'd just found happiness, found love again. Love. He hadn't told Lorna he loved her. Would she know? *Did* she know? Had she any idea how much she'd changed his life? He lifted a stone, feeling his strength wane, approaching its very limit. Beside him, one of his crew fainted, and panic rose in Jesse's gut at the very real and physical proof the end was coming. "Boss, it's no use." One of his men laid a hand on his arm, panting the words. How long had he been pulling stones alone?

The words came to him unexpectedly as the inevitable swept him. *Lord, be with my children, be with Lorna.*

Protect them when I am gone. Lord, thank you for them, for her. He closed his eyes and knew peace. Lorna had given him that, too. One of his men began to weep. No, he would not let them go like that, feeling alone and hopeless. He gathered his breath. "Do you know the story in Joshua of the sun standing still because Joshua prayed for it?" he began. "We must not be afraid to pray for the impossible at the eleventh hour or any hour."

It had taken dying to realize it. How much of his life had he wasted in anger at God? "Pray with me, if you can, or just pray in your minds. Whatever words you have will be enough. Our Father, who art in Heaven…" Jesse prayed out loud as long as he could, reciting every prayer he could remember—the Lord's Prayer, the twenty-third Psalm—and then just words, sometimes praying for deliverance, sometimes offering thanksgiving, praying for the families of his men, praying for his own family.

He wasn't sure he was making sense anymore when he heard it, the sound of voices. There was a shaft of light that speared his eyelids. The voices were too rough to be angels. Jesse found the strength to crack one eyelid open. Someone called his name. "Kittredge, are you in there?"

"Kinney?" Jesse croaked, his throat dry. He crawled forward toward the crack, toward the light. A hand thrust forward through a widening breach in the rock and Jesse grabbed it. A cry went up from the other side.

"Hang on, Kittredge. We'll have you out in a little while." That was Kinney, but in the next moment, there was another voice and the sound of someone scrambling over rock.

"Jesse." The feminine voice broke with relief. "Jesse, can you hear me? Are you alright? Is anyone hurt?" Lorna was there.

"I'm alright, Lorna."

"You'd better be," Kinney joked. "She's been at us since sunrise to get this rock moved."

"Be careful, Peter. I don't want the rest of the mountain to come down," Jesse warned.

"Too late for that," Peter called. "There's not much left to come down."

It was no easy task to extricate the men. Jesse handed each man through the small opening, one at a time. It was the largest opening they dared risk given the state of the mountainside. Their caution proved to be well warranted. As the last man went through, shale began to tumble into the little space his men had occupied.

"Jesse, hurry!" Lorna called out. "I don't think it will hold much longer."

He took a final look behind him and there it was, the gold seam Carrington had risked everything for. But the mountain was rumbling and Lorna was calling. He had much more than gold waiting for him on the other side. Jesse set his shoulder to the rock and gave a push into the morning, into Lorna's waiting arms.

"I thought I'd lost you," Lorna sobbed as they held on to one another. These were sobs of joy, of relief, of reunion. "Jack wouldn't come to look for you, but Kinney got some men together." She was babbling, his beautiful, usually coherent wife.

"Don't let her fool you." Kinney slapped him on the back. "*She* got the men together. If not for her, you would have been given up for dead long before this." Kinney jerked his chin toward the rubble of the northwest shaft. "I honestly don't know how we got to you. We never could have moved all that rock ourselves."

"Boss moved that rock." Jesse looked up to see them surrounded by his crew, some of them supported by others. "Boss kept moving rock all night after the rest of us couldn't. Never seen anything like it, and when that wasn't enough, then he prayed with us for deliverance."

He felt Lorna's eyes on him. "You prayed, Jesse."

He smiled at his wife. "I have it on good authority, that's what one ought to do when something needs doing. God came through."

Lorna grinned. "I told you, He always does. Let's go home. Our children are waiting." He liked the sound of that. Our children. Our home. Our life together. Jesse wrapped an arm around Lorna's shoulders and sent a private prayer heavenward as they walked.

There would be decisions to make in the days that followed about their future—to go back East, to stay here in the West—but they would make those decisions together and with God's guidance.

I am a blessed man, Lord. Thank you. Thank you for not giving up on me. Thank you for sending me Lorna and showing me the way home to you. She'd taught him to read, to write, love and to have faith. His education was complete but the journey was just beginning.

In the end, they chose to stay in the west. This was their home and it was a land rich in opportunity for those brave enough to claim it. And he was brave enough, thanks to the woman who stood beside him. She'd done more than change him. She'd saved him.

* * *

Jesse smiled at his wife as he handed her the pick-axe. Adam and Lotte stood nearby with lanterns in the interior of their newly acquired claim, registered with the state of California simply as Hope's Landing. "This is your doing," he grinned at Lorna. "You should have the first strike." After the disaster had shut down Carrington's, Lorna had convinced him it was time for them to move on. Actually, they'd prayed on it—he was still getting used to that, to having his faith back. They'd paid his debt to Carrington and bought the title to the little plot he'd found up in the hills. It was still a stressful time for Jesse. He hoped he wasn't wrong about it but Lorna was confident.

"Let's do it together," Lorna suggested, "The way we do everything."

He came up behind her and helped her heft the pick-axe. Together, they struck a promising area, metal clanking on stone while the children cheered. The great adventure had begun. He was determined to do it right; proper timbering, respecting the earth, and not digging too deep into the hillside. Perhaps he would let Adam dig with him, but school would come first. Both he and Lorna were determined the children would have that.

They were making more than a new life for themselves up here. They were making a new life for others as well. The men on Jesse's crew had been eager to follow him, despite the unknowns. Even now, just four months since the accident had destroyed Carrington's, houses were going up at Hope's Landing. The church had been the first building erected while they'd waited for the deed to go through. It had been a long winter, traveling between Woods River and Hope's Landing, using Woods River as a base, but now that spring had arrived, progress was faster.

Jesse knelt beside the rock, calling for Adam to bring the lantern near. He held up a rock and laughed. "That's no rock, that's a nugget." He passed it to Lorna and ran his hand along the revealed interior of the rock, letting out a low whistle. "Look at that, Lorna. A vein." The tension he'd been carrying these past months eased within him. He reached for Lorna's hand and gathered the children to him. "Let's pray. We have much to be thankful for."

* * * * *

Author's Note

I've always been interested in what compelled people to come west, especially knowing that the journey was dangerous whether it was three months on a clipper ship, or three months on a wagon train across the country. In addition to that danger was the reality that people left families behind knowing they would very likely not see them again because the distance was just too great and the travel expensive. And yet, people came west in droves looking for opportunities the east could no longer fulfill.

California was especially welcoming to women. In California, women could own businesses and land in their own names and women could initiate divorces. Women could also get jobs as teachers, something that was difficult for them to do in the east where most teaching jobs went to men. It is this economic freedom that appeals to Lorna Alderly as she decides to join the philanthropic society heading west.

Philanthropic societies like the one run by Mrs. Grace Elliott, were very popular in the mid-nineteenth century.

They organized wagon trains and passage on ships and helped people get settled into new towns and jobs. Many of the societies specialized in recruiting women. They were looking for women who were middle-class, educated and skilled, and who could afford to pay for their passage. This was often a hard sell because these women often didn't feel that going west was a step up for them. The women that were interested, however, tended to be uneducated and unskilled women looking to make a better life themselves. For information about these societies and women coming west, I enjoyed several resources, one of which was Marcia Zug's *Buying a Bride*.

Jesse and Lorna's story is set in the fictional town of Woods River, not far from Sonoma, a town that survived the gold rush. It still exists today.

Get 3 FREE REWARDS!

We'll send you 2 FREE Books plus a FREE Mystery Gift.

Both the **Harlequin® Historical** and **Harlequin® Romance** series feature compelling novels filled with emotion and simmering romance.

YES! Please send me 2 FREE novels from the Harlequin Historical or Harlequin Romance series and my FREE Mystery Gift (gift is worth about $10 retail). After receiving them, if I don't wish to receive any more books, I can return the shipping statement marked "cancel." If I don't cancel, I will receive 6 brand-new Harlequin Historical books every month and be billed just $6.19 each in the U.S. or $6.74 each in Canada, a savings of at least 11% off the cover price, or 4 brand-new Harlequin Romance Larger-Print books every month and be billed just $6.09 each in the U.S. or $6.24 each in Canada, a savings of at least 13% off the cover price. It's quite a bargain! Shipping and handling is just 50¢ per book in the U.S. and $1.25 per book in Canada.* I understand that accepting the 2 free books and gift places me under no obligation to buy anything. I can always return a shipment and cancel at any time by calling the number below. The free books and gift are mine to keep no matter what I decide.

Choose one:
- ☐ **Harlequin Historical** (246/349 BPA GRNX)
- ☐ **Harlequin Romance Larger-Print** (119/319 BPA GRNX)
- ☐ **Or Try Both!** (246/349 & 119/319 BPA GRRD)

Name (please print)

Address   Apt. #

City   State/Province   Zip/Postal Code

Email: Please check this box ☐ if you would like to receive newsletters and promotional emails from Harlequin Enterprises ULC and its affiliates. You can unsubscribe anytime.

Mail to the Harlequin Reader Service:
IN U.S.A.: P.O. Box 1341, Buffalo, NY 14240-8531
IN CANADA: P.O. Box 603, Fort Erie, Ontario L2A 5X3

Want to try 2 free books from another series? Call 1-800-873-8635 or visit www.ReaderService.com.

---

*Terms and prices subject to change without notice. Prices do not include sales taxes, which will be charged (if applicable) based on your state or country of residence. Canadian residents will be charged applicable taxes. Offer not valid in Quebec. This offer is limited to one order per household. Books received may not be as shown. Not valid for current subscribers to the Harlequin Historical or Harlequin Romance series. All orders subject to approval. Credit or debit balances in a customer's account(s) may be offset by any other outstanding balance owed by or to the customer. Please allow 4 to 6 weeks for delivery. Offer available while quantities last.

Your Privacy—Your information is being collected by Harlequin Enterprises ULC, operating as Harlequin Reader Service. For a complete summary of the information we collect, how we use this information and to whom it is disclosed, please visit our privacy notice located at corporate.harlequin.com/privacy-notice. From time to time we may also exchange your personal information with reputable third parties. If you wish to opt out of this sharing of your personal information, please visit readerservice.com/consumerschoice or call 1-800-873-8635. **Notice to California Residents**—Under California law, you have specific rights to control and access your data. For more information on these rights and how to exercise them, visit corporate.harlequin.com/california-privacy.

HHHRLP23

HARLEQUIN
PLUS

Try the best multimedia
subscription service for romance
readers like you!

Read, Watch and Play.

Experience the easiest way to get
the romance content you crave.

Start your **FREE TRIAL** at
<u>www.harlequinplus.com/freetrial</u>.